Loving a Borrego
Brother 2

Loving a Borrego Brother 2

Johnni Sherri

www.urbanbooks.net

Urban Books, LLC
300 Farmingdale Road, N.Y.-Route 109
Farmingdale, NY 11735

Loving a Borrego Brother 2

ISBN 13: 978-1-64556-044-9
ISBN 10: 1-64556-044-9

First Trade Paperback Printing March 2020
Printed in the United States of America

10 9 8 7 6 5 4 3 2 1

Distributed by Kensington Publishing Corp.
Submit Orders to:
Customer Service
400 Hahn Road
Westminster, MD 21157-4627
Phone: 1-800-733-3000
Fax: 1-800-659-2436

Loving a Borrego Brother 2

by

Johnni Sherri

Dear Readers,

Thank you for supporting me throughout this series as well as my other three-book series, *Love and the Game*. Your kind words on social media have truly meant a lot to me. Please stay tuned for my next series, titled *Heartbreak U!*

Love always,
Johnni Sherri

Chapter 1

Melo

"Please don't do this! Please!" I could hear my mother beg.

Being awakened by her fearful screams and pleas for help, I immediately got out of bed and tiptoed down the long hall. I found her kneeling on the kitchen floor with tears running down her face. Her hands were pressed together like she was praying for mercy. My father was towering over her, but I could only see his back—just a tall, dark image emanating fury and rage.

"You was gon' keep letting me think he was my son!" he hollered, only to hear her soft whimpers in response.

When she didn't answer, he got down on the floor and pulled her up close. With a tight grip on the silk nightgown she wore, he put her face right next to his.

"Answer me, woman!" he commanded. His eyes were bulging out of his head, and spit was flying from his mouth.

"I'm sorry. I'm so sorry, Raul!" she cried. Her thin body was trembling so bad you could tell she feared for her life. Her cheeks were red and her thick hair was wild, so I knew he had been slapping her around. I hated when he did that shit.

I wanted to yell out and make him stop, but I couldn't. My voice was somehow lost in that crucial moment. Although my body was frozen still, internally I was shaking like a damn leaf. Every muscle in my body was tight and tense. I could only stare at the scene before me. It was like watching a horror movie, preparing for the scene of death.

"You fucking slut! Can't trust my own fucking wife around my blood!" he yelled, now gripping her tightly around the throat.

She let out a few murmured sounds, choking before he finally released her from his grasp. Her frail body plopped to the tile floor. Then he stood up and began pacing back and forth with a gun cocked in his right hand. I hadn't seen it up until this moment, but now I knew why my mother was terrified.

My heart started to sprint its own race within my chest, and my stomach began to churn. Petrified, I stood there shirtless in my white briefs, wondering what my next move was going to be. That's when I locked eyes with my mother. Her beautiful eyes were light, like the color of honey, and in them I could tell that she wanted me to be quiet. They told me to remain still.

I was obedient, but then I saw him point the gun at her. He was shaking his head slowly, and I could now hear him weeping. His heart was breaking in that instant, and I didn't need to see his face to tell me that. It was the sound of his pain-filled cry that told me he didn't want to pull the trigger.

"Why?" he whispered. His voice cracked from hurt and confusion.

She looked up at him without an answer to give, only more tears. A few moments of silence passed between them, staring deeply into one another's eyes. Then something inside of him instantly snapped. He ran his free hand down his face before putting the gun directly to her forehead.

"Please, Raul. Pleeease!" she bawled in desperation. However, her cries fell on deaf ears because he pressed harder into her skull.

"Don't do this, Raul. Please," she begged again. Her voice was weak and strained from it all. She was so scared I could see a pool of urine puddled beneath her. Her silk nightgown was wet at the hem.

Then I took one step forward, hoping to stop the madness and prevent what I knew would inevitably happen.

Pow!

I was too late.

"Melo! Melo!" I could hear Raquel say with a shake to my arm.

I shot straight up in the bed with my heart still pounding from that dumb-ass dream. At least twice a week, I dreamt of my father shooting my mother in the head. It always seemed so real to me, but in reality, I knew the shit didn't go down like that. My mother killed her damn self. She blew her brains out right in front of me.

"Are you all right?" Raquel asked, genuinely concerned. My chest heaved up and down as I tried to catch my breath. "You were having that nightmare again?" she asked softly, looking over at me.

I nodded, taking in her beauty. Her brown shoulders were bare, and the white sheet was pulled up over her breasts. Inwardly I smiled as she wiped the sweat from my forehead with the tips of her fingers. I looked right into her light eyes, which resembled my mother's, before leaning over and kissing her lips.

"What was that for?" she scrunched her face and asked.

"What? I can't kiss you now, shawty?" I asked before stepping out of bed and stretching my arms wide, naked as the day I was born. The Borrego tattoo I had inked on my abs was proudly on display.

"I didn't say that," she mumbled, turning away.

Over the past few months, we'd slept together a count-less number of times, but she still acted shy. She acted like she didn't love this dick or know what to do with it, but that couldn't be further from the truth. She reached down to the floor to grab my T-shirt and quickly pulled it over her head before removing the covers from her body.

"I done seen everything you got, shawty. Why you keep acting shy wit' me, girl?" I asked, licking my lips. I was now standing directly in front of her, with morning wood. I loved fucking with Raquel. To know I could make her blush and feel so uncomfortable inspired me somehow.

"I'm not acting shy. Now would you please put some clothes on?" she snapped, looking away.

"Come. Let's take a shower," I told her, nodding my head toward the door. She rolled her eyes yet complied, following me into the bathroom.

After we showered and dressed, I caught Raquel singing in the mirror while putting her earrings back in her ears. Although it was just above a whisper, it made me smile because her voice was breathtaking. I asked her to sing for me all the time, but ever since that day she sang for me in the studio back at home, she refused. It had been a while since I'd heard the melodic sounds of her voice. I didn't even want to say anything to bring attention to the fact that I was listening to her, for fear she might stop singing.

I looked her over completely and noticed that she was wearing some low-cut black body shirt with ripped jeans. Being up under her sister Risa these past few months, she had changed her style, and I really wasn't feeling it. Raquel went from being my nerdy schoolgirl to being one of the hottest chicks on Clark's campus. She dressed way too sexy, and just the thought of another nigga looking at her, at what I felt was rightfully mine, made me want to fight, shoot, and kill.

"Where you going with that shit on?" I barked with a scowl on my face, looking down at her cleavage and exposed thighs through the tears in her jeans.

"I got class, Melo. Where else would I be going on a Tuesday morning?" her smart ass said with a roll of her hazel eyes.

"I just asked you a simple muthafucking question, shawty. You can chill wit' all the attitude."

"Look, I'm not your girlfriend, Melo. So don't try to check me," she sassed, moving past me to pack up her book bag.

After I broke her in the first time, I instantly claimed her as my own, but for some reason, she didn't want to admit that she was mine. I didn't know what that was all about, but somehow I knew I could show her better than I could tell her. I ain't never had to chase a bitch, and I damn sure wasn't about to start now. She was gon' learn though. She was definitely going to learn.

"Oh yeah? I'm not your boyfriend?" I questioned, turning to look at her with a smirk on my face.

"No. You're not," she said low, avoiding my stare.

"You sure?" I asked again, moving in close to her body, smelling that soft vanilla perfume that she loved to wear. With a lick of my lips, I reached down to cup my hand between her legs. Feeling that warm mound, I watched as she closed her eyes for a brief second and bit down on her bottom lip. I just knew I had her until her eyes unexpectedly flew open.

"I don't have time for the games, Melo. Now move!" she fussed, pushing past me again.

"A'ight. I'm not your man. Remember you said that shit," I said with a slick grin.

We headed out of my bedroom door and down the stairs where we could smell bacon and maple syrup. My nigga Fat Man had to be cooking because none of us in

the frat house other than him knew how to even boil water. When we got downstairs, Raquel followed me toward
the kitchen, passing through the living room, which was
littered with beer cans, red cups, and ashtrays full from
the night before.

As we approached the kitchen, I could hear Trey
Songz's "Nobody Else But You" playing on the radio. Fat
Man was the only nigga I knew to rep Trey Songz and his
love for R&B the way he did. He stood at the stove singing shirtless with his bubble belly hanging over his red
basketball shorts. A big gold rope hung around his neck
and draped down onto his chest, which was sprinkled
with little beads of black hair. From behind, it looked
like a pack of hot dogs permanently sat on the back of his
neck, but it was all good. That was my nigga. He was the
only one I really fucked with like that in the house other
than Dre.

"What up, Fat Man?" I said, dapping him up before
grabbing a piece of bacon off the plate.

"On your way to class?" he asked me, but his eyes were
fixed on Raquel.

"Yo, you asking me or Raquel, nigga? I'm over here," I
said, snapping my fingers to get his attention.

"My bad, bruh. How you doin', Raquel?" he asked,
softening his tone and licking his lips. He always flirted
with her, but I didn't get too mad because he mostly did
that shit to get under my skin. Plus, I also knew Raquel
didn't pay his fat ass no mind.

"I'm doing all right. Can I have some breakfast before I
go?" she asked.

"Nah, take your hungry ass on to class, my nigga. Only my
girl can eat up in this house, and that ain't you. Remember?"
I told her.

"Ooohh! You are so petty!" she shrieked, rolling her
eyes.

"I'll be that. But for real tho, you can see your way out," I said, walking over toward the counter that was full of food.

"Are you serious right now?"

"As a muthafucking heart attack," I replied calmly with my back facing her. I was fixing me a plate of bacon, eggs, home fries, and pancakes. My nigga could really throw down.

"Fine," she said before storming out of the kitchen.

"Yo, I think you pissed shawty off," Fat Man said with a laugh.

"She'll be all right." I shrugged my shoulders, shoveling another piece of bacon in my mouth. That's when we heard the front door slam. I shook my head and let out a light chuckle.

Like I said, I didn't chase after bitches, but I did want to find out what was up with her. I never heard of a girl losing her virginity to a man and not wanting to be in a relationship with him. That shit was unheard of in my world. Then again, Raquel was a unique individual all around. I shouldn't have even been surprised. She was going to make me work for it, and I already knew it.

Chapter 2

Romi

"When do you start?" Mama asked excitedly, sitting at the foot of my bed. Her awaiting green eyes gazed at me with delight.

"I start classes this summer. In June," I told her. I had finally applied to school and gotten accepted at the local community college. I didn't know what I was going to major in yet, but at least it was a start.

"Well, you already know you got someone to keep the baby while you're in class," she said with a proud smile. My parents were so happy I was finally getting my shit together. I was determined now more than ever to be able to support myself and the baby.

"Thanks, Ma. Ms. Calisa told me that she would babysit too," I said, sitting up Indian-style while flipping through my course catalogue.

"That woman has been such a blessing to me. You have no idea. She's like the sister I've always wanted. No offense to your aunt Marlene," Mama said with a laugh.

"Yeah, even after I told her that the baby wasn't Dre's, she still insists that she is going to be a grandma."

"Have you told Charles?" my mother asked low.

It came out months ago that my daddy's good friend Charles and I had slept together. Daddy nearly choked the life out of him at Raina's birthday party this past Fourth of July. Before the results of my paternity test, I even thought he could be the father of my unborn child. So these days we rarely, if ever, spoke his name, and when we did, it was always in a hushed, forbidden tone.

"No, and I'm not going to. I don't think it's his either," I said, watching her eyes grow wide. There was an uncomfortable silence in my room as she stared at me. Only the ticking of the clock hanging on the wall could be heard.

"Romi Renee Brimmage, I know you ain't sitting here telling me that you don't know who your baby's daddy is," she quizzed with her head cocked to the side.

I knew exactly who the father of my unborn child was, but that would be my secret to keep. Dre Borrego had taken me through so much shit this past year, between the on-again, off-again relationship, the accident, and now this new girlfriend of his, Brandi. When I came to the Borrego household to make things right with him that night, I had no idea he'd show up with another woman on his arm. I got so upset that I drove off and accidentally ran a red light. My car was slammed into by a sixteen-wheeler truck going full speed ahead. I ended up in the hospital, stuck in a coma for almost two months. Thank God, my baby survived. And now that it was all behind me, I just didn't want anything to do with him anymore. Even still, I was thankful for the support of his mother, Ms. Calisa.

"It doesn't matter, Mama. I'm raising this baby on my own anyway. Do I have your support or not?" I retorted, throwing my book to the other side of the bed.

My mother quickly stood up in a stance that had me slightly frightened. Although I was 20 years old, my mother still had that effect on me. She was old school and didn't take shit off of none of us girls.

"As my daughter, you will always have my love and support. Always! But let me tell you something, little girl. You have no idea how it feels to have your child questioning you about who their real father is. Day in and day out. The look in their eyes because they know a part of them is missing. While all along you have the answer but refuse to give it, because you know the heartbreak it will cause. I know what that's like. You don't. Remember, this is not about you, but it's about your child, Romi. It's about that baby growing inside of you," she scolded, rolling her green eyes before leaving my room with a hard shut to my door.

I lay back in my bed and pulled the covers up over my head, thinking about my mother's final words. I knew my son needed a father, but I really didn't want to deal with Dre. I was going to have to think long and hard about the whole situation. My mother was speaking directly from her experience with my sister Risa, but if you asked me, she turned out perfectly. If I could find someone half as decent as my father, I knew my son and I would be in good hands.

Suddenly, I felt my phone vibrate beside me. I released a throaty groan because I didn't want to be bothered. I was two weeks away from my due date, and I was growing more agitated by the minute. I had gained a total of thirty-eight pounds. My feet were swollen to the size of boxing gloves, and I hadn't had a good night's sleep in over a month. To say I was "over it" would have been an understatement.

"Hello," I said with a yawn.

"Hey, are you still coming with me to the mall?" my youngest sister, Raina, asked on the other end of the phone.

"Oh shit, I forgot," I muttered. "Why didn't you come in here and get me?"

"You and Mama were talking, and I didn't want to interrupt," she said.

"Give me about thirty minutes to get dressed, and then we can go."

We had plans to go the mall and walk this baby right up out of me. I was tired and miserable, so my mother suggested walking. There was no better venue than the mall for me. I could shop for the baby and a brand-new wardrobe for me that didn't include maternity clothes. Raina was game too, because ever since she started dating Damien, Dre's younger brother, she had stepped up her appearance. These days she loved shopping.

After getting dressed, I walked downstairs to see Daddy and Mama snuggled up on the couch, watching *Love Jones*. That was my mother's favorite movie, and although Daddy couldn't stand it, he would break down and watch it with her each and every time. As she rested her head back against his broad chest, I noticed that their fingers were interlaced. Complete envy overtook me as I watched their simple, uncomplicated love.

"You ready?" Raina asked. She wore a cream cashmere sweater with olive green jeans. Her hair was parted down the middle into two simple braids that hung to the middle of her back. The only trace of makeup on her face was the sheer pink gloss on her lips, and in her ears were modest one-carat diamond studs. She was a classic beauty.

"Yup, I'm ready," I said.

"Baby girl, don't let her drive. She's too big to be driving," my daddy called out.

"Damn. Thanks, Daddy," I mumbled in sarcasm with a roll of my eyes. Nobody needed to tell me how big I had gotten these past few months because I could feel every pound of it. I felt like a beached whale.

Raina laughed before saying, "Don't worry, I'm gon' drive, Daddy."

After we got into the car to head over to the mall, I rode silently, staring out of the window. The cold sky was appropriately clear and gray for the season. Bare winter trees with wide branches, along with green highways signs, flashed by us on the drive. I sat deep in thought, thinking about my life and the child I was carrying. There was a lot I needed to figure out inside my head.

"Have you decided on a name for the baby?" Raina asked, interrupting my thoughts.

"I'm thinking Thomas after Granddaddy, or maybe Ellison," I said low, still peering out of the window.

"Eww, Romi. Those are old names," she said.

"I don't know yet. I'm still thinking on it," I said with a shrug.

When we pulled up to the mall, the parking lot was so full that Raina had to drop me off at the door. As I stood behind the glass door of the mall entrance waiting for her to park, I witnessed couple after couple coming through holding hands. There was one particular woman who was just as pregnant as I was. She was tall, beautiful, and dark skinned with a curly 'fro. A small toddler squirmed in the stroller she pushed, and by her side was a tall, handsome man. Her husband, I assumed. With one look at her beaming face, you could tell she was truly happy and in love. That instantly made me think of Dre and the lonely journey of motherhood I was preparing for.

"Hey, you ready?" Raina asked, walking through the door.

I nodded and waddled behind her. She was walking way too fast for me.

"You're gonna have to slow down," I told her, already holding on to my big belly.

As we walked through the mall, we mostly shopped for baby things. I bought several cute little boy outfits. Mostly onesies that referenced a slogan with "Mommy" or "Grandma" on the front. Raina purposely overlooked ones that read like "Daddy's li'l Slugger" or "Daddy's li'l

Genius." She pretended as though she didn't even see them, although I knew she did. She didn't want to risk bringing up my situation with Dre or Charles only to upset me in the end. I appreciated her thoughtfulness.

"I'm hungry. You want to go to the food court and get something to eat?" she asked.

"Yes, and rest these feet," I told her, looking down at my swollen ankles. My feet were so huge I had to wear shoes two sizes larger than normal. I preferred slides that I could easily get my feet in and out of.

With only two weeks of pregnancy left, I didn't put much effort into how I looked. My chubby face was bare, with just a sheer coat of Carmex on my lips. I had on a red long-sleeved maternity top with skinny blue maternity jeans. And on my feet were a pair of black Naturalizer slides that could've easily been mistaken for orthopedic shoes.

When we got to the food court, I ordered two slices of pepperoni pizza, garlic knots, a side of spaghetti, and a garden salad. My appetite had picked up quite a bit these past few months. Raina only got one slice of pepperoni pizza and a bottle of water. She had a complex about her weight since she was chubby in her younger years, so I was used to her eating light. When we found a table nearby, we plopped our trays down and neatly arranged our shopping bags on the empty chairs.

"Mmmm," I moaned, taking a bite of pizza.

"Dang, you greedy. You didn't even say grace," Raina teased with a smile.

"You said it for the both of us. Now shut up and let me eat," I said, taking another bite.

While we sat there eating, my feet really began to throb. I pulled an empty chair beside me so that I could prop up my feet. However, my feet were so sore and my legs were so numb and heavy, I struggled to get them up. I bent down with plans on using both of my hands to lift one leg up a time.

"Let me help you with that," I heard him say.

I looked up and saw Dre standing before me, looking and smelling better than ever. He wore a red Armani T-shirt with a red Braves cap on his head. Diamond studs sparkled in each of his ears while a fancy diamond watch flashed on his wrist. I felt myself tingling at just the sight as I looked him over from head to toe. Then I remembered that I, myself, looked like shit. The first time seeing Dre since the grand opening of their father's new hotel, and here I was looking like a fat slob. I was mortified.

"I got it," I said low before bending back down, my face flushed with embarrassment.

He kneeled down beside me anyway, ignoring what I had just said, and placed his hand directly over mine. A spark of sorts occurred at the touch of our flesh. At first, I wasn't sure if he felt it, but then I looked up in his dark brown eyes. They were asking me, "Why? Why did all of this happen to us?" In them I could see that he still loved me just as much as, if not more than, I loved him.

We stayed in that position for what felt like a lifetime, merely speaking through our eyes, until I heard her voice.

"Dre, did you want sweet tea or lemonade?" Brandi asked in her usual soft, sweet tone.

She was standing there looking chic in a black leather motorcycle jacket and black skinny jeans. I could see her cute little toes polished in bright red from the black peep-toe leather boots she wore. Soft cinnamon-colored curls sat in a loose ponytail on the top of her head, while just a few wispy spirals mistakenly dangled in her pretty brown face.

"Lemme get a sweet tea," he responded with his eyes still connected to mine.

"Oh, I'm being so rude. How are you guys doing?" she asked, looking at Raina and then me.

"Doing good," Raina softly stated. I simply gave a half smile.

"I guess it won't be long now, will it?" she asked me.

"Two weeks," I responded, still looking at Dre.

Finally, he broke his gaze and lifted my legs up on the chair.

"Thanks, Dre," I said as he stood up from his crouching position.

"If you need anything, Ro, anything at all, just holla, a'ight?" he said. And with that, he walked off with Brandi at his side.

Chapter 3

Risa

As I sat in my car patiently waiting for the winter weather to subside, I saw a text come through on my phone. I looked down and sighed, seeing that it was from Micah. Without even reading his message, I turned the phone over and turned up my music. I was playing my Gretchen Wilson CD and listening to the words of "I Don't Feel Like Loving You Today." My sisters always made fun of me for liking country music, but those sappy lyrics were like none other when going through a heartbreak.

> *I don't feel like loving you today*
> *So don't you even try to change my mind*
> *The best thing you can do right now is just go away*
> *'Cause I don't feel like loving you today*

Although Micah sent me a dozen red roses every Monday since that dreadful night I caught him cheating, I still wouldn't speak to him. Even on those few occasions when he posted up outside my dorm in the cold waiting for me to leave for class, I refused to hear him out. I would walk right past him as though I didn't even see or hear him.

Micah Borrego broke my heart on one of the worst nights of my life, and I just couldn't forgive him. I'd been physically abused by my ex-boyfriend Zo for years, so when I finally met my Prince Charming, the one who did everything right, it broke me when I learned he was cheating on me. Not to mention, I got arrested for a crime I didn't even commit. I didn't know who murdered Zo. The only thing I knew was that it wasn't me. Although I didn't spend a single night in jail and all charges against me were dropped because another tape had surfaced of someone else entering Zo's apartment before me, I distanced myself from everyone. Well, everyone except my three sisters. I was emotionally damaged by it all.

Through the sounds of Gretchen and beads of sleet tapping against my windshield, I heard another text chime through. I rolled my eyes because I just knew it was Micah again. He texted me several times throughout the day, begging for forgiveness and professing his love. The only reason I hadn't blocked him yet was because I still loved him, and mentally I wasn't prepared for the finality of our relationship. Letting out another deep sigh, I decided to flip my phone over and read his messages.

Micah: Did you make it home in this weather?

Micah: Please just let me know that you're okay.

I guess it wouldn't hurt to let him know that I'm okay. After bouncing around the idea in my head for a few more minutes, I picked up my phone and started texting him back. That's when I suddenly heard a hard knock on my window.

"Ahhh!" I screamed out in fear.

"It's me. Open up," Micah said behind the cold glass. The icy sleet sprinkled down hard on his frame as I looked him over. He was layered down in his thick black coat with a black skull cap on his head. Even his hands were covered in black leather gloves. Just the sight of him gave me a headache.

Not wanting to let the cold in, I rolled the window down no more than an inch. "What do you want, Micah? Are you stalking me?"

"Why are you sitting out here in this weather?" he asked with a scowl on his face.

"I'm waiting for it to slow down a bit, and then I'm going to make a run for it."

"Nah. Unlock the door, and I'll make sure you get in safe," he said, reaching to open up the door.

"Look, we're not together anymore, so you don't have to do all that. As a matter of fact, where is Melody? Did she make it in all right?" I asked sarcastically, referring to his assistant, who he cheated on me with.

"I see you still on that bullshit after all these months," he said with a kiss of his teeth.

"What do you expect, Micah?" I asked softly. This was actually my first time talking to him about what happened that night, and I could feel my emotions starting to rise.

"Just let me in so we can talk," he said. Not even giving me a chance to respond, he immediately began jogging around to the passenger side of the car.

With my hands gripping the steering wheel, I closed my eyes, contemplating whether I should let him in. *I cannot be weak. I have to stay strong,* I told myself. *I will not cry, and most importantly, I will not let him touch me.* When I opened my eyes, I looked over to my right, realizing that I had left him out in the cold waiting to get in. Against my better judgment, I quickly hit the unlock button.

"Damn, you got it feeling good in here," he casually said before closing the door.

"What is it that you've been wanting to talk about, Micah?" I asked, getting straight to the point.

"I just wanted to say that I'm sorry, babe. I'm sorry for all the bullshit I put you through. I know I fucked up majorly, but this can't be the end for us. I love yo' ass way too much to just let it go. What can I do to make shit right between us again?" he asked in his deep, raspy tone while taking off his gloves.

"Wow," was all I could say.

"Wow, what?"

"Do me a favor and close your eyes for a minute," I told him. At first, he gave me a skeptical look, then he did as I instructed and closed his eyes.

"Imagine a cell phone to your ear. You hear my voice on the other end, along with another man's. You hear the man practically begging to get between my thighs. Lustfully begging to indulge in something you whole-heartedly believe is only yours. Then you hear me weakly try to fight him off, and that gives you just a glimmer of hope. But then you hear him say, 'Why not? We do this all the time.' After hearing that, your heart instantly drops to the pit of your stomach, but that's still not torture enough. Moments later, you can damn near hear him slurping and sucking all over me. All over your woman's body, and what's hurting you the most is that I sound like I'm actually enjoying it. Enjoying another man's tongue in my most sacred place. You begin shouting to the top of your lungs for the madness to stop, but I can't hear you, so the sex continues. Right in your ear," I said with tears in my eyes. "Now answer your own question. Would you be able to forgive me?" I asked, looking over at him for a response.

After releasing the clench of his jaw, he let out a deep sigh and ran his hands down his face. "Probably not," he confessed low.

"Then please don't ask it of me."

"What if I told I have a sex addiction?" he cut his eyes over and asked.

I let out a snort and rolled my eyes only to look in his face and see that he was actually serious.

"Be for real, Micah. You don't have no damn sex ad-diction. You're just like any other trifling-ass nigga who can't keep his dick in his pants. Just keep it real for once. Please!" I snapped.

"Shit, I don't know if I do, but I've been going to counseling anyway. I've never had a woman as perfect as you are. I've never loved another woman the way I love you, and for me just to fuck it up the way I did . . . there's got to be an explanation," he said more to himself than to me.

"Well, good luck with your counseling," I said with an attitude and rolled my eyes.

All of sudden, he reached over and grabbed my hand. I jerked my arm back out of his hold and looked at him like he was crazy.

"Let me just say this, and then I'll leave," he said, grabbing my hand once more.

"Fine."

"I love you, woman, and whether you believe it or not, you are my wife. I know I fucked up, and I can't just expect you to get over something like that, but I also know you love me too. Shit like that, like love, don't just go away because you mad, shawty," he said, looking deep in my eyes.

A brief moment of silence passed between us as I took in his words. Only the low sounds of Gretchen and tapping beads of sleet could be heard. I could feel our pulse beat in unison from our hands, which were still connected. He gazed into my eyes, waiting for a response, but my guard was still up. I couldn't speak. Then he reached over and gently tucked my hair behind my ear before breaking the silence.

"I'll give you your space, Risa, if that's what you need."

"You broke my fucking heart, Micah," I said with a cracked voiced. Tears suddenly began to flow down my face in abundance, and I was no longer emotionally in control. I had broken all of my rules, and now I was feeling weak all over again.

"Shhh, shh. I know I broke your heart," he confessed just above a whisper. He leaned over and thumbed away the tears from my eyes.

"I was battered and bruised when I met you, Micah. A damn damsel in distress, and I believed, I actually believed, you were my knight in shining armor," I cried.

"So you comparing me to a nigga who put his fucking hands on you," he said, raising his voice.

"I know you won't believe me. Shit, you don't have to believe me, but the pain you caused hurt me so much more than what Zo ever did. I actually loved you."

"Loved me?" he said, wounded by my use of the past tense.

"I just need time," I said again, looking into his dark brown eyes.

"Well, let me just walk you to the door. Please. Just let me get you out of this weather," he said with genuine concern.

I nodded and finished wiping the wetness from my face. He then came around and opened up my door before helping me out of the car. Carefully, we walked hand in hand up to the front door of my dorm. When we reached the lobby, he faced me and grabbed my other hand.

"Do you still love me, Risa?" he asked, now holding both of my hands in his.

I looked away, not wanting him to see the love in my eyes, but he wasn't having it. With the tip of his finger under my chin, he forced my head back to look at him.

"You know I still love you, Micah," I softly admitted. As soon as the words slipped out of my mouth, his lips rushed to kiss me. I didn't want to kiss him back, but the feeling of his soft mouth on mine made me weak. He pulled my body in close and tenderly parted my lips with his tongue. As our kiss deepened, I felt my eyes instinctively close and my knees buckle beneath me. We didn't care about the people coming through the door or watching us from afar. It was like we were the only two people in the room.

"Mmmm," he groaned into my mouth before pulling back. "Damn, I miss you," he said, staring into my eyes.

I bit my bottom lip and savored the sweet taste of his kiss because I knew it would be our last. I raised one of my hands and gently placed it to the side of his cold face before looking deep into his eyes.

"I just need more time," I told him quietly before walking away.

With my back pressed up against the elevator wall, I cursed myself the whole ride up to my room. How could I let him kiss me like that after everything he'd done? I was one weak-ass bitch, I thought. When I opened up my room, I sighed at the many unpacked boxes stacked in every corner. The day after I caught Micah cheating, my sister Raquel, Mama, and Ms. Calisa all went over to his place to get my things. That had been nearly two months ago. Yet I still hadn't found the energy to unpack.

I plopped down on my bed and stared up at the ceiling when, suddenly, I felt my cell phone vibrate. I looked over at the screen to see an unfamiliar number. Typically, I didn't answer calls from numbers I didn't recognize, but a strange feeling overtook me. I got a sense that it was important and that I should answer the call.

"Hello," I said with my eyebrow raised.

"Hi. I'm trying to reach a Risa Brimmage," a sweet voice said.

"This is she," I responded, trying to sound professional. I wasn't sure who was on the other end of the phone.

"Oh, ah, my name is Tisa Carter, and I believe that you may be my sister."

Chapter 4

Damien

On a cold winter's night, I found myself last in line to march up the hill. With a red mask covering my face, I looked up toward the full moon. Thick red gloves covered my fists as I locked my arms around the chest of the brother in front of me. Passing dorm after dorm, eight of us chanted and marched in unison. First, our left foot stomped together, then our right foot together, then our left, and then our right again. We marched still linked as one. I had no idea why, but I was anxious hearing the howling crowd as we approached. When we finally came to a stop, all standing side by side with our fists at our chins and our elbows out wide, I immediately scanned the awaiting crowd. Once I locked eyes with Raina, all of my nerves were instantly put to rest.

After each brother was slowly unveiled, it was finally my turn. The crowd was completely still and quiet. Just a few flashes of light from phones, either taking pictures or recording, could be seen in the darkness. Casually, my DP strolled over to me with a smirk on his face.

"Kolgate," he called out, using my line name. I gave a wide white smile that made all the bitches in the crowd swoon and cheer.

"Yes, Big Brother Kash Money!" I shouted out in response, seeing a frosted fog escape my mouth.

"Unveil yourself," he commanded.

Slowly, I removed the red mask from my face, then hollered out our call. The crowd around us began cheering so loudly that they even drowned out the sounds of me and my brothers. The next thing I heard was Drake, Lil Wayne, and Jeezy's "I'm Goin' In." My brothers and I immediately began moving to the beat. I was rubbing my hands together like I was trying to keep warm and rolling my shoulders like my life depended on it. Seductively, I ground my hips to the music while flicking the tip of my tongue. All the ladies went wild. That shit was an instant panty dropper because bitches were automatically assuming "what dat mouf do." Neither Micah, Dre, nor Melo danced or stepped, but I was a different breed of frat. I was a nasty li'l nigga and proud of it.

After the song was over, we strolled to the top of the hill, calling and chanting every step of the way. The probate show was finally over, so I rushed to go find Raina. That was my baby, and I was doing everything in my power to do right by her these days. I found her among the crowd standing with Raquel. Both sets of light eyes sparkled from the streetlights. Raina had on a white pea coat with a fuzzy white winter hat. Her long, pretty hair clung to the sides of her face, which was flushed from the cold. I rushed over to her and planted a long, deep kiss on her lips. Instantly, she grabbed the sides of my face and kissed me right back.

"Congratulations, babe," she squealed, pulling back with a big smile on her face.

"Thanks, beautiful. I'm glad you could make it."

"Of course. I wouldn't have missed it for the world," she said with her arms still wrapped around me.

The next thing I heard was Tina's annoying voice coming from behind me. "Congratulations, Dame," she said, reaching out for a hug.

I looked at her with a scowl on my face, then turned my attention back to Raina. I hadn't fucked Tina since the night Raina told me she was going to the homecoming dance with that fuck nigga, Codi. Just the thought of some other nigga cuffing Raina set my ass straight for good. Sure, I was backed up than a motherfucker not getting any pussy because she was a virgin, and crossing over wasn't going to make being faithful any easier, but I was determined to be a good boyfriend.

"Damn, it's like that?" Tina snapped.

"Yeah, shawty, it's like that," I coolly responded without even turning her way.

"Well, let me leave you to your high school romance," she said, snickering with her girls before walking off.

I shook my head at how petty she was. Then I looked down at Raina. She still had a bright smile plastered on her beautiful face, as though what Tina just said hadn't fazed her one bit. Every time I was around this girl, she amazed me. She made me feel like the luckiest guy in the world.

"Congrats, Dame," her sister Raquel said before giving me a hug.

"'Preciate it, sis."

I noticed that she kept staring across the yard with her face all scrunched up. I looked over and saw my brothers, Micah, Dre, and Melo, walking over toward us. Although Melo was technically our first cousin, we all considered him our brother since Mom and Pops raised him. When they saw me, they began making our sign with their hands in the air and shouting out our call. Melo then draped his arm over some pretty, light-skinned girl's shoulders. He was whispering in her ear and kissing the side of her cheek, causing her to laugh and blush. I didn't recognize her, but Melo pretty much had a different girl for every day of the week, so I wasn't surprised.

"What's up, li'l nigga? Congrats!" Micah said, dapping me up before bringing me in for a half hug.

"Thanks, big bro," I said before dapping up Dre and Melo.

I didn't know what was going on with Raquel, but she kept on clearing her throat and staring at Melo like he had two heads or something. Melo just acted like he didn't even see her ass. After hitting both her and Raina with a head nod, he kept whispering in ol' girl's ear. I didn't know what was up with them and why they were acting so weird.

"Where Risa at?" I asked Micah about Raina's oldest sister, his ex-girl.

"You got jokes, I see. You know she's not fucking with me like that no more," he said with a look of grief written on his face.

"Yo, why I gotta suffer just 'cause she not dealing wit'chu no more?" I half joked.

"Risa said that she had some studying to catch up on, but she wanted me to congratulate you, babe," Raina explained.

"Yeah, studying. I'm sure," Micah muttered sarcastically, shaking his head.

"Where the after-party at?" Dre cut in.

"Club Nixx. We got VIP," I told them.

"A'ight then, we'll meet y'all over there," he said before dapping me up. He and my brothers walked away, leaving me, Raina, and Raquel standing by ourselves.

"Oooh! I can't stand him," Raquel mumbled.

"Who? Melo?" I knowingly asked.

"It doesn't matter. Anyway, is Raina going to be able to get in since she doesn't have a college ID?" Raquel asked, changing the subject.

"It's already taken care of, shawty," I told her with a wink and a smile.

Later that night in my dorm room, I looked myself over in the floor-length mirror. I gave myself a wink and a smile of approval. I was dressed in a black leather motorcycle jacket and slim black Balmain jeans that were ripped at the knee. I wore a red Balmain T-shirt, and on my feet were bright red Balmain sneakers that were accented in gold. I rocked diamond stud earrings in both my ears and a thin gold chain around my neck. As always, my coal black wavy hair had just been freshly cut. I blew a kiss to myself in the mirror one more time before heading out the door.

When I finally reached the club with my line brothers later that night, the place was packed from wall to wall. We all rushed upstairs, eager to get into VIP, which was filled with smoke. The club owner had reserved the entire top floor just for my fraternity. Every table was stocked with three bottles and six shot glasses. There was one bottle of Patrón, one bottle of Henny, and the last, Cîroc.

Smiling, I leaned over the rail to take in the view of the partygoers dancing below. I kept looking in the crowd and at the door, hoping to see Raina or my brothers, but I didn't see any of them yet. All of a sudden, the DJ blared Kirko Bangz's "What Yo Name Iz?" and the crowd went wild. My line brothers and I immediately went into seduction mode. We put one leg up on the rail and began grinding our pelvises like dogs in heat. The ladies below looked up at us like we were gods while screaming and shouting our names.

When the beat dropped, we put our legs back down to the ground and began rolling our shoulders in unison like one big-ass sexy snake. I was going hard and singing them lyrics like I was that nigga Kirko Bangz himself.

> *All I wanna know girl what yo name iz*
> *I see them other niggas they be on that lame shit*
> *And I can take care of you and them girls you came with*
> *But first you gotta tell me what yo fuckin' name iz*

When the song finally went off, I spotted Micah, Melo, and Dre walking into VIP, dressed in all red from head to toe. Melo had the same light-skinned, pretty chick from the probate show on his arm, while Micah and Dre looked to be rolling solo. They dapped up several frat brothers before making their way over to me. After slapping hands and giving half hugs, we decided to take a couple rounds of shots.

"Toast to my li'l bruh. You one of the big dogs now," Dre said before we shouted out our fraternity call and downed our shots of Hennessy.

After taking one more shot, I looked back down in the crowd and saw Raina and Raquel walking in. My jaw instantly dropped at the sight of Raina. She was stunning with her long hair pinned around, curls cascading down the side of her pretty face. She wore a simple white halter minidress with white thigh-high leather boots. I didn't like the fact that her entire back was exposed or that she was showing that much of her thighs, but this was her first college party, so I knew she was trying to get her grown and sexy on. I couldn't be mad at her even if I tried.

Besides, her outfit didn't have shit on Raquel's. I had never seen Raquel look as sexy as she looked tonight. Her soft brown hair was styled in big, bold curls, and she wore a tight-fitting black cat suit that was sheer at the top. The only thing covering her apple-sized breasts was a black built-in bra with no back. I had to admit that her size-four shape looked like perfection that night. Black high-heeled pumps, simple gold jewelry, and red lipstick complemented her sexy style.

All eyes were on the girls as they made their way up to VIP. I immediately went over to get Raina before they could even cross the threshold. I knew I couldn't stop other niggas from looking at her, but I wanted to be at her side when they did. Her eyes lit up at the sight of me right before I grabbed her hand. Raquel followed close behind her as we headed over to my table, which was surrounded by my line brothers, along with Micah, Melo, and Dre. The girls both gave Micah and Dre a hug, and like always, Melo greeted them both with a simple nod of his head. He was laid in the cut with the same pretty, light-skinned girl.

"Ay, y'all, this my baby Raina right here," I proudly introduced her to my line brothers.

"Damn," Deon mumbled under his breath.

"My baby beautiful, ain't she?" I bragged, leaning over to plant a kiss on her neck. They all nodded in agreement before shaking her hand.

"Beautiful. You definitely are that," Deon said before kissing the back of her hand.

"Bruh. Really!" I said before giving him a look.

"My bad," he said with a laugh as his hands went up in surrender. "Yo, you got a sister, shawty?"

"That's one of her sisters right here," I said, pointing to Raquel, who was now just a couple feet away, looking over the rail.

"Damn, fa real?" Deon asked, eyeing Raquel from head to toe. I could tell that he was getting in mack mode from the way he licked his lips and rubbed his hands together.

"Yo, Raquel! Raquel!" I hollered out so that she could hear me over the music. She turned around with her eyebrows together and hazel eyes glowing in the dimly lit club. Raina and I both waved her over to where we were.

"What's up?" she quizzed.

"This is one of my line brothers, Deon. He wanted to meet you," I said.

They shook hands and immediately started talking. I didn't know if Deon's game was just that strong or what, but minutes later, Raquel was laughing at every other word this nigga was saying. I'm talking throwing her head back and exposing all thirty-two teeth kind of laughing. Raquel was mean as fuck, so I wasn't exactly sure what had gotten into her that night. She was definitely acting out of character. I glanced over and noticed that she had even allowed him to whisper in her ear while holding the small of her back.

Shortly after Deon and Raquel had gotten acquainted, Melo and his friend stood up and moved over closer to where we were. He had his arm wrapped around her tiny waist, and an unusual look was on his face. His eyes were cold like he was pissed, yet he was smirking like something was funny. I couldn't read him to save my life.

"We heading out," he said before dapping me up.

"A'ight, be safe. Thanks for coming through," I told him. He leaned over and gave Raina a hug, then stared at Raquel as she stood awkwardly next to Deon. He licked his lips and bit down on his bottom lip before smirking again.

"Come on, shawty. You got a lot of work to do," he told the light-skinned girl, but his eyes remained on Raquel. I didn't know what was going on with those two, but whatever it was, I knew it would soon come to light.

Chapter 5

Raquel

I was flirting with this Deon guy something heavy, hoping to make Melo jealous, but he actually seemed to be completely unmoved by the whole charade. In fact, the only thing that seemed to be getting his attention was the girl he had been parading around with all day. As soon as Melo left the club with that girl in tow, I could no longer concentrate on what the stupid guy in my face was even talking about. All I kept thinking was that Melo was taking her back home to have his way with her. The way I loved him to have his way with me.

"Ugh! Stop talking to me. Please!" I snapped at the idiot in my face, pinching the bridge of my nose. Deon's hot breath smelled awful, like a rank bag of Cheetos, and I just couldn't take it anymore.

I could tell he was caught off guard by my actions because he immediately jerked his neck back as if to say, "The fuck?" I didn't care, though. I immediately walked away from him and went right over to where Raina and Damien were now sitting. They were all hugged up and cozy on one of the white sofas nearby.

"Look, I gotta get out of here. Can you take care of Raina tonight?" I asked, looking directly at Damien.

"Uh, excuse me," Raina said with her hand raised. "You act like I'm not sitting right here. Where are you going?" she asked with an irritated look on her face.

"I just gotta get out of here, but here, take the keys to my dorm room," I said, digging into my clutch purse with trembling hands.

"Nah, she gon' stay with me tonight. I got her," Damien assured me.

I hugged my sister goodbye before rushing out of the club. As soon as I slid into my BMW and cranked up the engine, my lead foot was heavy on the gas. I knew Melo was only trying to prove a point, but I didn't think he'd take it so far as to actually sleep with another girl. Just the thought of him touching and kissing her the way he did me made we want to scream.

"Shit! Come on, come on," I muttered while tapping my fingernails against the steering wheel. I was at a red light and growing impatient. It seemed like I was getting stopped by every damn traffic light on the way, and my nerves were at an all-time high. I didn't know what I'd say or do when I got there, but I had to stop Melo or at least try.

When I finally turned down his street, I could see his lone car parked in the driveway. Instantly, my heart began to pick up speed. I was nervous because I didn't know if my heart could take him sleeping with another woman. Sure, I played all big and bad, but underneath it all, I was just as sensitive as the next female. Thus the reason I didn't want a commitment in the first place. I didn't do well dealing with my girly emotions.

Quickly, I reduced my speed so that I could get myself together. From a distance, it probably looked like I was creeping up to do a drive-by shooting in the night. When I finally pulled up, I could see that all of the lights were out in the house, all except the porch light and the TV glow from his bedroom window. I instantly killed the engine and took a slow, deep breath.

"Shit!" I muttered before getting out of the car and entering the cold. I was so nervous that not only were my hands trembling, but my stomach was starting to churn.

With my arms wrapped tightly around my chest for warmth, I made my way up the stairs of his frat house. Hearing a car ride by, I instinctively looked back just before turning around to ring the doorbell. Before I could even press the button, I heard noises coming from behind the door.

"Um, yasss!" I heard her softly moan. "Harder, harder!" she yelled out seductively.

I was crushed when I heard them having sex. My heart began to race, and I began to feel sick to my stomach, but I knew I wasn't leaving without a fight. Without him at least acknowledging my presence. I began banging wildly on the door and screaming at the top of my lungs. "Melooo!"

"Ooh, right there, Daddy," she moaned again.

I banged harder on the door, kicking and hitting with everything I had in me. "Open up this fucking door, Melo! Right now!" I shouted. "Melooo!"

I could hear their sex getting louder and louder, so I quickly thought about the jack in my car. Without a second thought, I rushed down and grabbed it out of my trunk. By this time, I was shaking like a leaf from all the rage I had inside. Instead of being cold from the thirty-six-degree weather we had that night, my body was now literally hot from head to toe. I was beyond furious but more so hurt by it all. Before I knew it, I was back at the top of the porch, using the jack in my hand to crash against the door.

"Open up this fucking door, Melooo!" I wailed one more time. Still, there was no answer. Only the loud, satisfied moans of this girl could be heard. Hearing her enjoy him the way I did made me instantly lose it. Without even thinking, I tossed the jack into the living room window, causing the glass to shatter.

Crashhh!

My unsteady hands quickly covered my mouth in shock of what I had just done. Then I looked up and saw Melo standing in the doorway laughing. I could still hear the sexy moans of the girl, but he was standing right in front of me, fully dressed. I looked down in his hand and saw that his iPad screen had porn on it. That's when I realized where the moans were coming from.

"Yo, you crazy as shit, girl," he said with a stupid grin on his face.

I couldn't even respond. Out of nowhere, I ran up to him and started wildly punching him in the chest. My face was suddenly covered in tears from all the emotions I had been trying to suppress.

"Why would you do that?" I cried, still trying to hit him.

He roughly pinned my arms down so that I could no longer fight, before pulling me into the house. "Calm yo crazy ass down, girl!" he barked with a scowl on his face. Melo didn't talk, yell, laugh, or even smile very much for that matter. However, right now, those were all of the things I brought out of him. He suddenly looked me in my face and realized that I was crying. His eyes quickly softened before he pulled me in close for a tight embrace.

"Fuck you crying for, shawty?" he whispered against my ear.

"Why would you do that?" I asked weakly, feeling his face pressed against my cheek.

He pulled back from me so that he could look me in the eyes before taking both of my hands into his. I watched his mind turn and wonder as his stance widened before me. He ran his tongue across his bottom lip, pulling it in between his teeth. His hazel eyes intently stared back into mine as he tried to find his voice. In the background, more sounds of porn could be heard coming from up the stairs.

"Look, I ain't never had a girlfriend before, but that's some shit I'm trying to do with you. You and I been kicking it pretty heavy these past few months, and I'm feeling you, shawty. I'm done playing games. Now either you in this with me or you not. If you not, then you can't be mad at me for fucking other broads."

I knew he was right, but I couldn't find the words to tell him so. All of a sudden, my voice was caught beneath the lump that had formed in my throat. Instead of saying anything, I stepped up and planted a deep kiss on his lips. His hands instinctively wrapped around me and slid down to my ass for a tight squeeze.

"Mmmm," he groaned into my mouth.

The whole way up the stairs, we continued to kiss while undressing one another. When we finally reached his bedroom, he kicked the door closed behind us before tossing me down to the bed. Lying back, I eagerly panted, watching as he pulled the white T-shirt over his head and quickly kicked the shoes off his feet. I took in his smooth caramel build, which was decorated in lean muscle and violent ink, before cutting off the TV. Yup, this slick-ass nigga had porn not only on his iPad but also on his TV, blaring it though his surround sound. The only source of light was now the small rays of streetlight shining through his bedroom window.

Within what felt like seconds, we were downright out of our clothes, and I was lying on my back with my feet in the air. Slowly, I could feel him entering me. His big, strong hands slithered up my thighs to tightly grip my waist just before he filled me up completely. I watched as he closed his eyes and bit down on his bottom lip from the pleasure he felt. Gradually, his hands slid up until they finally reached the sides of my face. He tenderly pressed his lips against mine while continuing to work his way in and out of me. In that moment, my entire being had been overtaken by his touch.

"Mmm," I moaned.

"Are you mine?" he whispered into my mouth.

I nodded as tears trickled down into my hair.

"Nah, lemme hear you say that shit. Are you mine?" His voice was low yet commanding.

"Yes, Melo. I'm yours," I finally admitted, wrapping my legs completely around him for a deeper connection.

Chapter 6

Micah

"Man, this some ol' high school shit," I told Timo while lighting up a blunt.

It was eight o'clock on a Saturday night when I found myself riding in the passenger seat of my best friend's Maserati. We were on our way to meet up with some girl he had met at the mall a few weeks ago. She didn't want to go out on a date with him alone, so she asked if she could bring a friend along. Timo agreed and, of course, asked me to be his wingman. I really didn't want to go, but lately, I had been so depressed without Risa. I allowed him to convince me to go just so I could get out of the house.

"Mane, it's gon' be straight, you'll see. Shawty said her girl is brown skinned with long hair. Slim with a fat ass, just like you like," he said, trying to gas me up.

"Bruh, I don't care what she looks like. I told you once before, unless her name is Risa Brimmage, I'm not interested," I declared before taking a pull on my blunt.

"Man, fuck that bitch," Timo snapped. He was still pissed about Risa knowing that his brother, Zo, had been killed. She didn't let him or anyone else know about it when she found him dead, and because of that, he wasn't fucking with her. Truthfully, I should have been mad at her for lying to me about it too. However, had I known the nigga was putting his hands on her, I would have pulled the trigger my damn self.

"Yo, you got one more time to call her a bitch before I fuck your ass up," I spat with smoke escaping my mouth. He glanced over at me on some playful shit, but after seeing my serious expression, he removed the smirk from his face.

When we finally pulled up to Maggianos, the place was packed. After getting valet parking, we made our way inside and headed to the front of the line. Timo gave the hostess our names, and since we had reservations, we didn't have to wait. We followed her as she led us to a nice, quiet table in the back. The place was dim with candles flickering throughout, giving the venue a romantic vibe. After we took our seats, I immediately grabbed the drink menu.

"Damn, you ain't gon' wait for them?" Timo asked.

"Nah, man, I don't know them girls. Shit, I need me a drink now. What's this girl's name anyway?" I asked, flipping through the menu.

"The girl I met at the mall is Bri. I don't know what her homegirl's name is, though."

After ordering a Hennessy and Coke, Timo and I chopped up it for about another ten minutes before he suddenly stood up from his seat. I looked toward the front of the restaurant, following his eyes. They immediately fell on a short, pretty, light-skinned girl with a purple bob cut. After dating Risa for about nine months, I recognized her friend Sabrina instantly. Once her eyes met Timo's, she looked behind her and waved for someone to follow. That's when Risa appeared.

She was dressed casually but sexy in a cream off-the-shoulder sweater dress. As she sashayed toward us, I noticed the tan peep-toe booties on her feet. I had just bought her those for Christmas, right before she walked out of my fucking life. Her silky hair was pulled up in a big bun, exposing her long neck, and her makeup was light and pink. For me, Risa was the epitome of beauty.

When she finally saw me, her eyes grew wide, and a frown was instantly etched onto her pretty face. However, I was sure her expression was no match for mine because I was beyond pissed. Before she could even reach the table, I went over and grabbed her by the arm.

"The fuck is you doing here?" I snapped with a firm grip.

"I guess the same thing as you. Now get your hands off me, Micah," she said, snatching herself away.

After rolling her eyes, she walked over to the table and quietly sat down. I wiped my hand down my face and let out a sigh of frustration before going over and joining them. Timo had an instant scowl on his face, so I knew he felt some type of way about seeing Risa. She gave him an apologetic look, but he wouldn't even look her in the eyes.

"Wow! So, this one crazy-ass coincidence, right? I didn't know that you were Zo's brother until Risa just told me," Sabrina explained, trying to address the elephant in the room.

"Look, Timo, I'm sorry for not calling you when I found Zo. For whatever it's worth, I truly hope they catch whoever did this to him. Is there any way that you can ever forgive me and we just move past this?" Risa cut in.

Timo cut his eyes at Risa and tightened his jaw. I guessed he wasn't ready to forgive and forget just yet, so he didn't say shit.

"And you! Don't be trying to set my girl up with no niggas, Sabrina. I'm dead ass," I stated, pointing my finger before taking a sip of my drink. I had to cut in to ease the awkwardness between Risa and Timo.

"It wasn't a hookup, Micah. I just wanted her to get out of the house and have some fun for a change. Damn!" she tried to explain with a roll of her eyes.

"Yeah, whatever. You heard what the fuck I said."

"Why are you even explaining yourself to this . . . this two-timing, lying, cheating, dirty-ass dog? We are not together, which means I'm free to get set up with anyone I want," Risa spat with her arms folded across her chest. Although she was sitting next to me, she sat at an angle in the chair so that her back was somewhat facing me. She was talking to Sabrina as if I weren't even in the room.

"Look, shawty, I'm not here to counsel these niggas. I'm here trying to see what's up with you and your pretty ass," Timo smoothly said to Sabrina, scooting in close before putting his arm around the back of her chair.

She smiled and blushed at his gesture. Timo always did have a way with the ladies. He was a light-skinned nigga with freckles covering his face. He had one lone dimple embedded in his left cheek, giving him the face of a baby. Growing up, all the girls loved his yellow ass, and from what I could tell, they still did. Being in the drug game, Timo never committed to just one woman, though. At 26 years old, he had two baby mamas, a main chick, and a side piece. And now that he was sitting here with Sabrina's wild ass, I was curious to see how things were going to play out.

"What are you ordering?" I leaned over and asked Risa.

She ignored me and kept flipping through her menu. Sabrina took notice and let out a faint snort of laughter.

"I'm getting the lobster fettuccine," Sabrina said.

"Well, I'm more of a ste—"

"Steak man. Yeah, yeah, we know, Micah," Risa muttered, finishing my sentence with an attitude.

I was getting ready to fuck her little ass up for having such a smart-ass mouth, but I knew she was still hurting, so I gave her a pass. After ordering our meals, the girls decided to also order a bottle of wine. By the time our dinner came out, Risa had already drunk two large glasses. I could tell that she was tipsy and loosening up a bit because she would occasionally talk to me. A few times throughout dinner, she even tapped me on the shoulder in a playful manner while laughing.

"Y'all ready to get out of here?" Timo asked, laying three crisp $100 bills on the table.

"Yeah, I'm ready," Risa said, attempting to stand up. As soon as she rose, she stumbled and fell back down into her seat.

"Nah, lightweight. You ain't driving nowhere tonight," I told her.

With her eyes barely open, she smiled at me, exposing the deep dimples in her cheeks. "Aw, look at my Micah Poo being all concerned about his wifey," she slurred. She was definitely drunk.

"Leave their car here, and we'll just drop them back off at the dorms," I told Timo.

"I don't want to go back there. I wanna go home to our place, Micah Poo," Risa drunkenly whined with her head now resting on my chest.

If a drunk man tells no tales, everything Risa was saying was true. However, being that I knew for a fact she wasn't sober made me cast all hopeful thoughts aside. After getting the girls in the car, Timo drove back toward campus so that we could drop them off. Sabrina rode up front in the passenger seat, while Risa rode in the back with me.

"Noo! I told you, I don't want to go back to that dump," Risa said. She was trying to sit up straight, but she was so drunk that she kept on leaning on me.

"Where do you want me to take you, then?" Timo asked. He had eased up on Risa a little throughout the course of dinner, and for now they appeared to be at least on speaking terms.

"I wanna go home," she whispered with a lazy smile.

"Yo, I'm not driving all the way back to Greensboro tonight, shawty," he said, looking at her through the rearview mirror.

"Bae, tell him to take us home," she slurred, rubbing her hand between my thighs.

"Yo, chill," I told her, removing her hand from my dick.

For the next minute or so, we kept going back and forth with her trying to grab my junk and me slapping her hand away. I finally had to pin her hands down just so she would stop. All of a sudden, she swung her leg over to straddle my lap in the back seat.

"Fuck is you doing, shawty?" I asked with a confused look on my face. I knew Risa was drunk, but if she didn't stop, I'd have to put something hard in her.

"Take me home and make love to me, Micah Poo," she whined with her eyes barely open. I was about to respond when, all of a sudden, an unexpected burp darted from her lips. When the faint stench hit my nose, I just looked at her with my head cocked to the side like, "The fuck was that?" She quickly covered her mouth in shame before both she and Sabrina fell into a fit of drunken laughter. Again, her deep dimples pierced the sides of her face. I could only chuckle my damn self, loving every inch of her amusing expression.

"Look! Where we going?" Timo impatiently asked from the front. He didn't find shit funny.

"Just drop me off at home, and I'll take her with me," I finally told him.

When we finally pulled up to my condo downtown, I literally had to pick her up bridal style and carry her inside. Her drunken limbs floppily dangled in my arms until I finally stood her up. The elevator ride up to the top floor was a long one because she kept on trying to kiss and rub all over me. Of course, I liked it, but at the same time, I wanted her to be sober while doing it. I wanted her to truly forgive me so I could fuck her senseless like I used to.

After entering my condo, I picked her up again and took her down the hall to my bedroom. She was half asleep by the time I gently placed her on my king-sized bed and stripped her out of her clothes. Once she was in nothing but her white lace bra and panties, I looked her body over and bit down on my bottom lip. I had to admit that Risa was sexy as hell. Her naturally perfect breasts sat up like implants even when she was lying on her back. My mouth began to water, and my dick instantly jumped as I admired her smooth dark brown skin. Without even thinking, I leaned down and planted a soft, wet kiss to her stomach. I French kissed all the way down to her navel, causing her eyes to flutter open and quiet moans to seep from her lips.

"Mmm, Micah, that feels so good," she whined.

I took it a step further and hooked my fingers underneath the waist of her panties before sliding them all the way down. As I held the lace thong underwear in my hands, I grew a little pissed looking at them. I hated that of all the underwear she had to choose from, she chose to wear these to go out on a date with a nigga she didn't even know. When I took her out on our first date, she wore some old, ugly cotton bloomers that completely covered her ass. Jealousy and rage instantly consumed me as the thought of her wearing sexy underwear for another nigga entered my mind. But when I glanced back down at her bald awaiting mound that was glistening from front to back, I immediately pushed all my anger aside. I gently lifted her ankle and began sliding the tip of my tongue all the way down her leg. Slowly, I twirled my tongue between the flesh of her thighs, causing her to shiver. I kissed all the way down until my mouth finally reached her pearl.

"Ahh! Mmm," she moaned again with her hands planted to the back of my head.

She was damn near pushing me up inside of her, but I wasn't complaining. Hearing that I could still please her made me instantly brick up. In fact, there was nothing I wanted more in that moment than to be inside of her. Firmly, I cupped her ass with the palms of my hands and began flicking my tongue faster against her. Her body immediately responded, and she began grinding her hips wildly against my face. Her moans grew louder and louder until she finally released, shuddering and trembling in my hold.

As I placed soft kisses to her inner thighs, I could suddenly hear her moans turning more into what sounded like whimpers. I looked up and saw that she was now crying with her hands shielding her face. Instantly, I felt like shit for taking it there with her when I knew for a fact she wasn't ready. I got up and gently pulled the covers over her half-naked body before kissing her on the forehead and quietly leaving the room.

Chapter 7

Romi

"Arrghh!" Grandma Lisa Mae screamed, tossing her Belk bag in the air.

"What's wrong, Mawmaw?" I rushed around the make-up counter and asked.

"I looked at my own damn reflection in this mirror. Literally scared the shit out of myself," she explained, clutching her chest.

"Mawmaw, you crazy. I thought something was really wrong with you."

"Something is really wrong. Shoot! You see all these bags and wrinkles on my face? Pores the size of potholes in Philly, chile," she said. My grandmother was a pure mess. I couldn't do anything but laugh at her.

Grandma Lisa Mae, my mother, Ms. Calisa, and I were all taking another walk through the mall trying to get this baby to drop when we made a quick detour into one of the department stores. While my mother and Ms. Calisa were looking at jewelry, Grandma and I were over at the MAC counter. I was beyond busted looking at this point. My light face was so swollen that it looked like it would burst from just the softest touch. My neck was even starting to have rolls in it, and my big, heavy belly hung so low that I literally had to hold the bottom when I walked. My pregnancy glow was now long gone, and at this point, I would have done anything to go into labor.

"You ready?" the makeup lady asked from behind the counter.

"Yes, ma'am," I replied before sitting up on the stool for her to do my makeup. Ever since I ran into Dre that day in the mall, I refused to walk around barefaced without my hair done. Sure, I was fat, swollen, and miserable, but I could still do my hair and makeup.

Grandma watched intently as the lady beat my face. "Damn. That looks good. You gon' have to hook me up after she's done," she told the makeup lady.

"Yes, ma'am. I'd be happy to do your makeup for you."

"You sure? I know I'm old and ugly now, but I used to look just like Vanessa Williams back in my day."

"You still are beautiful, Mawmaw," I told her truthfully with my eyes closed. The lady was now applying my eye shadow, so I was trying to keep completely still.

"Uh hmm. Tell me anything, chile," she replied, causing me and the makeup lady to laugh. Grandma knew that, even at 68 years old, she was still gorgeous. She simply fished for compliments because she liked it when someone would tell her how good she looked for her age.

After the lady applied a simple coat of pink lipstick to my lips, I pressed my lips together and gave my face a final glance in the mirror. I smiled because it was the most beautiful I had felt in a really long time. Both Grandma Lisa and the makeup lady admired my beauty from behind, giving me an added dose of confidence. After pushing the mirror back farther onto the counter, I hopped down slowly from the stool and grabbed the bottom of my belly for good measure. That's when I heard water splashing onto the floor. Quickly, I looked down at my pants and shoes, which were drenched, and I realized my water had just broken.

"Oh shit. I think my water just broke," I mumbled in disbelief.

"Lord Jesus!" Grandma Lisa Mae threw her hands up and said.

"Tell my mom and Ms. Calisa that we gotta go," I told her. I was expecting to be in pain when my water broke, but surprisingly, I wasn't.

"Ernie! Calisa! Come now, we gotta go!" she hollered out loudly in a panic. I was so embarrassed because the strangers walking by immediately turned around to stare at me. My grandmother was so loud that my mother and Ms. Calisa actually heard her, and they were at least twenty yards away.

They both rushed over to where we were and checked to make sure I was okay. Although I still wasn't feeling any contractions, I knew I had to go to the hospital. With one arm over my mother's shoulder and the other over Ms. Calisa's, I began wobbling out of the store. All of a sudden, my mother stopped walking, huffed, and turned around.

"Ma, come on! We gotta get her to the hospital now," she said.

"Damn it! Y'all just want me walking around here looking like the walking dead, don't you? Romi knew I was getting ready to get my makeup done, and now that she's looking all pretty and got her makeup done and shit, she hollerin' 'bout her water broke," she fussed.

"Come on here, Lisa Mae," I sassed back and said.

"Don't get cute, li'l girl! Remember, you and yo' mama gon' look just like this one day," she said, following.

After arriving at the hospital and being admitted, I quickly learned that I was already seven centimeters dilated. Painful contractions were now hitting back-to-back, and it was too late for an epidural. I wailed out in agony because the contractions were coming less than two minutes apart. My whole body was trembling from the pain, and my face was now covered in tears.

"Aarrghh!" I screamed, holding my mother's hand.

"Let me check her again," the midwife nurse said before pulling up the thin white sheet that was covering my lower half.

With latex gloves on her hands, she carefully reached inside my womb. I tilted my head down a little, careful not to push so that I could see exactly what she was doing. A sudden smile spread across her face, and a tinge of excitement filled her eyes. She pulled her hand out of me and quickly threw the bloody gloves in the trash. The room fell silent as we waited for her to speak. Only the fast beeping sounds of my baby boy's heart on the monitor could be heard.

"It's time to push," she said excitedly.

Ms. Calisa began lifting one of my legs while my mother lifted the other. They left Grandma Lisa Mae in the waiting room and told her to call my father and sisters. Closing my eyes, I took a few deep breaths to prepare for the agony I was getting ready to experience. I had taken a birthing class and watched a few videos of women giving birth, so I had an inkling of what I was in for.

"The next time you feel a contraction, I want you to push like you're trying to make a bowel movement," my midwife instructed.

I nodded my head, and no more than five seconds later, I felt a strong contraction. With all my might, I pushed down like she told me to. Feeling every muscle tear, tug, and pull open below, I squeezed both my mother's and Ms. Calisa's hands. I released the deep breath I had been holding before finally yelping out in pain.

"Ahhh!" I wailed, panting to catch my breath.

"That was a good one, Romi. Give me another one just like that," my midwife said.

Again, when the next contraction approached, they all encouraged me to push down hard. On the count of three, I sat up and bore down with my chin to my chest. With my teeth gritted tightly together, I strained, feeling that burning rip. The beads of sweat that were lining the edges of my face were starting to trickle down.

"Fuucckk!" I let out.

After only two pushes, I was beyond tired. My weak body was quivering, and I was starting to get discouraged. With chattering teeth, I let my head fall back onto the pillow and allowed my arms and legs to go completely limp.

"You can do this, baby," my mother said, pressing a cool cloth to my forehead.

"The baby is already crowning, Romi. I need one, maybe two more pushes," my midwife coached.

I looked up into my mother's smiling green eyes as she nodded her head in agreement. With the last bit of energy I had left, I leaned up, feeling that next contraction hit. My weak hands firmly gripped the backs of my legs as I clenched my jaws down tight. I gave one final push that felt like I was damn near splitting myself in half. That's when I heard his cry. It was faint yet strong, small but loud, all at the same time.

"Meet your son, Romi," my midwife said, placing his tiny body into my feeble arms.

I looked down into his perfect little face and instantly cried. My son was the mirror image of Dre Borrego, with the exception of his sparkling green eyes. His skin was already brown, and he had a tiny little beauty mark that could be seen underneath his left eye. Even through the tears, I smiled, thinking about the family marking that Ms. Calisa, Micah, Zaria, and now my baby all shared.

"Romi, please don't tell me—" Ms. Calisa started to say before covering her mouth in shock. She just stared into my son's face, shaking her head in disbelief.

"Ms. Calisa, please don't tell him," I said just above a whisper. Tears cascaded heavily down my cheeks.

She peered down at me with a look of disgust before grabbing her cell phone out of her purse and walking out of the room. My mother simply gave me a comforting look that told me everything would be okay. Clutching my baby a little tighter in my arms, I took in his scent one more time before passing him back to the nurse. No more than ten minutes after the baby's Apgar test, I heard a familiar deep voice entering the room.

"Is that my son?" Charles immediately asked without so much as a hello. As a matter of fact, he didn't even look at me. His eyes were merely examining every inch of my baby from across the room.

I hadn't seen Charles since my daddy beat his ass. Since then, it looked as if he'd aged another ten years. Worry lines were ingrained in his forehead, and deep creases framed the sides of his mouth. His dark chocolate skin was now ashen and gray, and his overgrown beard was unkempt. I guessed he had really been going through it these past few months.

Instead of answering his question, I hung my head down low in shame and covered my face with the palms of my hands. I just wanted this whole nightmare to be over and to be able to raise my child in peace. Suddenly, I felt my mother's hand on my shoulder. When I wouldn't look at her, she lifted my face with her hand.

"Tell this man the truth so he can leave. I don't need your daddy to come in here and whoop his ass again," she said, rolling her eyes.

"He's not your baby, Charles. I got a DNA test a couple months ago," I confessed.

He swallowed hard before tucking his hands into the pockets of his dress pants. A hint of relief spread across his face before he started for the door. I guessed there were no words left to share between the two of us. But before he could even make it out, Dre and Ms. Calisa walked in. Out of nowhere, Dre shoved Charles hard in the chest, causing me to shoot straight up in my bed.

"Dre, he knows that the baby's not his. Just let him go!" I shouted.

Ms. Calisa immediately got in between the two of them and firmly placed each of her hands on their chests. With their fists balled tightly at their sides and their jaws clenched, they both stood staring each other down like they were ready for war. They stayed like that for what seemed like forever, a silent fight between the male egos. Then, after a few moments of intensity had passed, I could see a devilish grin spread across Charles's face, showing that chipped tooth that I used to find so sexy. He glanced back at me for what I knew would be the last time before holding his hands up in surrender and walking out the door.

"Where's my son?" Dre barked, cutting his eyes over at me. His voice was harsh as he glared at me with cold eyes. He had one hand holding his motorcycle helmet at his side while the other was still balled in an angry fist.

I pointed toward my baby boy, who was now sleeping peacefully in the bassinet. Dre looked over at him, and his eyes instantly softened. I was waiting for him to walk over to see his son, but it was like his feet were planted in concrete and he just couldn't move. His hesitant face told a story of fear, love, and excitement all wrapped in one.

"Well? What are you waiting on, Dre?" Ms. Calisa asked, placing her hand on his shoulder.

I watched him take in a long, deep breath before making his way over. When he finally came near, he looked down at our baby boy, taking in his every feature. I could see him counting every finger and toe as he peered down with a closed-lip smile. His fingertips cautiously held the edges of the bassinet, almost like he was too afraid to touch him.

"Wash your hands and hold your son, Dre," Ms. Calisa told him.

He nodded his head before placing his helmet in the chair and going over to wash his hands. When she carefully placed him in his arms, I could instantly feel his nerves. Dre awkwardly held him in his arms, trying to get into a natural position, when our baby suddenly began to cry. Dre looked back at me with his shoulders awkwardly hunched and his brows raised.

"I don't know what I'm doing," he panicked.

"Here, bring him to me," I said.

Once he passed the baby to me, I opened up the front of my hospital gown and immediately began to nurse him like I'd been taught. Dre watched intently as the baby hungrily took my breast into his mouth. I merely stared down into his little angelic face, relishing the warmth and closeness of his touch. This was the happiest I had felt in a really long time.

"Well, at least now I know it wasn't me," Dre halfheartedly joked, gripping the back of his neck with his hand.

I looked up at him and smiled before he sat next to me on the bed, carrying a blended scent of winter and genuine leather.

"You two need some time alone with the baby," my mother quietly said before pulling Ms. Calisa out of the room with her.

"So," I said with my mouth twisted to the side. I was avoiding eye contact partly because I was ashamed and partly because I just didn't know what else to say.

"So?" Dre responded with his index finger snug in our baby's fist.

"This is our son," I finally let out, looking up into his handsome face. His dark, flawless skin was so smooth like melted fudge.

"So you lied?" he asked with a lick of his lips.

"Yes," I whispered shamefully. I couldn't even look him in the eyes.

"But why?"

"I just felt like you were playing with my heart, Dre, and I didn't want to hurt anymore," I explained, gently lifting my baby to burp him in the palm of my hand.

"But this wasn't about you, though. Shit, this wasn't even about us, Ro. This was about my son, my seed, and you lied to me."

My mouth went completely dry as I looked up into his dark, unsympathetic eyes. I felt completely stupid in that moment, thinking that I could keep our son's paternity a secret and keep Dre out of his son's life. I lifted my son, who was now sleeping, and tenderly placed him up against my breasts. Briefly, I allowed my eyes to close as I chewed on the corner of my mouth, mulling over exactly what I needed to say. I gradually opened up my eyes and sighed a deep breath.

"I'm sorry, Dre."

Chapter 8

Dre

"Where's Auntie's baby?" Risa cooed, entering the room with powder blue balloons in her hand. Raina and Raquel were trailing close behind her with wide smiles on their faces.

I wanted to be mad at Romi, cuss her out, and make her suffer for lying, but with just one look into her beautiful green eyes, I succumbed. It seemed like no matter what happened between us, she would forever have this fucking hold on my heart. I quickly stood up and gave Risa and Raina a hug. Raquel looked a little apprehensive at first, but then she also followed suit and showed me some love.

"Congratulations, Daddy! Ms. Calisa and Mama told us the good news," Risa said with a light, playful punch to my arm.

"Yeah," I responded, trying to hide the growing smile forming on my face. It was funny because at first I didn't even think I wanted a child, but now that my son was here, my seed, I couldn't be prouder.

"What's li'l man's name?" Raina asked while playing with his tiny feet.

"Damn, I don't even know. Shawty, what's my son's name?" I asked, glancing back at Romi.

She hunched her shoulders in response. "I haven't named him yet," she softly stated.

"Ooh! Name him Rashaud. I always did like that name," Raquel chimed in.

"Nah, you can name your son Rashaud. That ain't gon' be my son's name, shawty," I told her.

"What about Dillon?" Raina pondered, looking up with her finger to her chin.

"Nah, that's a white boy's name," I said, shaking my head.

"Well, Granddaddy's name is Thomas," Romi let out.

"Thomas?" Raquel and I questioned at the same time. Clearly, I was going to have to speak up before my son got some lame nigga's name.

"What about Armond? Armond Borrego," I said, looking at Romi for a response.

She smiled and nodded before saying, "I love it."

Before I could even take it all in, I heard the loud-ass voices of my brothers entering the room. Micah was the first one through the door, and he immediately came over with a full grin on his face, eyes filled with pride. He was dressed casually in blue jeans, brown leather Tims, and an army fatigues jacket. An olive green skull cap was molded to the top of his head. It was nice seeing him dress down for a change. Lately, he had been going hard at work, so usually when I saw him, he was in a tailor-made suit.

"I hear it's time to trade in that bike, bruh," he said, dapping me up before pulling me in for a brotherly hug.

"I'on know 'bout all dat," I coolly responded before dapping up Melo and Dame.

"Can't put a car seat on a bike," Micah said with a shrug. His eyes began to scan the room and instantly fell on Risa, who was washing her hands. He gave her a half smile but didn't say anything. Damien and Melo came farther in and hugged all the girls before making their way over to look at the baby.

"Damn. Li'l nigga look just like you," Damien muttered, peering down at my son, who was in Romi's arms.

My brothers and the girls all instantly laughed while I just smiled. There wasn't shit funny about it because he was damn sure was telling the truth. My son had my complexion, my mouth, and my nose. He even had unbroken life lines on the tiny palms of his hands that went straight across, just like mine. I let out a low snort of a laugh, thinking about how Romi was trying to keep this all a secret. There was no way in hell me or my mama wouldn't have been able to figure that shit out.

"Let me hold him," Risa said, reaching for my son.

She picked him up and held him gently in her arms. I had to admit that she had a natural maternal ability. Little Armond nuzzled against her and instantly went off into a peaceful sleep when she sank down into the rocking chair. I thought Micah noticed it too because he couldn't take his eyes off the two of them. My brother and I had had many late-night conversations about his relationship with Risa, so I knew in that moment that he was thinking about their future together.

"I wanna hold him," Raquel whined, leaning down to where Risa was sitting.

"Nah, shawty. Don't pick him up. You don't need to get no ideas," Melo cut in. His voice was low and stern.

She glanced back over her shoulder and gave him a hushed smile with her lips tucked in. Surprisingly, that nigga actually smiled back. It was a little smile, but a smile nonetheless. Suddenly, the door opened again, and this time it was my mother and father with Uncle Raul following. Uncle Raul just happened to be in the States that week handling some business with Timo, which was rare. After sending Melo to the States to be raised by Moms and Pops after his wife died, he didn't visit from Cuba very often.

"Man, they gon' kick all our asses out. Ain't there supposed to be a limit on how many people can be up in here?" Dame asked, lying back in the reclining chair with Raina on his lap. I assumed that was what I'd be sleeping on that night.

"Well, you know your daddy's got pull, so I think we'll be all right," my mother said, making her way over to see the baby with my father on her heels.

"What's up, Unc?" Micah said, pulling in Uncle Raul for a hug.

"Where's this new addition to our family?" he asked, looking over at Risa. His Cuban accent was thick, unlike my father's, who tried hard to hide it.

"Here, sit down, Ms. Calisa," Risa offered. She got up from the rocking chair and gently passed her the baby.

There were now eleven of us packed in that tiny-ass room, and there was hardly any room for us to maneuver. When Risa stood up to let my mother sit down, I could tell she didn't know where to stand. I watched as she slid past Micah, being careful not to brush her body against his and avoiding his stare. She walked to stand close to the door with her arms folded across her chest. Melo and Raquel stood next to her while Raina remained cuddled up with Dame.

We were all talking loud, excited over the baby, when Romi's grandmother, Lisa Mae, her mother, Ernie, and her father all walked in. It was a tight squeeze, but they ended up making their way over to see the baby one final time. The room quickly grew hot, and I was just ready for everyone to leave. Thankfully, no more than twenty minutes later, the nurse came in and kicked everybody out for the night.

"This has been one crazy-ass day," Romi said with a yawn. Her swollen face was bare as she looked at me with tired green eyes.

It was a little past ten that night in the hospital when we found ourselves alone in the cold room. Besides the TV, all of the lights were out. Little Armond was sleeping peacefully in his bassinet while Romi was lying back in the bed, struggling to keep her eyes open. Kicking the shoes off my feet, I melted back into the recliner and put my hands behind my head.

"Here, you want this blanket?" she asked, peeling off one of the many layers of blankets she had on top of her. She threw it over to me before trying to get comfortable in the bed.

"Shawty, stop fighting it and just go to sleep," I told her, fixing the blanket on top of me.

"I know, but I have to feed him again in an hour," she said. The doctor had told us that she had to feed the baby every two hours, even if that meant waking him up out of his sleep.

"I won't let you oversleep. Now just close your eyes and get some rest."

As though she had been waiting for permission, she instantly closed her eyes. She was curled up into a fetal position, and by the slow rhythm of her breathing, I could tell that it wouldn't take long for her to fall asleep. Just as I began to hear her light snores dance around the room, I cut the TV off and started to drift off to sleep.

No more than two minutes later, I could feel my cell phone starting to vibrate in my lap. My eyes instantly opened in the dark, and I looked down to see my girl-friend Brandi's pretty face appear on the glowing screen. I glanced over to make sure Romi wasn't awake, before getting up and tiptoeing out of the room. Feeling like I was sneaking, I carefully closed the door behind me before entering the hall. I gripped the back of my neck with my hand and let out a deep sigh.

"What's up?" I said, answering the call.

"Hey, baby. Where are you?" Her voice was sweet and warm as always.

"I um . . ." I hesitated telling Brandi where I was because I didn't want to hurt her.

"Hello?" she said as if our phone connection were breaking up.

"Yeah, I'm over at the hospital with Romi. She just had the baby and shit. Li'l man was like six pounds and seven ounces. We ended up naming him Armond . . . Armond Borrego," I said all in one breath. There was an awkward pause on the phone as I held my breath, waiting for her to respond. I knew she was most likely taking in my words, trying to understand because the last thing she heard was that the DNA test proved the baby wasn't mine.

"Borrego?" she suddenly asked just above a whisper.

"Yeah, he's my son," I said low.

"But I thought—"

"Nah, shawty, she lied," I cut in, shaking my head.

Another few moments of silence passed between us as she took in the news. Just the soft sounds of her breath-ing on the other end of the line were coming through. I couldn't take the tension anymore, so I said, "Romi and the baby are going home the day after tomorrow, so I'll get up with you then, a'ight?"

"Okay," she said softly before hanging up the phone.

Frustrated, I ran my hand down my face before quietly going back into the room. It was completely dark and still as I eased back down into the chair. After getting the pillow adjusted beneath my head, I pulled the covers up and closed my eyes.

"So how did Brandi take the news?" Romi quietly asked.

Chapter 9

Raina

It was late Saturday evening when I found myself lying on the couch watching the latest episode of *Bring It!* It had been thundering and raining on and off all day, which was always the perfect time for me to catch up on my recorded shows. Suddenly, I heard the doorbell ring. I didn't get up right away because I wanted to see who won the final dance battle. This was one of my favorite shows not only because I loved to dance, but because those young girls always taught me a move or two. When the doorbell rang for the second time, I huffed before getting up and going to the door.

I peeped through the hole and saw Risa standing in the rain. *She must have left her key,* I thought. I quickly opened the door and said, "Hey, sissy, where's your key?" That's when I heard a single clap of thunder. It was so loud and intense that we both jumped in place. I looked up at the gray clouds that were among the boiling sky, and I took in the cracks of lightning that flickered throughout. "Hurry up and come in," I told her.

When the door was fully ajar, I instantly noticed that Risa had cut her hair to her shoulders. "Oh my gosh, Risa, you cut your hair," I squealed, taking in her new look.

"No, uh, actually, my name is Tisa Carter. I was wondering, is Ms. Ernestine Brimmage home?" the girl timidly asked, stepping into the house. Her hands were nervously clasped together, and her face was tight, giving her a look of uneasiness.

I was completely confused, looking at this girl who looked exactly like my oldest sister. Hesitantly, I stepped back from her almost like I was seeing a ghost. "Mama!" I called out.

"What is it, baby?" my mother asked, entering the front room. She was drying her hands with a dish towel when she looked up and saw Tisa standing before her.

Her eyes grew wide before she gasped and covered her mouth with her hand. Instead of saying anything, she merely shook her head in disbelief. Unlike me, I guessed, my mother instantly recognized that this wasn't Risa. How, I just didn't know.

"Mama, do you know this girl?" I asked, still confused.

"Baby girl, this is . . . this is my daughter. Your sister Tisa," my mother said weakly as her eyes filled with tears.

"Your daughter?" I asked, confused.

My mother didn't respond. Instead, she walked over and gave Tisa a tight embrace, but I noticed Tisa didn't hug her back. She just stood there awkwardly with her hands down by her sides and a closed-lip smile on her face.

Suddenly the doorbell rang again, interrupting the uncomfortable silence that had fallen upon the room. But before I could even answer it, Risa walked in. She quickly gave me a hug, then went over and gave Tisa a hug as well. I was completely bewildered and speechless at this point. How did she know this girl well enough to give her a hug? Was I the only one who didn't know this Tisa girl?

"I thought you were going to wait for me before you came in," Risa said to the girl.

"I was, but my nerves got the best of me. I just couldn't sit in that car and think about it anymore," she said.

"Ah, hello! Does anyone care to explain?" I asked, looking from my mother to Risa.

"Uh, let me go get your father and sisters from upstairs," Mama said.

After Mama went to get the rest of the family, Risa led the way to the family room. I watched as Tisa followed her, taking in every inch of our home. She allowed her fingers to lightly skim the chair rail molding while looking up at every picture that hung on the walls. When we got to the den, she carefully chose the lone chair in the corner of the room.

"Would you like anything to drink?" Risa asked, looking over at Tisa.

"A bottle of water if you have it," she replied, clearing her throat.

As Risa got up to leave the room, Romi and Raina were walking in. They quickly got a glance of Tisa sitting over in the corner before they did a double take back at Risa. Confusion was written all over their faces, but Risa didn't say a thing. She simply bounced her eyebrows up and down, letting a tricky smile spread across her face before passing them.

"What the hell is going on?" Raquel asked, looking at Tisa for an explanation.

"I'll wait until Ms. Ernestine and Risa get back," Tisa said.

"This is some crazy-ass shit," Romi muttered, taking a seat next to me on the couch with li'l Armond strapped to her chest.

It was quiet in the room as we all waited for my father, Mama, and Risa to return. Tisa picked at her nails, avoiding eye contact with us, while Romi anxiously bounced her thighs. There were the occasional eye rolls coming from Raquel, but still, the room was silent. Then, out of nowhere, a thunderous boom filled the house. It was so loud that the baby instantly woke and started to cry.

Romi stood up and immediately began to bounce him in her arms. He was now 5 weeks old, and she had quickly learned how to soothe him in times like these. Raquel started softly singing Stevie Wonder's "These Three Words," which made Romi smile. She knew that Raquel was only trying to help calm the baby.

> *When was the last time*
> *That they heard you say*
> *Mother or father, I love you*
> *And when was the last time*

As Raquel continued to sing, I noticed that she was no longer singing alone. Tisa had stood up and begun singing right along with her, word for word. Her soprano voice was light but full of passion. She could sing just like Mama and Raquel. With her eyes closed and one hand clutching her chest like she was performing on stage, she continued letting the lyrics flow.

Raquel eyed her intently, but she never quit singing. In fact, she stood up directly across from her and sang even louder. Romi's eyes bounced back and forth between the two of them as they battled like they were on *The Voice*. When Romi glanced back at me, I could only shrug in response. Raquel was competitive when it came to her singing, so I wasn't surprised by her actions, but unexpectedly, Tisa had quickly come out of her shell after just a few melodies of Stevie Wonder.

They sang and sang until finally, we heard clapping hands entering the room. I looked and saw that it was my mother and father with Risa trailing behind. Raquel rolled her eyes at Tisa before taking her seat. Tisa thanked Risa before grabbing the bottle of water from her hands. Once everyone took a seat, we all stared up at Mother and waited for her to speak.

"I know you all are wondering what's going on, and I . . . I finally need to get this off my chest," my mother said low. My father stood behind her with his hands gently gripping her shoulders for support.

"Who is this girl, Ma?" Raquel cut in.

"My name is Tisa Carter. I reached out to Risa a few weeks ago after discovering who my real mother was and finding out that I had a twin sister," Tisa explained.

"What? How did this happen, Mama?" I asked.

My mother sat down on the ottoman and briefly closed her eyes, letting out a slow breath before she started to tell her story. "When I was in high school, I fell deeply in love with this guy named Monclaire. Monclaire Monroe," she stated firmly with a slight shake of her head. "Everyone around the way called Monclaire Money. I never did understand that, though, because the nigga was always broke. But anyway, the day we graduated from high school, he and I ran away to California together on a Greyhound bus. We had only been together for about six months, but back then you couldn't tell me that he wasn't my soul mate," she said, letting out a small snort of laughter.

"When we finally got to California, we had very little money, so we struggled. Struggled bad, sleeping in cheap motels, living on the streets, and practically begging for food. Life was just really hard for us. Monclaire looked for jobs day in and day out, but nothing ever turned up for him. We just couldn't seem to catch a break. As time went on and our struggle continued, Monclaire started to become violent. He took all of his frustrations out on me. Beating me and slapping me around for months on end. And right when I decided that I had finally had enough of his abuse and living on the streets, I found out that I was three months pregnant." She paused and shook her head, recalling the devastation she felt in that moment.

"Pregnant with twins," she finished saying. "So I stayed, but the beatings continued. Instead of sleeping on the streets, we started staying at homeless shelters, but life was still hard. Then, when I finally did give birth that November, I felt a newfound sense of clarity," she explained, pressing her hands together.

"Motherhood has that effect, ya know? I knew at that very moment that I had to leave. So I called my mother while I was in the hospital, and she told me that she would wire me some money for a bus ticket back to New Orleans. She told me to bring my babies home, and that was exactly what I planned to do. I couldn't raise two children out on the street, and most importantly, I knew I couldn't subject them to Monclaire," she said, wiping the tears from her face.

"My second night in the hospital was the night I was going to make a run for it. One of the nurses had given him a dinner pass for the hospital cafeteria that night, and while he was gone, I quickly packed my things. I didn't have much, just a few clothes and a pair of holey shoes, so it didn't take me long. The nursery wasn't too far from my room, so as I soon as I packed, I was headed straight for you girls," she explained, looking back and forth between Risa and Tisa.

"But when I got to the nursery, only one of you was there. They had taken Tisa off for a hearing exam, I believe. I went ahead and wrapped Risa up before placing her in the carrier they had given me, and I waited. I paced the floor over and over, watching the clock and waiting for them to return with my baby. But they took too long. All of a sudden, I could hear his voice approaching in the hall as he made his way back down to my room. I was so scared in that moment that I . . . I just didn't know what to do. Out of fear, I panicked and ran as fast as I could. Leaving my baby girl behind," she cried with a crack in her voice.

All of our faces were now covered in tears, even my father's. As he pulled her into his comforting arms, I could see her shoulders bounce as she bawled from having to recollect that painful memory. Over and over, she murmured the weeping words, "I'm so sorry," from within my father's hold. Her face was buried in his chest as he stroked her hair and repeatedly kissed the top of her head.

"Did you ever come back for me?" Tisa softly asked.

My mother pulled back from my father and looked Tisa right in the eyes. "I called the hospital as soon as I got to the bus station that night, but your father had already taken you. My mother and I even went out to California to find you on more than one occasion. Even Brad had some of his detective friends looking for you some years back, but we could never find a Tisa Monroe," she explained, walking toward her.

"I never knew Monclaire because he gave me up for adoption before I could even crawl. I was raised in Texas by my parents, Linda and Travis Carter," Tisa said, pulling a picture of her white adoptive parents out of her purse for us to see.

"So you were okay?" my mother asked, softly gripping her hand.

"I grew up just fine. I always knew I wanted to meet you one day, though," Tisa said.

I smiled at the thought.

Chapter 10

Risa

"Ma, why couldn't you tell me!" I shouted, storming out of the room.

When I finally met up with Tisa a week or ago, I couldn't deny her story. We looked almost identical, so she had to have been my twin. Then there was that picture I'd found all those years ago in my mother's trunk. It all made sense. The only thing that didn't make sense was my mother keeping it all hush-hush.

All these years, I knew there was a part of me missing, but I never could explain it. Hearing that my biological father beat on my mother the way Zo beat on me nearly broke my heart in two. I couldn't help but think that perhaps if she had shared her life story with me, I might have avoided Zo altogether.

When I reached the kitchen, I leaned down on the cold marble counter. My mind was racing a mile a minute, and my emotions were all over the place from the bomb my mother had just dropped. I knew I needed to get myself together and quick. Before I even had a chance, I heard my mother, Romi, Raquel, and Raina all coming in. Romi must have given the baby to our father because neither of them came into the kitchen.

"I'm sorry I kept all of this from you, Risa. I truly am, but I was only trying to protect you," my mother said, coming over to comfort me.

"Don't touch me," I told her, snatching away from her hold.

My mother instantly started to cry, and that's when my sisters chimed in.

"I get that you're upset, Risa, but don't be like that with Mama," Raquel snapped, rolling her hazel eyes.

"You just don't know what I've been through," I whispered. None of them knew the pain I'd suffered at the hands of Zo'mire.

"What you've been through?" my mother quizzed with her eyebrows together.

I took a deep breath and stared directly into my mother's eyes. "Zo beat on me for years, Mama," I confessed.

"He what?" she screamed, clutching her chest.

I nodded my head and just let the tears that had been threatening to fall finally flow down my face. "That accident in high school." I shook my head. "That was all him," I confessed weakly.

"Oh my God," my mother gasped in shocked, recalling those nights in the hospital. The emotions displayed on her face showed that she remembered the broken bones and all the bruises that had covered my body.

"Why didn't you tell us?" Romi asked, putting her arm around me.

"I thought he might try to hurt you guys if you got involved. You know how he and Timo got down back then," I explained. Timo and Zo were heavy in the drug game back then and were ruthless.

"We could have helped, Risa. You know better than to let a man beat on you," my mother scolded as though she had never been in my shoes.

I looked over and saw that Raina was now crying pretty hard. I thought this whole night had just been too much for her.

"I'm all right now, baby girl. It's all over," I said, trying to ease the hurt she felt for me.

She looked at me with an angry glare. "I'm just sick of this!" she shouted, throwing her hands in the air. We all looked at her, confused and surprised by her loud tone of voice.

"What's wrong with you ,chile?" my mother asked, looking at Raina like she had lost her mind.

"Y'all are what's wrong with me! The lying and the secrets is what's wrong with me! I thought we were supposed to be close," she said, letting her voice trail off. "First it was your affair with Mr. Charles. Then you lied about who the father of your baby was," she said, pointing her finger at Romi. "Then we find out we have a sister you've been keeping secret for the past twenty-one years. Who does stuff like that, Mama? For real?" she asked rhetorically with a frown on her face.

"Now we find out that not only were you the one to find Zo when he got murdered but that he also had been beating on you for all these years. What else are you hiding, huh?" Raina turned and asked me with a disappointed look in her eyes.

"Y'all, Raina's right. We're supposed to be as thick as thieves, yet y'all lying and keeping secrets," Raquel chimed in.

Raina cut her eyes hard at her. "Humph," Raina muttered, rolling her eyes.

"What's that supposed to mean?" Raquel asked.

"It means that you've been keeping secrets too. When were you going to tell me that you lost your virginity?

When were you going to tell me that you've been seeing Melo these past few months?" she asked with her hand on her hip.

Raquel's mouth nearly dropped to the floor before she let her eyes fall in shame.

"Oh my goodness. You lost your virginity? To Melo?" my mother asked with a confused grin on her face.

We all burst out laughing in that moment, even Raina. It was hard to visualize Melo being tender with a woman, but it was even harder to imagine Raquel's mean ass even allowing a man to touch her. They were an odd couple, to say the least.

"Yes, ma'am. The night I stayed with him after the party, it happened. And we've been seeing each other ever since," Raquel quietly confessed.

"Well, do you love him?" my mother took a seat and asked. She wanted all the tea, and my mother was not the type to beat around the bush. I guessed that's where Raquel got it from.

"Uh, I think I do," Raquel replied with a sheepish grin.

"Nah, either you do, or you don't," my mother said with her eyebrows raised.

We all watched Raquel intently, waiting for her next words. In a year, she had gone from the sister with no life of her own to the one sister who was having sex on a regular basis. I didn't have Micah anymore, so I found my sisters' love lives very interesting these days.

"I do," she finally admitted.

"You do what?" my mother asked. She wasn't going to make this conversation easy on her.

"I do love him, a'ight? I love him, but he doesn't know it yet," Raquel confessed with a shrug.

My mother smiled and shook her head. "Lord, I never thought I'd see the day," she said.

By this time, all five of us were gathered around the kitchen table, talking and laughing like old times. My mother gave Raquel the sex talk, making sure that she and Melo were using contraceptives. Eventually, we all chimed in, giving our two cents on the matters of love, sex, and relationships. Even Raina spoke on her and Damien's young, budding love. We talked so openly and freely with one another that night, I doubted there were any more secrets buried among us.

"Whatever happened to Tisa?" Romi finally thought to ask.

"Oh shit, I didn't even see her off," my mother muttered, completely disappointed in herself.

"No, ma'am, I'm right here," I heard her say.

I looked back to see Tisa leaning on the doorframe of the kitchen. She looked like she had been standing there for a while.

"Well, come on over here and sit down," my mother told her.

"No, I'm just enjoying watching you all. I never had sisters. Not even a brother. I grew up as the only child. It's just nice seeing how you all are with one another. Like a real family," she said softly.

I instantly felt bad for her. I didn't want her to feel excluded. After all, she was my twin sister and a part of this family. I immediately got up from my chair to try to get her to sit with us, but she realized what I was doing and instantly headed for the front door.

"You're leaving?" I asked, watching her step out onto our front porch.

"Yeah, I gotta run, but thank you for this," she turned around and said.

"Am I gonna see you soon?" I asked, looking past her to see drizzles of rain beneath the streetlights.

"I'd love that," she said, then gave me a closed-lip smile. With those last words, she got in her car and drove away in the rain.

When I went back in the house, the kitchen was now quiet and empty. My mother and sisters had all gone upstairs for the evening, leaving me behind. I didn't want to drive back to Atlanta that night in the rain, so I went upstairs to my old bedroom. As soon as I lay back on my queen-sized poster bed, I immediately checked my phone. I had a few texts and one specifically from Micah. It was his usual "I miss you" text. He sent them to me daily, so it was nothing new, but after the night I'd just had, I actually missed him too. He was actually the first person I wanted to tell about Tisa. I wanted to tell him my mother's story and fill him in on Raina's outburst.

Twisting my lips to the side, I pondered the idea. *Should I? Nah. Well? Maybe.* Cautiously, I let my fingers skim across my phone before finally I hit his contact and dialed his number.

"Hello," he said, almost sounding confused.

"Hey," I said softly.

"Risa?"

"Yeah, it's me," I said. I had the phone nuzzled between my ear and my shoulder while I picked at my nails.

"Damn," he mumbled in disbelief. "What made you call me?"

"Some crazy shit just happened, and you're the first person I wanted to call and tell about it," I said honestly.

"Talk to me," he said in his deep, raspy voice. I could hear him moving around, almost like he was sitting up to give me his undivided attention.

I smiled, loving the sound of his voice and the eagerness he expressed. "I will, but first, how come you didn't tell me that Melo took Raquel's virginity?"

He let out a deep, guttural laugh before finally filling me in on what he knew. I had to admit that I missed Micah something terrible. Was I ready to completely forgive him? No, but did I still want him in my life? Absolutely.

Chapter 11

Dre

Darkness had just begun to take the sky when I felt Brandi's arms wrapped tightly around me. We zoomed in the wind, seeing the green highway signs pass us by. It was late Saturday night, and we were headed out to dinner. I decided to take my motorcycle because Brandi always enjoyed riding on the back.

When we pulled up to A-Town Wings, I parked my bike and allowed her to hop off first. She took the helmet off her head and shook out her curly brown hair. Once I hopped off, we started to head inside. I felt her gently reach over and grab my hand. Without even thinking, I pulled away. She jerked her head back, letting a confused look take over her face.

"My bad," I told her, taking her hand back in mine.

After getting us a table, I went up to order some wings and fries. I loved the traditional hot wings, while Brandi liked the lemon-pepper ones. When I glanced back at her sitting at the table, I noticed that she was nervously biting her nails. She never did that before, and I could tell that something was off. As a matter of fact, our whole vibe that night was off. Lately, I had been spending a lot more time with Romi and the baby, so this was actually one of the first nights in a good little minute that we'd been able to spend a moment together.

Over the past several weeks, my feelings for Romi had started to resurface. I had been staying at the Brimmage family home just about every weekend with her and the baby. Although we weren't fucking, every night that I was with her, we would lie together in the bed cuddling with li'l Armond. It was an indescribable feeling being with just the two of them. Shit just felt like that was where I belonged.

Quietly I took my seat across from Brandi, waiting for our order number to be called.

"Dre," said softly, breaking the awkward silence between us.

"Sup," I said, looking at a group of pretty girls walking through the door.

She glanced back to see what had my attention, then frowned. "Dre!" she said again but louder.

"Yo! What's up," I said again.

"Tell me, how's the baby?"

"He's doing good. Getting fat, drinking that breast milk and shit," I said. I knew a creepish smile probably spread across my face, thinking about how big Romi's titties had gotten.

"And your baby mama, how's she?" she asked with a slight attitude.

"Ro straight," I simply said, not wanting to talk much more about her.

"When can I meet your son?" she finally asked.

My eyes grew wide. "Uh, I'on know," I said. Truth be told, I didn't know if I really wanted to Brandi to meet my son.

"What's going on between us, Dre? Ever since the baby was born, I feel like we've been growing further apart."

I sighed and ran my hand down my face. I really wasn't ready to have this conversation with her. In fact, all I wanted to do was take her out tonight to get her off my back, then head straight back over to Romi and the baby. Looking into her pretty brown face, I could see that she was waiting for me to respond.

"Look, I don't know what to tell you, shawty. A nigga's priorities are different now."

"Do you still love her?" she whispered.

I paused with a chuck of my chin, knowing full well who she was referring to. Carefully, I thought about my next words. "I'll always love her. That's the mother of my son."

"You know what I mean, Dre. Are you still in love with Romi?" she asked, flipping her curls with her hand.

I simply shrugged. It was the only thing I could think to do in that moment so that I didn't have to lie to her.

"What that hell was that?" she asked, shrugging her shoulders to mimic me.

I clenched my jaw out of frustration, then said, "Yeah, I still love her, a'ight?"

"Table number five! Table number five! Your order is up," the man at the counter hollered. I was saved by the bell. Without even finishing our conversation, I got up to get our wings and fries.

When I got back to the table, I set our food down and slid back into my seat. I immediately started eating in hopes that she wouldn't continue with the conversation.

"Are you breaking up with me?" she asked.

Shit! "To be truly honest with you, I don't have time for a girl right now. I'll be starting my senior year of college in a few more months, then I'll be working full time for my pops. On top of that, I need to fit li'l Armond into the equation because he's most important right now. I didn't want it to come to this, but yes. I think we should take a break for a while." I grabbed another hot wing and put it in my mouth before staring up at the soccer game on one of the TVs. I was doing anything I could do to avoid looking into her sad eyes. She was such a sweet girl that I hated breaking her heart.

"Well, since you're prioritizing and making equations and whatnot," she snapped, fumbling through her black leather satchel, "please fit this in too," she said, placing a positive pregnancy test in front of me.

Fuck!

The very next morning, I headed right over to see Romi and the baby. I would have gone there last night, but the bomb Brandi dropped on me fucked my head all up. With a grip on my jeans, which were slightly sagging, I jogged up to the front door and rang the bell. No more than a few seconds later, Mrs. Ernie came to the door with her pink bathrobe still on.

"You're here early," she said, letting me in.

"Hey, Ma. Where my baby at?" I asked, giving her a kiss on the cheek.

"Armond was crying on and off all last night, so I think both of them are still sleeping," she said.

I instantly felt like shit for not coming over, because I knew I could have helped Romi with the baby throughout the night. Quickly, I rushed up the stairs and opened up her bedroom door. She was sleeping on her back with a couple of pillows propped under her head. Lying on top of her breasts was li'l Armond, who was fast asleep. After kicking off my shoes, I eased down into the bed beside them.

"Good morning," she said with a groggy voice.

"My bad, did I wake you?" I whispered.

"I heard the doorbell ring," she said.

"Go back to sleep and get some rest. Your mama told me you had a rough night," I said.

"Yeah, we did."

"Well, I got him today. You just get some rest," I told her.

We both closed our eyes and slept for another two hours before the whimpering sounds of li'l Armond woke us up. She immediately changed his diaper and started feeding him. After breastfeeding the baby, Romi went to go jump in the shower. When it was just me and him in the room, I held him in my arms and started to talk to him.

"What's up, li'l man?" I asked, rubbing on his tiny hands. "You may be getting a little brother or a little sister soon. Don't tell Mommy yet, though," I whispered, looking down into his emerald green eyes.

He started to squirm in my arms and scrunch up his cute little face. I stood up from where I was sitting, hoping to soothe him, but he instantly started to cry. Softly, I rocked him until a foul stench hit my nose.

"Oh, no you didn't, li'l nigga," I muttered, looking down at my son.

I laid him down on the changing table and quickly checked his diaper. Sure enough, it was filled up with a stinky green paste.

"This how you do Daddy? Huh?" I said, playing with his belly. I bent down for a diaper and some wipes that were stacked beneath the changing table. When I came back up, I immediately started to change his diaper the way Romi showed me how.

"There, all done, stinka butt," I said, carefully holding him up in the air. "You gon' have to learn to only do that shit when Mommy's around, okay?"

He smiled at me like he knew exactly what I was saying. That's when I heard Romi clearing her throat behind me. I turned around to see her smiling with a white towel wrapped around her naked body. Her hair was wet, and her bright, beautiful face was bare.

"You're so good with him, Dre. It's kinda sexy, you know?" With a hint of sex in her eyes, she seductively took the tip of her index finger between her teeth.

"G'on wit' all that, girl," I said with a smirk. I was dark as shit, but Romi still had a nigga blushing.

We both sat down on the bed, and she began to put lotion on her smooth, pretty legs. My mouth instantly started to salivate, and I could feel myself getting hard. I hadn't had sex in what seemed like a lifetime. Not that I didn't have options, I just wanted to solely focus on my son. Romi stood up and slowly took off her towel so that she could put lotion on the rest of her body.

I licked my lips and allowed my eyes to roam her figure from head to toe. "You can't be getting all naked and shit in front of my son, Ro," I told her, biting down on my lower lip. I still had my son in my arms, so I was trying to be on my best behavior. Shawty was definitely testing the fuck out of me right now, though. Her body was more beautiful now than it was before she got pregnant. Her hips were wider, her breasts were fuller, and her stomach had returned flat.

"Dre, can you help me put some lotion on my back?" she asked, still fully nude.

"Why you playing games?" I asked, scanning her body and licking my lips. I got up from the bed and headed toward her bedroom door.

"Dre, where are you going?" she asked, but I kept going. After closing her bedroom door behind me, I walked downstairs and gave the baby to Mrs. Ernie, who was in the kitchen. She was happy to see li'l Armond and immediately took him right out of my arms with no questions asked. I ran back upstairs and entered Romi's room.

"What was all that shit you was saying now?" I asked, unzipping my jeans.

She laughed, lying back on the bed with her thighs spread wide. She bit down on her bottom lip and motioned with the tip of her finger for me to come hither. I pulled the shirt over my head and dropped my pants to the floor before eagerly climbing on top of her.

I tried taking her breast into my mouth, but she quickly pushed me away and shook her head. I knew that was for the baby, but I couldn't help myself in the moment. While kissing her neck, I gently inserted two of my fingers inside of her to inspect her "after baby" pussy. She was still tight and wet the way I remembered. *Damn, shawty got that snapback.*

After pulling my fingers out, I quickly slid them into my mouth to taste her. It was the same sweet flavor as before. I reached down to stroke my length before working my way inside her. Her tight, wet walls felt like heaven on earth. Closing my eyes tight, I let out a low, deep groan, letting it be known that I was enjoying every stroke. In that moment, I knew there was no place else I'd rather be.

Chapter 12

Raina

On the second Saturday in June, I sat at my vanity, brushing my long hair over my shoulder. It was finally the day of my high school graduation, and I had twenty minutes left to get ready before it was time to go. I painted my lips with a sheer pink gloss and pressed my lips together. After putting my pearl stud earrings in my ear, I looked my face over one final time in the mirror before getting up from my seat. I kept it simple and wore a fitted white dress with white Michael Kors sandals.

"You ready?" Raquel asked. I turned around to see her standing in the doorway of my bedroom.

"Yeah, I'm ready. You look cute," I said. She wore the dark pink maxi dress she bought while we were at the mall last week. She had been home for the summer for the last three weeks, and I was enjoying having her around.

When we walked downstairs, Mama, Daddy, Romi, and li'l Armond were all sitting at the kitchen table. Daddy sat in his nice navy blue suit, which he wore to all of us girls' graduations, drinking a cup of coffee. Mama sat next to him, playing with li'l Armond, who was sitting in a rocker chair that sat on top of the kitchen table. She wore a simple cream sheath dress with her hair in an elegant twisted updo. I glanced at Romi, who was filing her nails. She wore a lavender sundress with a light blue diaper bag draped on her arm.

"Your high school graduate is finally ready!" I said.

Romi turned around and smiled. "Good. Now let's go, because my baby is getting cranky. I need that car ride to put his little butt to sleep."

Mama and Daddy rode in their truck with the baby while the three of us rode in Raquel's BMW. Risa was riding with Tisa, and they were going to meet us there. I felt a text message come through on my phone. I looked down, seeing that it was from Damien.

Dame: Hey, beautiful! You excited for your big day?

Me: Yep. Can't wait to see you!

Dame: You already know. I'm gon' be there front and center, cheering for my baby.

Me: Seems like just yesterday we were at yours.

Dame: Shawty, don't even bring that shit up. I'm a new man since that day.

Me: I know you are. I love you.

Dame: I love you too, beautiful.

When we arrived at the Coliseum, I immediately had to rush inside to line up with my class. After running up two flights of stairs with my cap and gown draped over my arm, I pushed the double doors open to see none other than Codi. He was standing against the wall next to big Rob, looking as handsome as ever in his red cap and gown. As soon as he saw me, he smiled and nodded for me to come over.

"Hey, y'all," I said, walking up to them.

"Hey, Rain. You finally gon' let a nigga take you out?" Big Rob said with a smile. He had begun changing his look. He no longer sported his Afro. Sitting underneath his red cap were short dreadlocks that fell just below his ears.

"Sorry, Big Rob. I already told you that I got a man."

"Well, when that nigga mess up, just know I'm here, a'ight?" he said with a wide smile, exposing the gap between his two front teeth. I just laughed and shook my head.

"Nah, when that nigga messes up, Raina knows who to call. Ain't that right, ma?" Codi asked, running the tip of his tongue across his bottom lip.

"He's doing good right now, y'all. I don't think he's gonna mess up this time around."

After Damien and Codi fought the night of home-coming, everyone around school knew all my business. Somehow they even knew about Damien and Tina still messing around at the time. At first, I was embarrassed to still be in love with him after what he did, but seeing how much he'd changed and how much I believed he truly loved me, it made me not even care about what everyone else thought.

Codi came and draped his arm over my shoulder. "You know I could love you ten times better than that nigga ever could, don't you?" he whispered in my ear.

I looked up into his bright, handsome face and gave a small smile. "Maybe you could, Codi, and maybe I'm just a fool, but I love him."

"Well, I'm here, ma. That is, if you ever change your mind," he said, kissing my cheek.

After we all lined up and went into the auditorium, I looked up, spotting my entire family in the crowd. Even Mr. and Mrs. Borrego came with Dre, Melo, Micah, and of course, Dame. As soon as our eyes met, I smiled. He puckered up his lips to give me an air kiss and winked his eye at me. I waved and blew a kiss right back.

I sat down in my seat, which was right next to Keke, my best friend since freshman year. She gave me a hug and told me how excited she was. Moments later, after the ceremony began, we listened to Bradley Montgomery give his commencement speech on the big stage. I was so excited that I just couldn't stop smiling. We both stood proudly in our crisp white caps and gowns, cheering loudly and clapping our hands along with our fellow classmates as Bradley let out those final words to his speech. "Your time is limited, so don't squander it by living someone else's life. Don't let the sound of others' ideals drown out your own inner voice. And always," he said, "always have the audacity to follow your heart and live out your own dream."

Principal Ryland came up behind Bradley and shook his hand before taking the microphone. "Now, for our Most Outstanding Senior Awards," he said, clearing his throat.

"Codi Taylor is not only our star quarterback, but he is also a straight A student. He has received both an engineering scholarship to MIT and a full football scholarship to Ohio State. Codi has also put in more hours of community service than any other senior this year. It gives me great pleasure to announce Codi as one of our Most Outstanding Seniors this year. Please come up to the stage, son," he said.

I watched as Codi strutted with confidence up to the stage. Through the loud claps and cheers of the crowd, I could hear a faint booing. I prayed that was not Damien. When I looked up to where they all were in the crowd, sure enough, he had his hands circled around his mouth, hollering out, "Boo." Thank goodness the other cheers from the crowd pretty much drowned him out. I then mouthed to Micah, "Tell him to stop." Seconds later, Micah slapped him on the back of his head and then pointed to me when Damien looked at him.

"Next, I would like to honor our final Most Outstanding Senior Award recipient. This young lady not only has a 4.3 GPA and is the captain of our majorettes, but she also became the president of our student government body this year. This upcoming fall, she will be attending

Clark Atlanta on a full scholarship for dance. I am so proud to announce one of the sweetest, smartest girls here at Greene County High, Raina Brimmage," Principal Ryland said.

The crowd started to cheer, and I was smiling so hard that my face was actually hurting. I walked to the stage and stood next to Codi before Principal Ryland handed us our awards. I looked up into the crowd to see my entire family up on their feet. Damien and his brothers were all whistling through their fingers, and Romi, Risa, Raquel, and Tisa were shouting out loud. I felt so happy making them all proud.

As Codi and I began walking off the stage, he grabbed my hand to help me down the steps. I thanked him and took his hand. Surprisingly, when we go to the bottom, he pulled my hand up to his mouth and kissed the back of it. I gave Codi a closed-lip smile and pulled my hand back. I knew for sure that Damien had seen that, and I didn't want him acting up on the day of my graduation.

When the ceremony let out, I walked outside and over to where I told everyone I would meet them. Dre had the baby strapped to his chest as he stood next to Romi. They were holding hands, looking like the perfect little family. Micah stood next to his mother and father while Risa and Tisa stood with our parents. Ducked off to the side by their lonesome were Melo and Raquel. He stood behind her with his hands wrapped around her waist and his face pressed against her cheek. Even I had to admit they were cute.

Of course, the first person to approach me was Damien. "Congratulations, beautiful," he said low, coming up to give me a hug.

I tightened my embrace around him and looked up into his eyes. "I know you saw Codi kiss my hand," I said.

"Yeah, I saw that fuck nigga."

I shook my head. "Babe, please don't start nothing."

"I'm not. I know who your heart belongs to just like he does," he said, staring past me.

I turned around to see what he was glaring at, and sure enough, it was Codi. Codi chucked his chin up and squinted his eyes. A smug grin slowly spread across his face.

"Clown-ass nigga," Dame mumbled before giving Codi his middle finger. He then threw his arm over my shoulder and kissed me on the forehead before we walked over to meet up with the rest of the family.

Chapter 13

Damien

"Damn, y'all. Hurry the fuck up!" I yelled out to my brothers.

It was early in the morning, on the third of July, when we pulled up to my father's private jet. While they were all still getting their luggage out of the truck, I was impatiently waiting for them at the top of the stairs. We were on our way to New Orleans to surprise Raina for her eighteenth birthday. Her mother had sent her and all of her sisters out there for a week of bonding or some shit like that. I couldn't wait to see my baby's face when she saw me. Truth be told, all of the girls would be surprised because no one knew that we were even going, except my parents and Mrs. Ernie because they had to keep li'l Armond.

"Damn, li'l nigga, be patient. Baby girl ain't going nowhere," Micah said, referring to Raina as he climbed the stairs to the jet with a suitcase in his hand.

He pushed past me with a shove of his shoulder before going inside. Melo and Micah were coming up next. As soon as I saw that they were boarding, I quickly went inside and grabbed a window seat. My father's jet had all-white leather seats, a private bedroom, two bathrooms, and a bar area. His personal flight attendant was already standing in the aisle with a tray in her hand. She was carrying some fruit and four glasses of champagne mimosas. Pops really knew how to live.

"How you pulling all this shit off?" Dre asked, sitting down across from me. Melo sat quietly behind us while Micah sat on the other side of the plane.

"Pops hooked me up with all his connects in New Orleans. So a nigga got some tricks up his sleeve. You gon' see," I told him, smirking with a stroke of my chin.

"Yeah, a'ight. And don't be trying nothing with baby girl either. Just because she eighteen don't mean she ready," Micah preached from across the aisle. He acted more like her older brother than mine some days.

"'She may be young but she ready,'" I sang low, rubbing my hands together. Dre heard me and shook his head before cracking a smile.

When we finally touched down to the private lanes at Louis Armstrong airport, I gathered up my belongings and stepped out of the jet. The sun was so bright, I immediately had to put on my Gucci shades. The brutal heat and humidity in the air instantly covered my face. It was so hot there a nigga damn near felt like he was suffocating. I looked down the steps and saw the black Maybach that was waiting for us. Quickly, I jogged down, anticipating the coolness of the air conditioning inside.

Pops had rented us the penthouse suite at one of the finest hotels in downtown New Orleans. It had four bedrooms, four baths, a kitchen, and a living room. As soon as we arrived in the hotel lobby, I noticed the fancy marble floors and all the crystal chandeliers hanging from the ceiling. I had to admit that this was some real upscale shit, but it was comparable to one of Pops's hotels. I knew he had his eye on New Orleans for when he opened up his next hotel, and this hotel here would definitely be his competition.

"I got this room here," Micah said, making his way to the biggest room in the suite.

I kissed my teeth with a chuck of my chin. "Nigga, I invited y'all down here. How you gon' just up and take the biggest room?"

He ignored me and closed the bedroom door behind him. Melo and Dre both chose a room as well, leaving me with the last one. It was a nice, clean room, so I really couldn't complain. It had a thick white down comforter on the bed, big fluffy white pillows stacked against the headboard, and sheer white curtains framing the window. Even the adjoining bathroom had all-white marble tile.

I immediately dropped my bags to the floor and went over to look out the window. The city view was full of tourists walking up and down the narrow streets below. Suddenly, I heard a tap on my bedroom door. When I glanced back, I saw Dre standing there with his arms out wide, holding the doorframe.

"Yo, what's the plan for tonight?" he asked.

"I don't want to go out and end up running into them. That'll fuck my whole surprise up," I said.

Micah tapped Dre on the arm before walking into the room. He sat down on the edge of my bed with his legs gapped wide. "We ain't gon' run into them tonight. They probably gon' be listening to jazz music, eating beignets and shit," he said.

"Not Romi's wild ass. She couldn't wait to get out here so she could shake her ass and party. Her first time away from the baby in five months, too. Shiidd!" Dre said, shaking his head. The three of us laughed, thinking about Romi's crazy ass.

"It's an all-white masquerade party at that club right across the street tonight," I said, looking out of the window at the nightclub. "Y'all trying to roll to that?"

"It's whatever. As long as we get out for a little bit to-night, I'm good," Micah said before standing up to leave. Dre nodded his head in agreement before they both left the room.

***

It was around eleven o'clock when we stepped out, immediately feeling the sticky summer's night air of New Orleans. I was looking fly in my all-white Robin's jeans, V-neck white tee, and a fresh pair of white-on-white Jays on my feet. Since none of us had a mask, we decided to go the hood route. We threw on white Gucci shades and wore all-white fitted Braves caps on our heads. To further disguise ourselves, we tied white bandanas around the lower half of our faces. Thankfully we were in all white, so we didn't come off looking like some L.A. robbers or gang bangers.

Luckily I'd called ahead and gotten our names on VIP because the line was wrapped around the building. Since we were Borregos, it wasn't a problem at all. In fact, they wanted the DJ to announce us, but I declined. I didn't want to take the chance of Raina and her sisters knowing that we were here. I was already feeling uneasy being out in the city as it was, even though we were only across the street from the hotel.

As we climbed the stairs to VIP, I scanned the dancing crowd. I looked down, seeing a sea of white on the dance floor. The smoke-filled place was packed from wall to wall, looking like damn near every nigga in NOLA came out wearing their Sunday best. I bobbed my head as Migos's "Bad and Boujee" blared throughout the club. As we took our seats, Melo was the first one to fire up a blunt.

"Are you guys going to need bottle service tonight?" a pretty, dark-skinned waitress came over and asked. She had on a white sequin leotard, a white masquerade mask, and white five-inch stilettos, all of which complemented her midnight skin. Her long black hair was up in a high ponytail that swung down, reaching the top of her ass. I glanced over at Micah, and he was eyeing her sexy body over from head to toe. *This nigga!*

"Yeah, three bottles of Henny and a bottle of Ace if you have it, sweetheart," he told her, licking his lips.

I shook my head. He was the main one preaching to me about treating baby girl right, yet he was really the one who couldn't keep his dick in his pants. As the girl walked off to go get our drinks, I watched his lust-filled eyes follow her.

"You gon' holla at shawty or what?" I leaned up and asked over the music.

He let out a deep sigh and said, "Nah, just something pretty to look at. You know I'm trying to get my baby back."

I nodded my head, knowing full well that he was talking about Risa. When they were together, they were inseparable and appeared to be the most perfect couple. I probably would have even put money on the fact that they would be married with kids one day. I guessed shit wasn't always what it seemed.

"Yo, pass that shit!" Dre hollered over the music to Melo.

"Where yo' shit at?" Melo asked.

"I ain't got none, bruh. Just got a lot on my mind right now. You passing that shit or nah?" Dre asked.

Melo scrunched up his nose, then reluctantly passed over the blunt after taking one last pull.

"Fuck going on wit'chu?" I asked, noticing the stressed look on Dre's face.

"Brandi's pregnant," he confessed, running his hand down his face.

"Damn, for real?"

He slowly nodded his head before lowering his face into the palms of his hands.

"Nigga, you need to learn how to strap the fuck up. Safe sex is the best sex," I sang.

"Damn, bruh. Does Ro know?" Micah asked, cutting me off.

"Nah, I gotta tell her, though," he said.

"Well, don't do that shit this weekend. Don't be fucking up my plans for baby girl," I said.

Micah laughed and shook his head. "This li'l nigga swear he getting some ass this weekend." We all fell out laughing, even Melo.

Then I watched Melo's low red eyes fall back on the dancing crowd. "Yo, ain't that the girls right there?" he pointed and asked.

I looked down to where he pointed, and sure enough, all five girls were on the floor dancing. I was getting ready to tell the fellas, "Come on, let's roll out," but when I saw Raina bucking and shaking her ass stripper style, all that birthday surprise bullshit went right out of the fucking window. She had on some white romper that damn near had her ass cheeks spilling out the bottom. While Raina wasn't a big girl, she had more curves than her sisters. Well, more ass to be specific. The more she shook her behind, the more heated I became. Then to add insult to injury, there was a group of niggas surrounding her and her sisters, gawking while they danced. In that moment, I just lost it.

"Where you going, li'l nigga?" Micah asked when I hopped up from my seat. I ignored him and headed straight downstairs for the dance floor.

Chapter 14

Raina

I was twerking like my life depended on it to Big Sean's "Moves" when I suddenly felt someone come up behind me. I immediately stopped dancing and tried to pry off the death grip they had on my waist. When I turned around, I nearly jumped out of my skin, seeing this guy with a white bandana wrapped around the lower half of his face.

"Why you stop, beautiful?" he leaned down and whispered in my ear.

A huge smile instantly spread across my face, hearing Dame's sexy voice. I quickly pulled down the bandana and kissed his lips. He wrapped his arm around my waist and held me close as we French kissed in the middle of the crowd. When I finally pulled back, breaking our kiss, I took the shades off his face.

"What are you doing here?" I squealed.

"I should be asking you that. You the one down here shaking ya ass with this little shit on," he said with his lips twisted to the side, fingers lightly tugging at the hem of my shorts.

"I'm just dancing and having fun, babe," I told him with a light laugh.

"Yeah, a'ight. Fun! That's what you call it," he said, cutting his eyes at me. For some reason, I loved it when he got jealous like that.

"Hey, Dame. What are you doing here?" Risa came over and asked, giving him a hug.

"I came down here to surprise my baby for her birthday. The fellas are with me," he said, pointing up toward VIP.

She looked up and saw Micah leaning over the rail, wearing his all white. "Damn, it's like déjà vu," she muttered, recalling the very first time she laid eyes on him back at the club in Atlanta.

"Y'all just couldn't let us take a girl's trip without y'all, could you?" Romi came over and asked, giving Dame a hug.

"Nah, not this time," he joked with a big white smile.

"Hey, big head," Raquel said before giving him a hug. "Where's your brother at?"

"Which one?" he asked with a smirk, knowing full well she was asking about Melo. She playfully punched him in the arm. "Your man is upstairs," he told her. She mouthed, "Thank you," before making her way through the thick crowd.

"What's up, Tisa?" He reached out to hug my other sister as well. This was only his second time meeting her, but he instantly treated her like he did the others. She was family.

After the girls all went up to VIP to see the guys, it was just me and Damien on the dance floor. "What was all that shit you was doing down here? Come on, let a nigga see you twerk something," he said, playfully smacking me on the booty. As if on cue, the beat suddenly dropped, and I could hear the slow, sexy sounds of Chris Brown's "Privacy."

Dame came from behind and wrapped his arms around me so that our bodies were tightly melded together. I could feel a light prickle from his mustache when he buried his face in the crook of my neck. Together, our hips began to sway instinctively to the music, slow and sensual.

> *I need your body in ways*
> *That you don't understand, but I'm losing my patience*
> *'Cause we've been going over and over again*

"*Girl, I just wanna take you home and get right to it,*" he softly sang against my ear.

My panties instantly grew moist, hearing him sing so sexily and, surprisingly, on key. I closed my eyes and ground my body up against his. I could feel the hardness beneath his jeans press up against my booty, causing my breathing to get shallow. As the song continued, I let my arm reach up to softly grab the back of his neck, ensuring that there was no separation between us.

With my head resting back on his shoulder, he placed sweet, wet kisses to the curve of my neck. Our sweat-covered bodies were still grinding seductively to the music as if we were the only two people in the club. We stayed like that, dancing with each other for the next hour or so until the club lights were completely cut on and it was finally time to go. It was one of the most fun-filled nights I had ever had.

"Y'all staying with us tonight?" Micah quickly asked. I knew he was just asking because he wanted Risa to stay the night with him.

"Yeah, you staying with me tonight, beautiful," Damien said to me with a wink.

"I'll just go back to the hotel. I don't want to be the fifth wheel," Tisa said.

"Girl, please. I am not letting you go back there by yourself. And besides, you aren't going to be a fifth wheel. I'm single, remember?" Risa told her.

Micah rolled his eyes but didn't say anything.

"We got a pullout couch," Dre chimed in.

"I guess that'll be fine until the morning," Tisa said.

We all walked across the street to their hotel and went up to their beautiful penthouse suite. Our hotel rooms were nice but nothing like this. This was pretty much a luxury condo. The first thing I noticed was the floor-to-ceiling windows. I walked over and took in the busy metropolis. It was a beautiful sight to see with all the city lights glowing near and far. Sitting just above the skyscrapers, I could even see a few twinkling stars that accented the pitch-black sky of the night.

Damien came next to me and casually draped his arm around my shoulders. "Happy birthday, beautiful!" he said, kissing me on the cheek.

"Thank you, Dame," I said, realizing that it was now, in fact, my birthday.

He took me by the hand and proceeded to guide me into his room.

"Where y'all going?" Micah asked, stopping us dead in our tracks.

"Where it look like we going? Damn nigga, stop cock blocking," Damien mumbled.

Micah got up and walked over toward us. "Don't let this li'l nigga talk you into something you may not be ready for, baby girl," Micah whispered. Damien cut his eyes hard at Micah and shook his head.

"You just mad because Risa's sliding into that pullout bed with her sister," Damien said, nodding his head toward the living room. Sure enough, Risa was getting under the covers on the pullout sofa. As if to rub salt deeper into Micah's wound, she and Tisa both had on white T-shirts of his to sleep in. The only reason I held in my laugh was seeing the sad, almost pathetic look on Micah's face.

Damien gripped my hand a little tighter and pulled me along into his room. He closed the door behind us and instantly began taking off his shirt. Immediately my eyes began to roam his beautiful brown muscles, which were covered in ink. When he reached up to pull the shirt over his head, I noticed that he had gotten a new tattoo on his rib cage. In black cursive writing, it read, "Dame and Beautiful."

"Dame! What's this?" I squealed, sliding my hand across his smooth, tatted skin.

"This was one of your birthday presents," he said, giving me a wink and a smile. "You like it?" he asked.

"I love it, babe. I can't believe you actually did something like this." I stood on my tiptoes for a kiss.

"Why not?" he asked after pecking my lips.

"I don't know, it's just so . . . permanent."

"My love for you is permanent. So, like I said, why not?"

"Love?" I questioned with a big, goofy smile on my face.

"Yeah, love. I love you, Raina," he said softly, looking down into my eyes. "And don't you ever forget that shit." He leaned down and kissed me so deeply that I didn't even get a chance to respond. Our tongues danced in each other's mouths for what felt like an eternity. The kiss was so passionate that I actually felt my knees buckle beneath me, and I was finding it extremely hard to even breathe.

"You wanna jump in the shower?" he asked, breaking our kiss.

"Yes, pl . . . please," I stammered, still catching my breath. My skin was sticky from the club, and my hair was puffed up from all the humidity. A shower was exactly what I needed.

I was in the shower for a good ten minutes before I heard Damien step inside the bathroom.

"I put a towel and one of my T-shirts out here for you to sleep in," he said before leaving and closing back the door. *My boyfriend is the sweetest.* That was so funny, me calling him my boyfriend. Just a year ago, he was completely scared of that label.

After we had showered and gotten in bed, we both lay quiet in the darkness. I let my head rest on his muscular chest as I snuggled underneath his arm. Softly I skimmed my fingers up and down his bare chest and abs, feeling every rise and fall of the air he breathed.

"What's wrong?" I asked, breaking the silence.

"Ain't nothing wrong, baby. I'm just glad I got you in my arms tonight," he said in a quiet tone.

I sat up and peered down into his handsome face. "I love you, Dame," I confessed.

"You didn't have to say that. I already know you love the kid," he said. His cocky white smile cut though the darkness like a star in the night.

"You are so arrogant. I swear," I said, rolling my eyes. He reached up underneath my T-shirt and tickled my sides. I let out a series of girlish giggles, feeling like I was about to pee myself before he flipped me over onto my back and rested between my thighs.

"You're so beautiful, baby," he said with his eyes roaming every inch of my face. I could tell he actually believed the words he spoke, making me feel like the prettiest girl in the world. I leaned up to kiss him, sliding my hands down into his Armani boxer briefs. Just as I started to feel the prickle of his low-cut hair, he asked, "Are you sure you ready for all that?"

I nodded my head, but that wasn't good enough.

"Nah, let me hear you say that shit. Are you ready?" he firmly asked. "If you not, I'll wait."

"I'm ready, Dame," I said just above a whisper.

He lifted my shirt over my head and quickly tossed it to the floor. As he placed tender kisses to my neck, I could feel his lips ease their way down onto my breast. A soft moan seeped from my lips as he took one of my nipples into his mouth. "Mmm," I moaned. My heart began to race as he traced my body with the tip of his tongue. I closed my eyes, feeling his warm mouth connect to my stomach.

Before I even got a chance to prepare myself, he buried his face deep in between my thighs and slid his tongue up and down my center. It was an unforgettable sensation, to say the least.

"Mmmm," I moaned again, only this time louder. I could feel my back robotically arch as he palmed my cheeks in hands. His tongue was still hard at work, flicking fast, when I felt an unusual feeling arise.

"Ohh myy Gawwdd!" I hollered out, feeling my very first orgasm surface. My legs trembled on the tops of his shoulders as he placed tender kisses to my inner thighs.

"Feel good?" he asked. I nodded my head, feeling exhausted and completely out of breath.

He pulled his body up so that he was now hovering over me. Lovingly, he kissed me on the mouth. At first, I was skeptical because he had just been down there, but then I decided to go along with it. Surprisingly, I actually enjoyed the taste of his tongue. After one last kiss to my lips, he leaned over and grabbed something off the nightstand. I could hear the noise of the wrapper, so I instantly knew it was a condom.

"You had this all planned out, didn't you?" I asked, smirking.

"I have a condom with me every time I'm around you, shawty. A nigga never wants to be unprepared when it comes to your pretty ass," he said. He pecked my lips one more time before he reached down between us and rolled the condom up his length. "Just relax, a'ight? I got you," he whispered in my ear, slowly inserting himself inside of me.

"Ssss," I hissed, feeling that initial painful tear. Every muscle in my body had tightened in that moment.

Damien didn't stop though. He just kept working himself slowly in and out of me. "Just relax. Look at me, baby. Tell me you love me," he said, inching his way inside.

"I . . . I love you. Ahh, it hurts," I whined.

"It will start to feel good in a minute. I promise," he said, thrusting his hips into me.

"Ahhh, Dame, it hurts," I whined again, feeling like my center was damn near ripping down there. I looked off to the side, feeling tears in my eyes.

He softly grabbed my chin and turned my face back so that I could look at him. "Shh," he cooed. "Look at me, baby," he whispered, kissing the tears that were falling from the corners of my eyes. When he finally filled me up completely, he stopped moving. From the city lights coming in through the window, I could see him biting down on his lower lip. His eyes were shut tight, and gratification was written all over his face. "Fuck. You feel good as shit," he hissed before kissing my neck.

He started moving in and out of me again, but this time with ease. Although I doubted his words at first, he was right. It was starting to feel good. He gently grabbed me around my throat with one of his hands and used the other to firm up the grip he had on my waist. I could tell that he wanted to be as deep inside of me as he possibly could. By the pleasure-filled look on his handsome face, I knew he was fully enjoying my virgin body.

"Oooh, Dame!" I moaned. With increasing speed, he stroked deeper and deeper. And with every thrust he gave, I found myself loving the feeling more and more.

"Feel good, baby?" he mumbled against my mouth with his eyes still closed.

"Yaass. Mmmm," I said, trying my best to answer.

All of a sudden, he pulled out of me, catching me completely off guard. It was just starting to feel good. "Turn over," he instructed. I instantly got scared because I didn't think I was ready to try a new position, but I still did as he asked.

I was lying flat on my stomach when I felt him pull my legs apart. He slid back inside while resting on top of me. With every long stroke he gave, my nerves started to subside. The feeling of him inside of me was one I didn't think I could ever get tired of.

"Mmmm," I moaned again, hearing the sounds of our wet bodies collide.

Suddenly, he sat up, straddling the backs of my thighs. In that position, he continued to work his way in and out of me, occasionally smacking my backside. "Damn, that ass," he groaned. The sound of him grunting and groaning turned me on even more because I knew that my body was pleasing him. My body was exceeding his every expectation.

All of a sudden, my center began to throb, and I knew another orgasm was near. With every thrust, stroke, and lash he gave, the sensual urge to release grew stronger and stronger. "Ooooh, Dame!" I hollered out loud. "Wait, I'm about to . . . Aaaaah!" I wailed, feeling that tension between my thighs explode into a warm ecstasy just before wetting up our sheets.

Chapter 15

Risa

"Next stop, Canal Street," the driver shouted.

Just moments after sunrise, I found myself riding on the streetcar alone. With the side of my face resting against the warm glass, I looked out at the sight of downtown. Although I had been in the city for the past three days, there was something special about seeing New Orleans at this time of day. The crowded and vulgar metropolis of the night before was now quiet and soft. The traffic was normal and steady, and the trash that littered the streets just hours before had already been swept away. We even passed the same gray-bearded fellow who could be seen on the very same corner every day of the week, holding his cardboard sign.

When the streetcar finally came to my stop, I got off and walked down Decatur Street toward the French Market. It was already eighty-five degrees outside, and the humidity was almost unbearable. Somehow, one last taste of a French-style crepe made it all worth it. I had slipped out of bed early this morning while everyone else was fast asleep. I was the only early riser out of the bunch. Plus, I really needed some "me" time.

"Let me get two crepes with strawberries please," I said to the small Asian lady behind the counter.

"That will be ten dollars and eighty-two cents," she said. I reached down and fumbled in my purse before I suddenly realized that I must have left my money on the streetcar. I had taken it out because I knew exactly how much the crepes were going cost. Unfortunately, I left the rest of my money back at the hotel.

"Oh shit," I muttered. I was so embarrassed and even more so upset that I wouldn't get to eat my crepes.

"Let me get that," a deep, raspy voice said from behind. Before I could turn back to look at him, I saw his big, strong hand and the sparkling diamond Rolex on his wrist as he passed the lady a crisp $20 bill. I turned around, instantly knowing exactly who that voice and hand belonged to. When my eyes fell on Micah's handsome face, he simply smiled.

"Micah, what are you doing here?" I asked, looking confused.

With a happy grin on his face, he ignored my question. I couldn't help but think how perfect his bright smile was against his smooth, dark skin. After getting his change back from the little Asian lady, he handed me my crepes. Tucking both hands into the pockets of his jean shorts and rocking back on his heels, he looked me over while licking his lips. He was casually dressed in a white fitted tee, jean shorts, and white boat shoes. I had to admit that he looked very sexy.

"What are you doing here?" I asked again, trying to sound firm.

"I just wanted to spend some time with you, Risa," he said. He licked his lips again and removed a hand from one of his pockets before affectionately touching the ends of my hair. "Is that a'ight with you?"

When he looked down at me with those piercing dark brown eyes and that lone beauty mark on his face, I instantly grew weak. I had been acting all big and bad these last few months. As long as I didn't see him, I was fine. Out of sight, out of mind. But whenever I would come face-to-face with him like this, I instantly wanted to forget about the past and be held in his arms. I wanted him to kiss me and even make love to me the way he used to. I hated that I felt that way.

"I guess," I finally broke down and said. I could feel myself about to start fidgeting, so I took a small bite of a crepe.

"You sure?" he asked, slowly moving into my personal space. The intermingling smells of his light sweat and Burberry cologne remained stagnant in the morning's heat. I swore I could feel my internal temperature rise one single degree at a time with every second that passed, further making me despise that he still had this effect on me.

"Uhh, well, uh, yeah, I guess it's fine," I stammered, fanning my face.

He let out a light chuckle as if he knew he was getting me all hot and bothered. "Cool. Let's walk down to the flea market then," he said, and just like that, I was back under his spell. I no longer cared about the money I left on the streetcar, or anything else for that matter.

Micah and I spent pretty much the whole day laughing and talking about our current lives. We had even experienced our first beignets from Café Du Monde together. We sat in the very back corner of the café while he listened to me fret over whether I'd actually get into law school.

"Well, I applied to Harvard, Yale, and Emory. I should find out my fate within the next week or two. Of course, Harvard is my first choice, but I guess I wouldn't mind going to Emory, just to be closer to my tinka-tink," I said, referring to li'l Armond.

"Ain't no doubt in my mind that you gon' get into Harvard," he said, leaning up to gently thumb away the powdered sugar from my cheek. "But of course, I want you to stay here. With me."

"With you?" I asked, raising one of my eyebrows.

"You know what I mean," he said, sitting back in his chair with a smirk on his face.

I shook my head and tried to change the subject. "What's Miss Zaria been up to?" I asked, referring to his daughter.

"She's doing good. You should call her some time, or better yet, hang out with us on the weekends I have her."

I laughed. "Keesha didn't tell you, did she?" Keesha was his daughter's mother.

"Tell me what?" he quizzed with his eyebrows pulling together.

"I've been getting Zaria every other Saturday for the past, what, three months maybe?" I asked more to myself than him.

"You what?"

I let out a little laugh. "Yeah, I was missing my baby, so I got Keesha's number from your mom. She'll either drop her off to me on those Saturdays, or I'll pick her up. I assumed Zaria would have told you about it. That's weird."

"Her trifling-ass mama probably told her not to. Shit, with her staying with me every other weekend and then staying with you on the opposite weekends, that means Keesha ass gets a child-free weekend every fucking weekend!"

"When you put it that way, you just might be right," I said, shaking my head. Keesha was a trip. I should have known she was up to something, but I just figured she was being nice because I wasn't with Micah anymore. "You aren't going to take away my weekends with her, are you?"

"I guess not. I mean unless you don't mind spending time with the both of us."

"We'll see," I said before taking a final sip of my coffee.

"You ready to get out of here?" he asked.

"Yeah, let's go."

As we trekked from street to street, he naturally held my hand. At first, I pulled back, but as the day went on, it just felt right. Occasionally we'd stop to shop or watch a street show. We sat and watched one man wearing a silver suit and a painted face pop and lock to the urban beats of his boom box. Micah was trying to impress me, so he, of course, he had to break dance too. It was an awful sight to see, but we both laughed like there was no tomorrow. Truthfully, I had forgotten just how fun he could be.

Once we were near where the hotel was, I noticed Micah glancing down at his watch. It was getting late and time for us to head back for Raina's birthday surprise. Dame wanted us to all be ready by eight o'clock, and it was now a little after five. He was so excited about his surprise for her that I surely didn't want to be the one to ruin it.

"It's time for us to head back, isn't it?" I asked.

"Yeah, but I'm not ready to go back," he said, pulling my hand up for a gentle kiss. I smiled at his simple act of affection. That was the one thing I would never get tired of, his romantic gestures.

"I enjoyed today too," I said.

"Will you let me take you out when we get back to Atlanta?" He interlaced his fingers through mine.

"I don't know. I'm kind of enjoying us being . . . just friends," I said, continuing to walk along.

With his hand still attached to mine, he stopped midstep and cocked his head to the side. The way he turned and twisted his lips, I knew he was calling my bluff. "Friends, huh?" he asked. I stood just a few steps in front of him, nodding my head. I refused to look him in the eyes, but he yanked me back, forcing our gazes to lock. "You want to be just friends, right?" he asked low, wrapping his arms around my waist. When he leaned down to kiss me, I immediately closed my eyes.

We stood there in the middle of a busy sidewalk, kissing while pedestrians walked right on by. I didn't even care. I was simply enjoying the familiar taste and feel of his tongue in my mouth. This was the hard part about being around Micah. He could literally make me weak with just one simple touch.

"Mmm," I let out a soft, unintentional moan.

"Friends, right?" he whispered again into my mouth.

I pulled away a little, savoring the flavor on my lips and nodded. "Yeah, let's just take things slow, okay?"

I tried to continue walking, but he wouldn't let me. "You know I would never hurt you again, don't you?" he whispered, gripping my waist to hold me in place.

"And how do I know that?" I looked up and asked, using my hand to shade my eyes from the bright New Orleans sun.

"Because I've learned my lesson. I know I make it look easy, but I'm for real struggling out here without you baby. For all the wrong I've ever done to you, I promise to spend the rest of my days on this earth making it right. I love you, Risa, and us not being together, not having you by my side, shit is killing me," he confessed, peering down at me.

His sincere eyes pleaded and tugged at every string attached to my broken heart. But I honestly didn't know if I was willing to take a chance on Micah again, so I didn't respond. I merely stood on my tiptoes to peck his lips, gently caressing the sides of his face. I pulled back and stared him in the eyes. "I love you, Micah, but I can't make you any promises right now. I've been through so much in just a short period of time that I think I just . . . I just need a break from it all. I need to focus on my career right now. I hope that you can understand that."

His head slightly dropped in defeat, but then he slowly nodded his head. "I completely understand, baby. I'm here whenever you're ready."

Chapter 16

Damien

We found ourselves all wandering down Bourbon Street just before nightfall stretched across the sky. As we traveled down the wild, crowded path, sipping Hurricanes through a straw, we could hear angles of music traveling from all different directions toward us. The collective sounds of jazz, blues, rock, and rap all blared as people partied in and out of the street.

"Yo, it's wild as shit out here," Dre said with one arm draped over Romi's shoulders. It was the first time out there for all of us, so we were just taking in the bright lights, bars, and strips clubs that were damn near at every other door.

"Ooh, y'all, I wanna dance," Romi said with a little twerk.

"Shawty, I think you've done enough dancing these past few days. It's time to sit your pretty ass down somewhere so you can get back home to my son," Dre told her seriously. We all burst into laughter as she rolled her green eyes.

"Yeah, it's definitely too many niggas out here for me. Yo, where the hell we going?" Micah asked. He and Risa were actually holding hands, which totally threw me off because just yesterday, she was giving that nigga the cold shoulder.

"We're almost there, y'all," I said excitedly. My baby had her arm looped through mine, and she was dressed to kill. The tight-fitting gold dress she wore fit her body like a glove, and the sparkly gold heels on her feet accentuated the perfect muscles in her calves. In fact, all the girls were dressed up and wearing high heels this night. It was funny as shit to see them walking down Bourbon Street all dolled up, avoiding piss and potholes at every other step.

After adapting to the common stench of urine and vomit that was floating in the New Orleans air, I told everyone to cut into one of the bars. Anita Baker's "Body and Soul" seductively played on the set as we entered. It was a small, smoky hole-in-the-wall with only a few rickety pub tables lining the edge of the dance floor. However, that dance floor was completely packed. In the back, there was even a small stage set up with band equipment.

"Yo, you brought us to this shithole? This supposed to be baby girl's big birthday surprise?" Micah said, looking around the place with his nose scrunched up. I gave him a wink, letting him know that I had more tricks up my sleeve.

While the rest of the crew all headed over to the bar, I grabbed Raina's hand and led her straight to the dance floor. I pulled her in close and wrapped my protective arms around her, burying my face in the crook of her pretty-ass neck. I closed my eyes, enjoying that faint smell of lavender as she gently melted into my embrace. Rhythmically, we swayed to the beat of each other's heart while the soft sounds of "Body and Soul" could still be heard. That was that baby-making music that Moms and Pops would always play back at the house. The way Raina ground her hips into me with each melody that played, I could see why they loved this song so much.

When the song was finally over, I gently lifted her

chin with the tip of my finger and looked into her eyes. I gave her a confident grin before kissing her sweet lips. Instinctively, she sealed her eyes tight and slipped her tongue into my mouth. I was completely gone over this girl. I went from "never kisses bitches" to tonguing down my queen every chance I got. I could now officially say that I was a soft-ass nigga, the same as the other soft-ass niggas I used to clown.

"Good evening," an old man on stage abruptly said into the mic. As the bright spotlight beamed directly down, I could slightly see a band setting up behind him. He wore brown plaid pants with suspenders and a musician's hat on his head. He even had an old guitar draped across his chest as he spoke to the crowd.

"Are y'all having a good time tonight?" he yelled out to the audience.

"Hell yeah!" I could hear some of the people say.

"Nah, I didn't hear y'all. Let me ask it again. I said, are y'all having a good time tonight, baby?" he asked with that special Nawlins twang.

"Hell yeah!" the crowd all roared.

"Well, I have a special surprise tonight. It seems we have a birthday girl in the building. Ms. Raina, where you at, sweetheart?" he said. He looked out into the crowd, searching with his hand hooded over his eyes.

I stood there pointing so that everyone could see her while she covered her face from embarrassment. The loud chants and cheers from our crew behind us egged me on even more. I pulled her hands from her face and put her hand up high in the air before kissing her blushing red cheek. She looked at me with wide eyes and a shocked smile on her face. After holding out my arm for her to take, I then escorted her to the front just below the stage.

"Here she is," I said.

"Ms. Raina baby, somebody wants to wish you a very happy birthday," the old man said before walking to the back.

All of a sudden, the spotlight on the platform grew dim and soft, allowing us to clearly see the rest of the band on stage. They began playing a soft, slow instrumental version of "Happy Birthday," using just a keyboard, saxophone, and guitar. Suddenly from stage right, a sexy leg adorned in a red high-heeled shoe peeped from the curtain, teasing the crowd. Everyone whistled and cheered, anticipating the sight of this lady.

Raina cut her eyes over at me, wondering what this was all about, but I simply gave her a smirk and a shrug. When her eyes fell back onto the stage, Grandma Lisa Mae appeared from behind the curtain wearing a red strapless sequined gown with a long slit up the side. Her long sandy brown hair cascaded down her back as she sashayed to the center of the stage. Wrapped, almost dangling, just below her shoulders was a red feather boa that matched the bright red lipstick she wore. As I watched this ageless beauty stand in front of the mic with her green eyes glittering back toward the crowd, I couldn't help but think that this was what Raina would look like fifty years from now.

"I want to wish my granddaughter Raina a very happy birthday tonight, y'all," Grandma Lisa Mae said into the mic. "And I want to thank that fine young thang hanging on her arm tonight, too. He called me up and said, 'Grandma, what can I do to surprise my baby?'" she continued, causing the crowd to ooh and aw. "She got a keeper, y'all, that's for damn sure. Look at that little nigga. Fine as shhhi . . . Woo weee," she hollered out, fanning her face while moving her hips in a circle. The crowd erupted in laughter.

"Well, suga, this one here is just for you," she said, pointing at Raina. She cleared her throat and gave a little wink to Raina just before she opened her mouth to sing. "'Happy birthday to you. Haappy birthday to youuu. Haaappppy biirthdayyyy, dear Raina. Haaaappyy biiirthdayy tooo youuuuu!'" The blues-like flair she put on the simple song had the crowd instantly on their feet and going wild. Ms. Ernie told me that Grandma Lisa Mae used to be a jazz and blues singer back in the day, but never in a million years did I imagine anything like that. I looked down at Raina, and she had tears pooled in her eyes as she and Grandma Lisa Mae blew kisses back and forth to one another.

"And that's not all we got, y'all," Grandma Lisa Mae said into the mic.

Raina cut her beautiful light eyes over at me once more, wondering what else I had up my sleeve. I simply shrugged and smiled again.

"Coming to the stage, *Bring It!* Coach D and the Dancing Dolls," Grandma Lisa Mae dramatically introduced before exiting the stage.

"Oh my Gah, Dame. You didn't," Raina squealed, bouncing up and down as she held me tight.

All of a sudden, what sounded like the beat of a thousand drums emanated from the stage. Colorful lights flickered about as a small marching band began parading before us. Then about eight or so girls came out dancing to the beat, wildly swinging their hair like I'd seen Raina do a dozen times before going out on the field. The last one out on stage was their leader, Coach D. She strutted out in a sexy red and silver cat suit, then stood right in front of the other girls with her hands on her hips.

With a hard strike of the drum, they all began dancing their routine, gyrating, splitting, and bucking all together as one to the sounds of the band. When I glanced over at

Raina, she had her hands pressed to the sides of her face, watching in pure amusement. My baby loved that show *Bring It!* Even more so, she loved to dance. So I'd figured this would be the perfect gift.

As time went on that night, Raina got a chance to meet Coach D and the Dancing Dolls. They took pictures, and she even got a chance to dance with them on stage. My baby was a star, and she always shined no matter who was dancing beside her. She told me that she would remember this night for the rest of her life, and just that statement alone made a nigga feel some type of way.

After Coach D and the Dancing Dolls left the bar, the DJ went back to playing that baby-making music. As Grandma, Tisa, Romi, and Dre were all over at the bar having a drink, Raquel sat on Melo's lap at a table near the dance floor. Risa slow danced with Micah, allowing her arms to gently clasp around his neck while laying her head on his chest. They were doing a slow-ass two-step like they were at a middle school dance and shit, while Raina and I were grinding our bodies to the beat. My sweaty form adhered to hers like glue as we practically fucked right there on the dance floor. With my arms tightly enclosed around her waist, we seductively moved chest to chest, pelvis to pelvis, and thigh to thigh to the rhythm of Ro James's "Permission." I was hard as a rock, so I knew she felt that big motherfucker poking at her. Just one night of sex with Raina and I could no longer even be close to her without thinking about the pussy.

> *Tonight I wanna be a little me on you*
> *Ooh yeah*
> *With your permission*
> *I wanna spend the night sipping on you*
> *You know what I'm talking about baby, yeah*

As the music continued to play, I kept grinding into her, exploring with my hands. I rubbed all over her fat ass while tonguing her down in the middle of the dance floor. Our sweat-covered bodies remained that way, connecting for several songs like we were the only couple in the room. When we all finally left the bar that night and headed back down the brick path, I looked up just in time to see loud, bright bursts of color scatter across the sky. Then I glanced over, seeing Raina's light eyes twinkle with delight as she looked up toward the fireworks.

"Damn. Happy Fourth of July, beautiful," I said, placing a tender kiss to her cheek.

She looked over at me and smiled. "Happy Fourth of July, Dame."

Chapter 17

Raquel

"Damn, Quel, hurry up!" I heard Melo yell.

I was in his bathroom, putting the final touches on my hair and makeup while he impatiently sat on the edge of his bed. This would be my first time meeting his father, Raul, when he would actually introduce me as his girlfriend. It's true that at first I wasn't keen on the title, but now that our relationship was out and on full display, I'd had a change of heart. These days, whenever we were out in public, I would make him hold my hand. No matter where we were, I'd pucker up my lips for him to give me a small kiss, and on those nights we'd spend apart, we'd talk on the phone for hours until we finally fell asleep. I was loving the feeling of being in a real relationship.

Melo's father was in town on business again and had invited us to lunch. Lately, he had been coming over to the States from Cuba at least once a month. I didn't know why, but I was kind of excited to meet up with him. Melo rarely talked about his father, so I saw this as an opportunity to learn more about my man, about who he was and where he came from.

All of a sudden, the bathroom door flew open, and through the mirror, I could see Melo standing in the entrance with a pissed look on his face. "You ready?" he asked sternly without a hint of a smile.

"Almost. I just wanna look perfect, bae," I told him, applying a thin coat of black mascara to my lashes.

"Why? That nigga done seen yo' ass before," he said, coming up behind and wrapping his strong, tatted arms around me.

I turned my head and gave him a little peck before I said, "Just five more minutes, okay?" He shook his head with a sigh of frustration before walking out of the bathroom.

When we finally reached Benihana that afternoon, Mr. Raul was already seated at a quiet table in the back. I felt bad because we were fifteen minutes late and he was waiting alone. With a closed-lip smile, he waved us over to join him before pushing his glasses up onto the bridge of his nose. Melo grabbed me softly by the hand and led the way.

I looked Mr. Raul over as he stood up from the table and put his hand out for Melo to shake. He was a man of average height and size. A clean gray business suit hung on his slender frame. There was no tie hanging from his neck, only a white dress shirt that had two buttons undone at the top, exposing the straight gray hairs on his chest. His aging skin was the color of red clay, and the fine hairs on the top of his head were the blended colors of salt and pepper.

Melo shook his hand before Mr. Raul brought him in for a half hug. "How's it going, son?" he asked, letting that thick Cuban accent roll off his tongue with ease.

"Shit, I'm making it, Pops," Melo said with a scratch to his ear. "You remember my girl, Raquel, right?" he asked, pulling me in front of him. I simply smiled.

"Of course, of course," he said, opening his arms wide for a hug. I really didn't like hugging nobody, but I forced myself to since this was Melo's dad.

"Come on, let's have a seat," he said, motioning his hand toward the table.

We all sat down and scanned the menu before ordering our food. I ordered the shrimp while Melo and his dad ordered the steak. Throughout the course of dinner, I noticed that Mr. Raul kept staring at me. He wasn't being discreet about it either. It was an awkward, almost creepy stare that I just couldn't read. He was making me so uncomfortable that I had even started to fidget in my seat. I even cleared my throat several times to get Melo's attention, but he never said anything. Luckily, Romi texted me pictures of the baby, so I kept my head down, texting back on my phone.

"How are you liking it at Clark, young lady?" Mr. Raul asked, forcing me to look at him.

I looked up, pulling my eyes away from the screen before clearing my throat once more. "Oh, I love it. Straight A's for a second semester in a row," I bragged.

He casually studied my face before giving me a smile. "And she's smart, too," he said, bouncing his eyebrows.

"Yo, why you keep looking at her like that?" Melo finally spoke up.

"Her eyes, son," he said calmly, trying put Melo at ease. "Her eyes remind me so much of your mother's." He took a small sip of wine before biting down on his bottom lip.

"Yeah, they do," Melo said low before tightening his jaw.

My emotions were torn. I was partly flattered because I knew it was a compliment hearing that my eyes remind-ed them of his deceased mother's, but picking up on the sadness in Melo's voice made me feel apologetic for some reason. He told me once before that I reminded him of his mother. Now hearing his father repeat those exact same sentiments confirmed the thought.

"I just wished she would've never . . ." Mr. Raul started to say before taking another sip of his red wine.

"Did Melo tell you about his nightmares? Well, the dream where you actually shoot her in the head?" I asked before taking another bite of my shrimp.

Mr. Raul's eyes grew wide, and out of nowhere, I could see the red wine fly from his mouth, soaring across the table. With several punches to his own chest, he began to cough and choke uncontrollably.

"Damn. You all right, Pops?" Melo asked, wiping the wine from his own clothes.

Mr. Raul nodded his head and stood up from the table. He tried to speak, but his coughing was so bad that he couldn't release the words from his throat. With one hand held up high signaling that he was okay and the other clutching his sunken chest, he walked away to the men's bathroom. That's when suddenly I felt a hard smack to my thigh.

"Fuck you tell him that shit for?" Melo snapped with sullen hazel eyes.

I shrugged my shoulders. "I mean, I didn't think it was that big of a deal. It was just a dream, right? Why's he all bent outta shape?" I asked, rolling my eyes. Yes, I knew that it might have been in poor taste to mention the nightmares Melo had been having about his mother, but sometimes whatever came to my mind just came flying right out of my mouth. Shit, I couldn't help it. The way Mr. Raul acted was very peculiar. I was willing to bet there was more to Melo's mother's death than the story I'd heard.

"Pops don't like talking about my mom. Period. Especially the way she died. So don't bring that shit up no more, a'ight?" Although I had a lot more questions, I nodded my head out of respect for Melo and his father.

A few minutes later, Mr. Raul was walking out of the bathroom and heading back over toward the table. "Now, where were we?" he said, sliding back in the booth. He took off his glasses and began cleaning the lenses with the corner of his white dinner napkin. "Ah yes, Kizzy," he said, calling Melo's mother's name.

"We ain't gotta talk about her, Pops," Melo cut in, firmly gripping my thigh underneath the table to keep me quiet.

"I think you two should come to Cuba for a visit. I have lots of pictures of Kizzy and special things around that remind me of her back at home," he said with a smile.

"Ooh yeah! I've never been to Cuba," I sat up and said excitedly. A trip out of the country was like music to my ears.

"Um, I'on know, Pops," Melo said.

"Pleassee," I whined, batting my eyes little. Melo just shook his head at my dramatics.

"Yeah, I see now that you have your hands full, son," his father said with a laugh. I simply rolled my eyes.

Later that evening after dinner, Melo dropped me off at the local music studio near campus. An up-and-coming artist by the name of Traxx had specifically requested for me to sing on his first official track. Previously, Traxx had done a bunch of mixed tapes and a few featured hooks on other rappers' songs, but nothing big. Based on our phone conversation, he was really trying to get his name out there, and he thought I was just the person to help him do it.

When I walked into the dark, smoke-filled studio, the smell of weed instantly hit my nose. A crazy beat was blaring from the speakers as hints of red and green light flickered on the soundboard. After hearing me enter, Traxx immediately spun around in his chair and gave a lazy smile. His shiny gold teeth beamed against his midnight skin. On the top of his head was a messy ball of black and honey blond dreadlocks. Several gold chains draped heavily from his neck while his hands sparkled in the night from all the gold and diamond rings he wore.

He removed the dangling blunt from his lips before standing up to greet me. "Mane, you Rock-kel, right?" he said slowly, extending his hand for me to shake.

"Yep, that's me."

He walked over and cut on the lights, allowing me to take in his whole appearance. I had seen him on YouTube before, but this was my very first time seeing him in person. He had a black teardrop tatted underneath his left eye that was almost invisible against his dark complexion. Two nicks were sliced in each of his eyebrows, complementing his dark, slanted eyes. While a two-inch scar lined the edge of his left jaw, he had a broad African nose and full, kissable brown lips. His angular face was interesting, to say the least. I looked him over once more, taking in his small gold hoop earrings, extra-long white tee, and black skinny jeans.

"Mane, I see ya over dere checking a nigga out," he said with a slow country accent. His gold teeth peeped through the part of his lips as he grinned. He slowly licked his lips as I watched his low red eyes form a smile.

"Uh, no-no," I quickly told him with a shake of my head. I held my hand up, rolling my eyes because I did not want this nigga getting confused. He simply laughed at my response.

Then he waved me over to have a seat next to him. After hitting a few buttons on the mixing board, he said, "Shawty, listen to this right here."

That same crazy beat started playing again, but this time I could actually hear his lyrics playing along with it. At first, Traxx was just rapping along, bobbing his head casually to the beat. But when the beat finally dropped, he took it to a whole other level. His hands gripped the top of his head as he continued to bop to the sound. He rounded his back while bouncing his shoulders. With his hand waving high up in the air, I could feel his eyes burning a hole in me like he was trying to see if I was feeling the track.

I couldn't front, the track was dope, so I was vibing to it too. I was bobbing my head to the beat when, all of a sudden, he spun my chair around to face him. He grabbed the bottom of my seat and pulled me closer to him. Our knees touched as he continued to rap, almost like he was singing the lyrics specifically to me. Physically, Traxx wasn't my type, but I couldn't lie, he could definitely spit.

"Right here is where I need you to come in at," he said, tapping my leg.

I closed my eyes and took in the sound. My mind raced a mile a minute as I tried to find the words. *I got it.* Singing the first thing that came to mind, I sang, "I don't need you to lie to me, I just need you to vibe with me." He gave an approving smile, showing those gold teeth again.

"I don't need you to side with me, I just need you to ride with me," I sang.

Traxx let out a light chuckle before cutting off the mixing board. Although he was grinning from ear to ear, I couldn't quite read his expression. I was praying that he wasn't going to clown my lyrics. With his fist held up to his mouth, he shook his head. "Yuh, yuh! You did that shit, gul! We 'bout to make beautiful music together, baby!"

Chapter 18

Micah

I lay back on the blue suede couch across from my fine-ass therapist, Dr. Fatima Jackson, this Friday evening. She was a tall, dark-skinned beauty with a short Halle cut. Her high cheekbones, slanted eyes, and thin lips made her look like a runway model. Not to mention, this woman had class and style.

I did notice, however, that with each passing appointment, her style of dress grew sexier and sexier. Today she had on a pink silk blouse with buttons going down the front. A tight heather gray pencil skirt clung to her small hips, and on her feet were high silver pumps. Now I realize to most people that shit doesn't sound sexy at all, but it definitely was.

She didn't have the traditional two buttons at the top of her blouse undone. Instead, she had the top four buttons undone. Her shirt was open so wide, I could actually see the dark chocolate flesh between her breasts and the black lace bra she wore. Seductively she would play with the pearl necklace around her neck while crossing and uncrossing her long, colt-like legs as if she wanted me to see up underneath her skirt. Then, whenever there were moments of silence during our session, she would pretend like she was thinking. She'd take the stem of her eyeglasses and put it in her mouth, allowing me to see her pink tongue twirl around.

I didn't know if she was just testing a nigga because of everything she knew I was going through with Risa, or if she just wanted to fuck. Either way, I stayed on my best behavior and avoided looking at her sexy ass. Whenever I was in her office, I always lay down on the couch and stared up at the ceiling, saying small silent prayers throughout the hour. Believe it or not, that shit actually worked.

"Mr. Borrego, can you tell me a little bit about your first sexual experience?" she asked. I glanced over, noticing that she was looking at me over the top of her eyeglasses from where they sat low on her nose.

"Sure," I said, folding my hands on the top of my stomach, focusing my eyes back up toward the ceiling. "I was like fourteen at the time, and even though I didn't live in the hood, you couldn't keep my bad ass out the projects," I said, letting out a small snort of laughter. "Me and my nigga Timo used to ride our bikes down to the Freemont projects just to play ball and talk to girls and shit. One day during the summer, we were on the basketball court playing a game of two on two. They were some older niggas we were playing against, but we knew we could take 'em. Apparently some older girls over on the bleachers watching made a bet. It was three of them: Sade, Meeka, and I think the other girl's name was Nasha.

"After we won, the three girls walked over to us in the center of the court. It was Meeka and Nasha up front walking with these sneaky-ass smiles on their faces while Sade lagged behind. When they approached us, they told us that Sade had bet against us, and just for losing the bet, she had to fuck one of us. My nigga Timo had already lost his virginity, but I hadn't done it yet. I glanced behind Meeka and Nasha to get a better look at Sade, who had her hands on her hips, rolling her eyes. Shawty was a short, pretty, brown-skinned girl with a ponytail full of long black hair. Instantly, a nigga was sold," I said, shaking my head.

"I remember as soon as we left the basketball court that day, we headed right over to Meeka's house, and since her mama wasn't home, we did it right up in her bedroom. I never told Sade I was a virgin that day, but of course, she already knew. She was seventeen and more experienced, so I just lay back and let her take the lead. Shit, I don't think a nigga lasted more than two minutes." I let out a chuckle, glancing over to see Dr. Fatima's reaction.

She had a smirk on her face. "Hmm. I see, Mr. Borrego," she said, uncrossing her legs. She undid one more button on her blouse and fanned her face like she was burning up. "It's so hot in here," she said seductively, biting down on her bottom lip.

Dr. Fatima was a fucking trip because they had the air conditioning on blast in that bitch. I knew it couldn't have been my story that got her ass so hot either, because I didn't even go into any sexual details. When she got up from her chair and walked over to lock the door, I figured she was about to be on some bullshit. I quickly sat up in the chair, ready to bounce, but when I looked up, shawty's blouse had been tossed to the floor. She stood there looking sexy in her black lace bra and high-waist pencil skirt.

"Fuck nah," I mumbled, running my hand down my face. When I tried standing up from my seat, she pushed me back down to the couch and quickly straddled me. "Fuck is you doing, shawty?"

She ignored my question and immediately started kissing on my neck while winding her hips on my lap. I closed my eyes from frustration, letting out a deep sigh before pushing that bitch right up off of me.

"Micah," she said with a confused look on her face, lying back on the couch.

"Micah? The fuck happened to Mr. Borrego?" I shook my head and walked right out the door. In that moment, I decided that today would definitely be my last day going to therapy. If I could reject Fatima's fine ass, I knew for a fact that a nigga had been cured.

As I drove over to Keesha's condo to pick up Zaria, my phone started to vibrate. "Yo," I said, answering the call on Bluetooth.

"Mane, this bitch done slit all my muthafuckin' tires. I'm standing out here stranded, bruh. Where you at?" Timo asked. I could tell just by his tone that he was beyond pissed.

"I'm on my way to pick up Zaria. Now, who did you say slit your tires?"

"That crazy-ass bitch Sabrina," he snapped, referring to Risa's best friend. Wherever he was at, I could hear cars passing by in the background.

I started laughing, thinking about Sabrina's senseless ass. The very first night I seen them at the restaurant together, I knew he had met his match. "Nigga, what did you do? She ain't just gon' slice your tires up for no fucking reason."

"Pshhh! Man, fuck that bit—" he started to say.

"What happened?"

He let out a deep sigh. "I got caught slipping. She caught me out with Sherika and the kids. Straight pulled up on us all nonchalant and shit in the grocery store like, 'Hey, baby.' When I said hey back, Sherika instantly started popping off at the mouth. Telling her how we one big happy family and she's just a homewrecker. Told Sabrina how we still be fucking three to four times a week and all'at. Tal'm 'bout I'm her man and ain't nobody gon' change that shit. Blah, blah, blah," he mocked, trying his best to tell the story.

I know I shouldn't have, but I laughed my ass off. Just picturing Sherika's ghetto ass getting into it with Sabrina had a nigga's stomach hurting. "Damn, bruh, you sho' know how to pick 'em," I said with a chuckle.

"Fuck you, nigga. You coming to get me or nah?" he said.

"Yeah, I'll swing through. Where you at?"

"Down here off Peters Street, right down from Pearl's," he said.

"A'ight, be there in twenty," I told him before killing the line.

As soon as I hung up with him, I dialed up the one person I knew I could depend on when it came to my baby.

"Hello," she answered. Just the soft sound of her voice made me regret all the dumb shit I had pulled in the past.

"What's up, sweetheart? How ya doing?" I asked, smoothing out my raspy tone.

"I'm doing fine, Micah. How are you?" Risa asked.

"Doing all right. You busy?"

"Just getting a mani-pedi, but I'm almost done. What's up?"

"I need your help with something."

"Okay?"

"I'm supposed to pick up Zaria for the weekend, but Timo just called and told me that your girl slashed all his fucking tires. Now I got to go pick that nigga up. Can you get Zari for me and take her back to my place?" I asked, knowing she still had a key.

There was a brief moment of silence on the phone before she finally said, "Sure. I'd be happy to."

After ending the call, I headed over to get Timo. Sure enough, when I pulled up on Peters Street, that nigga's Maserati was sitting right on the ground. He was outside, pacing the sidewalk with his phone up to his ear, wearing a pissed look on his face. From the way he was yelling,

I knew whoever was on the other end had fucked up majorly with him. When he saw me pull up, he quickly ended the call and hopped into my truck.

"'Bout time, nigga," he said with a scowl on his face.

"I can let yo' ass right back out on Peters if that's what you want," I told him. He wasn't about to talk shit to me when I was the one doing that nigga a favor.

"Damn, my bad, bruh. Bri just got my head all fucked up. Where my baby at?" he asked, turning around to look in the back seat.

"Nah, Risa picked her up for me," I said, smiling. I could finally talk to Timo about Risa without him getting all bent out of fucking shape. Although he was still looking for Zo's murderer, he no longer blamed her for what happened to him.

Timo shook his head. "Shawty just can't stay away from yo' ass, can she? And you using my niece as bait in the process."

"I'm not using her. Risa loves my baby. As a matter of fact, she gets her from Keesha on the weekends that I don't have her."

"Damn, Keesha living it up, ain't she? She gets to party every fucking weekend?"

"That's the same shit I said, but Risa was like, 'Don't take away my weekends with her,'" I said, trying to imitate her feminine voice.

"You damn sure have a keeper, that's for sure. Shawty trying to get her law degree, and she don't mind helping take care of Zari either. Yeah, you fucked that shit up fa real fa real, my nigga."

I clenched my jaw hearing him say that. He wasn't telling me shit I didn't already know. I told myself the same shit on a daily basis, so the last thing I needed was to hear it from his ass too.

"I'm trying to get her back, but she's on that 'let's just be friends' bullshit right now."

"I'm throwing a pool party and barbecue next weekend at my crib. I'll have Sabrina invite her. You just make sure you roll through too," he said.

"Sabrina? I thought you wasn't fucking with her no more," I said, making him smirk.

"Mannn, I can't stay away from that crazy-ass girl to save my life," he said, shaking his head.

After dropping him off at his house that night, I headed back home to my condo. It was a little before nine o'clock, and it had just begun to get dark outside. When I entered my place, all the lights were off, but the TV in the living room was still on. I looked down on the couch to see Risa lying there asleep with Zaria sleeping on top of her. I picked Zaria up and went to go put her in the bed. When I got back to the living room, Risa was sitting up and putting on her shoes. She had on those teeny burgundy cheerleader shorts that I loved with a gray Spelman T-shirt. Her hair was in a simple ponytail, and her beautiful face was bare.

"You don't have to go. You know you can stay in the guest room," I suggested.

"No, I need to go. I have some studying to do tomorrow," she said, standing up and stretching.

"Well, thank you," I told her, pulling her in for a hug.

She hugged me back and said, "It was no problem at all, Micah. We actually had a good time."

When I walked her to the door, we quietly looked into each other's eyes. It was like she didn't want to leave, and I knew damn well I didn't want her to. After a few seconds passed, she pushed back whatever was running through her mind and said, "Well, I guess I'll talk to you later."

"Yeah, talk to you later," I said, watching her walk away.

Chapter 19

Romi

Last night, Dre drove all the way home from school just so that he could go with me to li'l Armond's six-month checkup the very next morning. Of course, he stayed the night with us, and before eight o'clock the next morning had even rolled around, the aroma of Mama's pancakes and bacon was already floating in the air. After getting out of bed and getting ourselves dressed for the day, we all headed downstairs for breakfast. When we entered the kitchen, Dre was tossing li'l Armond high up in the air, causing him to giggle. He had the most adorable laugh I had ever heard.

"All right now, you gonna make him throw up," Mama fussed.

"Nah, he knows not to pull that mess with Daddy. Don't you, stinka butt?" He kissed li'l Armond's chubby cheek.

"So when do you start school back up again?" Mama asked me as she set plates of food down on the table in front of us. My mouth watered at the sight of her home-made buttermilk pancakes stacked up high on the plate.

"The week after Labor Day," I replied.

"Yeah, about that. We need to figure some shit out," Dre said, cutting his eyes over at me.

"Figure what out, Dre?" I asked, totally confused.

"I want you and Armond to move to Atlanta with me."

I looked over at my mother, and I could tell it was killing her to keep her mouth shut. She didn't say anything, though. She merely walked away from the table and went over to stand in front of the kitchen sink.

"I have school, Dre, and a whole support system here. I can't just up and leave," I told him.

"Shawty, this driving back and forth shit is for the birds. I need to see my son every day, not just on the weekends, and I need to see you, too," he said, hooking his finger under my chin.

I looked up into his dark, piercing brown eyes, taking in the sincerity behind them. Before I could say anything else, he pressed his lips against mine and said, "But we'll talk more about it later, a'ight?" I simply nodded my head in response.

After breakfast, we headed over to the pediatrician's office in Dre's brand-new black Benz Concept GLA. He had finally put that bike of his to rest, and I couldn't have been happier. At first, I thought the motorcycle was sexy, but now that we had li'l Armond, all I could do was think about how dangerous it was. I didn't know what I would do if something ever happened to Dre.

As we rode quietly, listening to Bruno Mars on the radio, I stared out of the window. All of a sudden, I could hear his cell phone start to vibrate. After he looked down at the screen, I noticed that he quickly hit the ignore button. I let out an unintentional sigh before returning my gaze to the window.

"What's wrong?" he asked.

I looked over at him and shook my head, giving a closed-lip smile. As we continued to ride, I kept thinking about my future with Dre. We were spending every weekend together as a family, and we practically talked every day, all day, either by phone or by text. Dre and I were actually getting along better than we ever had, but honestly, I didn't know if we were in an actual committed relationship or not. I was just too afraid to ask. After everything we had been through, I didn't want to take one step forward only to take two steps back.

He told me that he broke it off with Brandi months ago, but because I was a snoop by nature, I would still go through his phone. From what I could see in his call log, he and Brandi still talked several times a week. I could tell that he had been deleting all of their text messages, too, which was also a red flag. Of course, I was pissed about it, but how could I be? He never officially made me his girlfriend even after li'l Armond was born. And even though we acted like a couple now more than ever before, he had yet to say the words.

When we pulled up to the doctor's office, Dre parked the truck and hopped out. While I grabbed the diaper bag, Dre unlatched li'l Armond's car seat carrier from the back. He was sound asleep, so we didn't even bother taking him out. As we walked up to the front door, Dre gently grabbed my hand.

"You sure everything's all right?" he asked.

"Everything's fine, baby," I told him with a half smile.

He brought my hand up to his mouth before placing a tender kiss to the back of it. We continued walking into the building, holding hands. He carried li'l Armond in the carrier with his free hand while I carried the diaper bag in mine. I knew if I were to even consider moving to Atlanta with him, I needed more clarification on the status of our relationship. I also needed to know what was up with him and Brandi, but right now wasn't the time. My focus needed to be on li'l Armond, and in that moment, that was exactly what I planned to do.

Later that same Friday night, I found myself sleeping over at the Borrego family home. Mrs. Calisa really

wanted to spend some time with us and the baby. Since
Dre was always spending the weekends over at our house,
I thought it was only fair. When I rolled over in the bed,
I noticed Dre wasn't there beside me. The alarm clock
on his nightstand read 11:48 p.m. Ever since I'd had the
baby, I couldn't help but turn in early. Usually, Dre did
too, which was why I was surprised when he wasn't fast
asleep in the bed next to me.

I slid out of bed and slipped on my red cotton V.S.
nightgown before tiptoeing down the long hall. Of course,
I checked on li'l Armond first, who was sleeping peacefully in the nursery Mrs. Calisa had set up just for him.
Glowing stars were rotating on the dark ceiling above,
while a sweet lullaby played softly in the background. I
peeked down into his crib, making sure to see the rise
and fall of his little chest, before quietly stepping out.

As I began walking down the stairs, I could hear Dre
and his mother talking. At first, I couldn't make out what
they were saying, but as I walked farther down the steps,
the sounds of their conversation started to become clear.

"You need to tell her, Dre," Ms. Calisa said.

"I know I do. But I just . . ."

"You just what?" she asked.

I knew I was wrong for eavesdropping, but I was
curious as to what they were talking about. Instead of
going right into the kitchen, I stood on the bottom step
and continued to listen in on their conversation.

"I don't want to lose her this time, Ma. It's like things
are finally going good between us. And I know for a fact
if I told her, it would fuck up everything we trying to
build. I just can't do that to her. And I ain't doing that to
Armond," he snapped.

That definitely got my attention. If I was unsure before,
I definitely knew now that he was talking about me. I
took one more step but instantly stopped in my tracks,
hearing his mother's voice.

"You don't have to leave li'l Armond behind or even Romi for that matter, but you do have to do what's right, Dre. I can't look at her one more day and keep this secret from her. You've known about this for months now and had more than enough time to tell her. You're going to have a new responsibility coming your way very soon, so I'm gonna need you to step up and be a man about it," she said.

What the hell was she talking about?

"Either you tell her or I will," she pressed in a stern tone.

I didn't know why, but I was feeling nervous all of a sudden. The palms of my hands were literally sweating, and I was slightly trembling. With every step I took, my heartbeat grew faster and louder from within my chest, and my stomach churned. When I approached the kitchen entrance, I just stood there looking at Dre, who had his face buried in his hands. He sat on a barstool next to the marble kitchen counter, looking stressed, while Mrs. Calisa stood across from him, downing a glass of red wine.

"Dre," I said softly, entering the kitchen.

When he looked up, I saw that his eyes were bloodshot. I'd never known Dre to cry, so I figured that he was most likely tired or majorly stressed.

"Hey, baby, did we wake you?" he quickly asked, opening up his arms for me.

I walked over and wedged myself in between his legs before hugging him tightly around the neck. After closing my eyes and taking a long, deep breath, I said a quick, silent prayer. I prayed for the courage to ask about this so-called secret he had been withholding, and I also prayed for strength to deal with whatever answer he gave.

Pulling back from our embrace, I looked him directly in the eyes and tenderly placed my hands to the sides of his smooth dark brown face. "Now, what is it that you need to tell me, baby?"

Chapter 20

Dre

"Shawty, what you talking about?" I asked, trying my best to look confused. I knew Romi must have overheard my conversation with my mother, but I wasn't ready to talk. Hey, I wouldn't even be a man if I didn't at least try to weasel my way out of having this conversation.

"Go ahead and tell her now, Dre," my mother said, leaning forward on the counter.

I let out a deep sigh before running my hand down my face. When I opened up my mouth to speak, the words just wouldn't form. "I . . . I just . . . ." I stuttered.

Romi looked from me to my mother.

"Tell her, Dre, or I will," my mother said firmly.

After a hard swallow and another deep breath, I finally let it out. "Brandi's pregnant, Ro."

She covered her face with her hands and shook her head, crying out, "No, Dre. Please. Why do you keep doing this to me?"

I felt like shit hearing her cry like that. Softly, I tugged at the hem of her nightgown before removing one of her hands from her face. "Hey, hey. It happened before we even got back together, Ro. Before li'l Armond was even born, shawty," I explained, looking into her green eyes, which were filled with tears.

All of a sudden, a confused look was etched across her face as she tried processing what I had just said. I could see her mind rapidly working and calculating as she tried to figure out exactly what it all meant. "How far along is she?" she asked.

"Six and a half months. I'm gonna have a daughter," I told her, taking both of her hands in mine.

"Why did you wait all this time to tell me, Dre? After everything we've been through, why?" she asked with a cracked voice, sniffing back her tears.

"I fucked up. I just didn't want you to run this time. You got my son now, and you know you got my heart, Ro," I said, pulling her in close.

As she stood between my legs, allowing her arms to loosely drape around my neck, she looked me square in the eyes and asked, "Does Brandi know that I have your heart?"

"She does. When I told you I broke it off with her months ago, I did. I do go check up on her throughout the week, though, and I've been going to all of her doctor's appointments because she's sick."

"Sick? What's wrong? Is the baby okay?"

"The baby's fine for right now, but she's got that pre-eclampsia shit. She's on bed rest and everything," I said, running my hand down my waves. I felt bad that Brandi was going through all of this shit during her pregnancy.

"Take me to see her," Romi softly said.

"Nah, shawty, she can't get upset right now. Stress is definitely not good for her condition."

"I'm not going to upset her, Dre. I just want us to move past this so that I can be there for her if she needs me. After all, our children will be brother and sister, you know?" she said with a little shrug.

My mother walked around the counter and came over next to us. "You two can make this work. Just keep that same mature attitude and continue to love one another, okay?" She wrapped her arms around the both of us for a group hug.

"We got this, Ma. We got this," I joked.

My mother slapped the back of my head before she said, "Shut up, boy! If it weren't for me, you'd still be running around here sneaking between your two baby mamas."

"Ughh! Baby mama. I hate that phrase," Romi said, rolling her green eyes.

"I hate it too. What are you gonna do about that, Dre?" my mother asked, cutting her eyes at me.

I knew what she was hinting around to, but I needed to make sure shit was in order before I took it there with Romi. I'd loved her since the very first time I laid eyes on her back at the mall, so there wasn't a doubt in my mind that she was the one for me. But currently, I didn't meet any of the husband qualifications, so there wasn't even a need to apply for the job. Shit, with one year of college left, a single bedroom in the frat house, and a new baby on the way with my ex, a nigga didn't need to be walking down nobody's aisle.

I let out a small laugh under my breath before I said, "Yeah, we'll see."

The very next morning, as promised, Romi and I headed over to Brandi's place. She lived in a small one-bedroom apartment about thirty minutes from our home back in Greensboro. Although the entire ride there was quiet, Romi and I held hands on the middle console. When we finally got there, I pulled in a parking spot close by her door. When I looked over at Romi, she was chewing on the corner of her mouth.

"You ready?" I asked, gently squeezing her hand.

"Yes. I'm ready," she said just above a whisper.

After making our way up to Brandi's apartment door, I knocked hard three times. When Brandi didn't answer the door, I immediately began worrying about her, because her car was parked out front. Although I was somewhat ashamed to pull out my key in front of Romi, I had no other choice. I pulled it out of my pocket and quickly opened up the door. Romi cut her eyes over at me, but she didn't say shit.

"Yo, Bran! Brandi, where you at?" I hollered out, entering her apartment.

Before I could even make it into her living room, I saw her wobbling down the hall toward the front door. Although Brandi was a beautiful girl, she had been looking terrible these past few months. Her buttery brown skin was now ashen, and dark circles had begun to form around her eyes from the preeclampsia. Unlike Romi, whose long black hair grew several inches during her pregnancy, Brandi's curls had started to fall out, and her hair was becoming very thin.

"I'm coming, Dre," she said, holding her belly.

"How you feeling, shawty?" I asked, helping her down onto the sofa. I glanced back at Romi, who awkwardly stood next to the front door with her hands clasped behind her back. I knew this was extremely uncomfortable for her to see me and my pregnant ex-girlfriend, but it was truly the reality of our situation.

"I'm feeling all right today," Brandi responded, shifting in the chair in an attempt to get comfortable. "Romi, please have a seat. Make yourself at home," Brandi said.

Romi sat down on the couch across from Brandi, and of course, I sat next to her. I didn't know how this conversation was supposed to go or who was supposed to even get it started, but I decided to break the ice. "When's your next doctor's appointment?"

"Oh, it's next Thursday. They want to see me every week now until the baby comes," Brandi said. She looked over at Romi and then back at me. "What is it that you guys wanted to talk to me about?"

Romi cleared her throat and crossed her legs. In that moment, I took the deepest breath I possibly could, praying that she would stay on her best behavior. The last thing Brandi needed was to be stressed the hell out, and honestly, I didn't need to be put in a position where I was going to have to choose between the health of my baby over my girl. As my mind started to race, I wondered, *what the fuck did I do, bringing Romi's ass here?*

"To be honest, I'm the one who wanted to talk," Romi started to say, interrupting my thoughts.

"I see," Brandi said, folding her arms across her chest.

"I just found out that you were pregnant last night, and I wanted to let you know that . . . if there's anything I can do for you . . . while you're pregnant or even after the baby is born, for that matter, I'm here."

My neck jerked back, hearing such sincere words leaving Romi's mouth. My shawty was finally growing the fuck up, and I couldn't have been prouder of her.

"That's so sweet, Romi. I thought you were gonna come try to tell me to stay away from Dre or something crazy like that," Brandi said.

"No, I know he needs to be there for you and his daughter. I'm learning to trust him again," Romi said, letting out a small laugh.

"Dre and I haven't been together like that since before Armond was born. Trust me, you have nothing to worry about. Even when Dre and I were together, I knew his heart still belonged to you. I just thought that, with time, things could change," Brandi said low, letting her voice trail off.

Hearing Brandi say that made me feel terrible inside. She was a sweet girl and didn't deserve half the shit I put her through. Even when we were together, I knew I still had love for Romi, but I just couldn't admit it. Like a sucker, I strung Brandi along, and even to this day, she didn't resent me for it. For that alone, she'd always have a special place in my heart.

"I know our children are going to be brother and sister, so I just wanted to make sure that we're cool, you know?" Romi said.

"Absolutely. Thanks for reaching out to me like this. It means a lot."

"Well, unless y'all got some more hugging, kissing, and making up to do, I'm ready to bounce. You ready?" I looked over at Romi and asked with a smirk on my face.

"Making up to do? Nigga, you need to be the one making up. You're the one who got us in this situation in the first place," she fussed, standing up from her seat.

"I know, right. Got us having project twins and shit," Brandi said. I cut my eyes at Brandi and just shook my head. I couldn't do shit but laugh because it wasn't really like her to cuss.

"A'ight, y'all, damn. I know I messed up. Now let's hurry the fuck up and get the hell up out of here before y'all have another *Waiting to Exhale* moment on a nigga." Both of the girls fell out laughing.

I escorted Brandi back down the hall to her bedroom and made sure she was straight before Romi and I headed out the door.

"Well, that went better than I expected," she said, smiling as we got into the car.

"Shit, you and me both, shawty." I leaned over the console and pecked her lips. For a 21-year-old, I still had a lot on my plate, but seeing my two baby mamas get along definitely gave a nigga some hope. Things were looking up, and I could only pray that they continued to stay that way.

Chapter 21

Risa

"Ooh! Don't you look hot," Sabrina said, casually entering my dorm room. Unfortunately, I was still living on campus, completing my summer law program.

"Thanks. But . . ." I said with my voice trailing off. I stood in front of the floor-length mirror, admiring my slender frame. I was dressed in a red two-piece bikini, preparing for this pool party Sabrina had invited me to. Although I had to admit I looked good, mentally I was talking myself out of going. It had been a little over nine months since Micah and I had broken up, and still I wasn't sure if I was ready to mingle with other guys. Especially not in a bikini.

"But what? You look so fucking sexy in that bikini, boo. Stop being such a grandma all the damn time," she said.

When I turned around from the mirror, Sabrina had her lips twisted to the side, and her hands were on her hips. I let out a deep sigh before looking her over. "I like your swimsuit too, though. That's cute, girl," I told her.

She had on a black one-piece bathing suit that was sheer between the breasts. A sheer black sarong was neatly wrapped around her waist, while black kitten heels adorned her tiny feet. The purplish bob cut she used to wear no longer existed. She now rocked auburn hair, which had grown a little past her shoulders. She wore it in wet curls, which I assumed was for the pool.

Gold stud earrings with a gold beach bag thrown over her shoulder completed her look.

"Are we ready to get out here or what?" she asked impatiently, shifting her weight to one hip.

"Whose pool party is this again?" I quizzed.

"Again, it's just a friend of mine, Risa. Stop overthinking everything, damn! Loosen up and have some fun for a change," she snapped.

"Fine," I huffed, grabbing my red beach bag off the chair.

Sabrina threw on her Chanel shades and tossed her hair behind her shoulders before heading out of the room with her chin held high. Sabrina was my girl, but I swore she could be such a diva at times. Once I put my cover-up on and fixed my ponytail in the mirror, I went out the door right behind her. When we both got outside, the six o'clock sun was still beaming down bright. It had to have been at least ninety degrees in Atlanta that day. After clicking the alarm on her Jeep, Sabrina quickly let down the top so that we could let the winds of late summer blow in our hair.

After a thirty-minute ride, we were finally driving up a cobblestone driveway, approaching a huge mansion in Sandy Springs. I could hear the booming sounds of Biggie Smalls growing louder in the air as we drove up toward the home. I sat back, taking in the view, admiring the large, manicured lawn. The grass was neatly cut with stylish stripes of green, while beautiful flowers lined the driveway in various shades of pink, purple, and gold. To my right, there looked to be over fifty cars precisely parked on a vacant lot beside the house, and to my left, I could see a large man-made pond. This home was nothing short of amazing, and I hadn't even stepped a foot inside.

"Wow, whose house is this?" I asked, getting out of the Jeep and looking up to admire the brick home. The savory smell of barbecue smoke drifted in the air.

"You'll see. Now come on," she said, pulling me along.

When we entered through the wrought-iron gate, there were white Christmas lights hung up high, lining the perimeter of the enormous backyard. Although nightfall had yet to take the sky, the beautiful decorations instantly caught my attention. The yard was loud and packed, full of people both in and out of the pool. When I glanced up, I saw that the DJ booth had been set up on the massive back deck that stretched the full length of the house. Half-naked people were dancing on it like it was a dance floor at the club.

After noticing the six white cabana beds sitting around the edge of the pool, I immediately walked toward the last one that was vacant. "Come on, let's go grab that seat," I told Sabrina.

"You go ahead. I'll be right over in just a minute," she said before handing me her bag and walking off.

After heading over to the cabana bed, I quickly put our bags down on the seat beside me. Before I could even get my cover-up off good, I heard the deep voices of men approaching me from behind. I threw my cover-up down on the bed and quickly turned around. My eyes were greeted with the sight of two men standing before me. One was a tall, light-skinned man who had sleepy dark brown eyes and a head full of long, curly brown wet hair. The other was a little shorter and had a smooth, dark complexion. Both of them stood there shirtless, with tiny beads of water garnishing their muscular physique, as though they had just jumped out of the pool.

"You wanna go for a swim, Miss Lady?" the light-skinned guy asked, scanning my body with his eyes.

I let out a small laugh, blushing, I was sure, before I said, "No, not yet." I slipped off my flip-flops before getting down and lying back in the cabana bed.

"Well, how about a dance then?" the other one eagerly asked with a wink of his eye.

"No, thank you. Maybe later," I said, wishing now that they would both leave. However, to my surprise, they both made themselves at home and sat down on the edge of the bed near my feet.

"Well, I'd love to keep you company," the light-skinned guy said, licking his lips. He tried to take my bare foot in his hand, but quickly I pulled my legs back just in time.

"What? I can't give you a foot rub, Miss Lady?" he asked with a smirk on his face.

I was completely thrown off by his aggressiveness, but still, I smiled in an attempt to be polite. "No, no, thank you. Really, guys, I'll be sure to get up with you two later on. But right now, I'm just waiting on a friend and trying to relax," I told them.

Right as they both stood up to leave, I saw Micah walking up behind them. Although I was confused as to why he was even there, I instantly got distracted by how sexy he looked. He had his hair freshly cut and edged up to perfection. Large diamond studs sparkled in each of his ears, bouncing off his smooth dark chocolate skin. The white tank top he had on clung to the muscles of his chest, while the board shorts he wore allowed me to see the long, meaty print of his dick. My mouth instantly started to water. I took my bottom lip in between my teeth, allowing my eyes to slowly travel his perfect physique. I hated to admit it, but just the mere sight of him had me wet between the thighs.

"The fuck y'all over here talking about?" he barked, taking me out of my trance.

"Borrego, right?" the light-skinned guy knowingly asked before extending his hand for Micah to shake.

Micah just ignored him and slipped his hand into the pockets of his shorts while his eyes remained fixed on me.

"Come on, man, let's go get us a plate while the food still hot," the short, dark-skinned guy said, tapping the other one on the shoulder.

"Grab a bottle of Dasani while you're over there, too," Micah mumbled. "Thirsty-ass niggas."

After they walked off, Micah moved our beach bags out of the way and sat down on the bed next to me. I could feel his dark eyes looking me over as he slowly scanned my body with his jaws clenched tight.

"And what the fuck you got on?" he asked with a scowl on his face.

"Ah, well, hello to you too, Micah," I said.

"Hey, Risa. How you doing? You doin' all right? Cool. Now again, what the fuck do you have on?" he snapped.

"It's a bathing suit, Micah. This is a pool party, right?" I asked, shrugging my shoulders.

"The fuck kind of bathing suit is that? That little-ass shit you got on might as well be underwear, Risa. And then you sitting over here wondering why these clown-ass niggas smiling all up in ya face," he fussed, slicing the air with hands.

Instantly, I grew pissed, hearing his harsh words. I didn't know who he thought he was talking to, but it damn for sure wasn't me. Quickly, I shot up from my seat and placed my hand on my hips. "Look, Micah, if I wanted to hear my daddy's mouth, I would have taken my ass back home to Greensboro. And despite what you might think, I can say, do, and wear whatever I please. You are no longer my man. Remember?"

"Yeah. Sure. Whatever your ass say. Now put this shit on before you piss me the fuck off," he growled through gritted teeth, throwing my cover-up at me.

Just as the cover-up was about to smack me in the face, I caught it and flung it back hard at him. Micah had officially made me mad with all of his cussing and jealous behavior. He had never talked to me like that before, and it completely caught me off guard. Before I lost all control and attempted to choke the life out of him, I turned around and stormed off. As I trekked toward the house, I passed by Sabrina while she was sitting lovingly on Timo's lap. I rolled my eyes at her sneaky ass before I headed inside the house. I merely needed a minute or two to cool down and to just get away from Micah. The crazy thing was, though, I didn't even have to turn around or hear him to know that he was hot on my trail. I could feel his powerful presence following me, one angry footstep after the other.

Chapter 22

Micah

Timo said he was going to get Sabrina to bring Risa to the pool party on some ol' "get Micah and Risa back together" type of mission. But as soon as I spotted her through the crowd, I saw some lame-ass niggas smiling all up in her face. I sat back and watched for a while, wanting to see how she would react. Specifically, I wanted to know exactly how long she would even allow them to remain in her presence. However, as soon as they sat down with her on the cabana bed, I forgot all about spying and instantly shot up from my seat.

From the way her deep dimples pierced the sides of her face, I knew she was blushing. That's what really pissed me the fuck off. Here I was unable to hardly eat, sleep, or breathe because we were apart, but somehow, she was still functioning, finding ways to actually smile and shit. Risa stayed on my mind morning, noon, and night, yet here she was all "kee-keeing" it up in the next nigga's face. I mean, yeah, I knew I fucked up, but somewhere in the back of my mind, I always thought we'd get past everything.

As soon as I walked over and scared those fuck niggas off, I studied every inch of her body with my eyes. The first thing I noticed was how skimpy her bathing suit was. *Damn, she's beautiful as fuck. Smooth brown body just sitting there like an unwrapped Hershey's Kiss, ready for a nigga like me to eat.* Just the mere thought of all these niggas out here seeing how sexy she looked caused me to snap. I asked her what the fuck she had on, and when she responded with a smart-ass mouth, I fucking lost it. My possessiveness of her was something I couldn't control. Oftentimes I didn't even want to.

"Look, Micah, if I wanted to hear my daddy's mouth, I would have taken my ass back home to Greensboro," she sassed. "And despite what you might think, I can say, do, and wear whatever I please. You are no longer my man. Remember?"

Before I knew what was happening, I threw her cover-up in her face, demanding that she put that shit on. When she slung it back at it me and stormed off, I knew I had fucked up. "Shit," I muttered, immediately going after her. Once I went up on the back deck, I saw Sabrina and Timo all cuddled up, looking like they were in love. "Where she go?" I asked.

Timo simply nodded his head toward the house.

I quickly entered and shut the French doors behind me. When I looked around the crowded living room and in the kitchen area, Risa was nowhere to be found. For a second, I thought she might have gone out the front door, but when I looked out the window I didn't see her, and Sabrina's Jeep was still parked.

As I climbed the spiral staircase, I looked down on the entire first floor, trying my best to spot her in the crowd, but I still couldn't find her. When I finally hit the top step of the second floor, I began opening up every door I saw, but I was still coming up empty. The last door I opened was to one of the guest bedrooms. I still didn't see her in there, but before I could close the door, I heard a sniveling sound.

Walking in quietly, I tried to follow where the sound was coming from. At first, I checked the adjoining bathroom, but no one was in there. I didn't know why, but I even checked underneath the bed. Scanning the space once more, I noticed that there was one other door in the room. I walked over and pushed it open. When I entered the empty walk-in closet, my eyes finally fell on Risa. She was sitting down in the back of the closet with her knees pulled up tight to her chest. Her head was hanging down, and I could hear her sniffing back tears. Just the sight of my baby crying because of my stupid-ass actions nearly broke a nigga's heart in two.

I walked over and dropped down to my knees in front of her. She slightly raised her head, but when her red eyes met mine, she put her head back down. I gently lifted her face and looked her right in the eyes. "Baby, I'm so sorry. A nigga just can't breathe without you, Risa. I'm tired of being around your pretty ass and not being able to touch you," I whispered, stroking her face with my thumb. "Not being able to kiss you and claim you as my own. Can't you see that a nigga's struggling out here without you? I love you," I said, holding her face in my hands.

Tears fell from her eyes as she nodded her head. I leaned down and softly pecked her lips. As I pulled her close to me, I could feel her body start to relax. She rose up on her knees and began to kiss me back. While sucking on her bottom lip, I slid my hands down to her soft, round ass. "Mmm," I groaned in her mouth.

My lips gradually found their way to her neck, and I began planting slow, wet kisses on it. "Damn, I missed yo' ass," I whispered between kisses. I untied her bikini top, causing it to fall to the floor, before taking her breast into my mouth. Gently grazing the tip of my wet tongue back and forth over her nipple, I caused her to shiver and moan. When I tried laying her back on the floor, she stopped me. She stood up from her kneeling position and pulled me up from the floor with her.

I thought for sure she was gonna hit me with that "let's just be friends" bullshit again, but surprisingly she started pulling my shirt off over my head. When it was completely off, she began kissing all over my chest. Her soft hands slid down into the front of my board shorts, and she began to stroke my length. What shocked me the most was when she dropped back down to her knees and freed my dick from my shorts.

"Shit," I hissed, feeling her warm mouth wrap around my hard muscle. My eyes immediately closed and my hands instantly went to the back of her head as she bobbed up and down. This was the first time in months since I had gotten my dick wet, so a nigga didn't even know how to act. When she began working her hands around my shaft and snaking the tip of her sloppy, wet tongue across the head, my toes instantly started to curl. "Fuck, girl," I murmured, quickly lifting her from the floor. I wasn't ready to bust yet. I wanted to feel inside of her first.

"I guess you missed a nigga too," I said low as she wiped the corners of her mouth with her hand. She nodded her head and smiled. Taking her face in my hands, I kissed her lips again, but this time with more aggression. After sliding her bikini bottoms off, I slowly dipped my fingers inside of her wetness, which got me even more excited. "And you wet as fuck, too. Mmm," I groaned in a low tone.

"I'm so horny, Micah," she whined as I pressed her back against the wall. I slid down to my knees, and as soon as I felt her soft-ass thighs wrap around my neck, I immediately started returning the favor. I gently latched on to her pearl and began tongue kissing her pussy like there was no tomorrow.

"Mmm, Micah," she moaned, grabbing the back of my head. I began flickering my tongue fast against her, just how I knew she liked it before I felt her legs start to shake.

"Ahhh. Mmm," she wailed as she released.

I quickly stood up and spun her around so that she was now facing the wall. She spread her legs, anticipating what was about to come, before craning her neck back around to kiss me. I kissed her lips and rubbed myself back and forth over her slippery, wet entrance.

"Stop playing, Micah, and just put it in," she whined impatiently.

"Nah, tell me you love me first," I teased, still rubbing my head back and forth over her slit.

"Umm, I love you, baby," she moaned in a whisper.

Hearing her say that shit was like music to my ears. I slid inside of her with ease and bit down on my bottom lip, relishing the feeling. Her body felt incredible, and I couldn't believe that I had fucked all this up over Melody's ho ass. I decided to take my time, slowly grinding in and out of her as I worked my hips.

"Ahhh, Micah," she moaned as I firmly pulled her ponytail back. Her back arched perfectly for me as I went up and down, stroking her from behind. I reached around and softly grabbed her throat, pressing deeper inside of her. The sounds of our wet bodies slapping against one another as I pounded her from behind made a nigga feel weak.

"Come on, throw that shit back on this big muthafucka," I told her, grabbing ahold of her hips. Submitting to my command, she began to forcefully buck back against me until she could no longer take it.

"Ohh my Gahhhh, Micahhh!" she wailed.

Hearing her reach her peak had me on the verge of cumming right after. I was so tempted to fill her up with my seeds in hopes that she would get pregnant, but I knew that would be a fuck nigga's move, so I pulled out and came in my hand instead. "Fucckkk!" I groaned.

She spun around and looked me in the eyes, smiling, before we both burst out laughing. "You came quick," she said, covering her smile with her hands.

"Shit, you did too," I said, kissing her lips.

"Micah—" she said low, as her face slowly changed into a more serious expression.

Just by the way she said my name, I knew she was going to say something to piss me off, so I immediately cut her off. "Nah, I don't even want to hear that bullshit you getting ready to spit. I've learned my lesson, shawty, and I've suffered long enough. We back together now, and that's the end of the fucking discussion."

She softly placed her index finger over my mouth and put her other hand up to my heaving chest to calm me down. Her beautiful eyes gradually softened just before she let out a long, deep breath. "Micah, I'm leaving for Harvard in two weeks."

Chapter 23

Damien

It was a late Tuesday morning in September when I found myself finally moving into the frat house. Since Dre had moved into a luxury condo with Romi and the baby, his room at the frat house was up for grabs. I quickly jumped at the opportunity. All my brothers had gotten a chance to live in the frat house during their years at college, and I wanted to follow in their footsteps. While Micah was busy at work, and Dre was busy with his family, Melo offered to help unload my things. Raquel and Raina claimed they were helping out too, but by the way they were sitting around and shit, I really couldn't tell.

"Y'all gon' help do something or just sit there and look pretty all day?" I stopped and asked, standing at the front door. Raina and Raquel were sitting down on the living room couch laughing and talking without a care in the world. When they both ignored me, I sucked my teeth and headed back outside for another box, letting the screen door slam behind me.

After jogging down the steps of the porch, I walked into the driveway where Melo was ready to hand me another box out of the small U-Haul truck I'd rented. "One more trip and we should be done," he said, using his cutoff white tee to wipe the sweat off his face.

He grabbed another box from the truck and followed me inside the house. When we entered the door, he quickly dropped the heavy box to the floor and went over to give Raquel a hug.

"Ughh, Melo! Stop playing," she said, trying to avoid his sweat.

"Gimme a kiss, girl," he said, puckering up his lips. She kissed him back before rolling her hazel eyes with a smile.

We all headed upstairs with the final two boxes in hand before entering my new room. It wasn't nothing to write home about, but it was big enough to fit a queen-sized bed and had an adjoining bath. Besides, I wasn't there for the bedroom, I was there for the turn up. Everybody knew that my frat threw the best house parties, and I couldn't wait to be a part of it.

As Melo sat on the window seat with Raquel in his lap, I watched Raina delicately run her fingers across the wooden furniture, taking in the old, faded blue wallpaper. A bed, nightstand, and dresser all came with the room, and apparently, Dre hadn't cleaned up shit before he left.

"You need to dust, babe," Raina said with a scrunch of her nose, looking at the dirt on her fingers.

"G'on ahead and hook that up for me," I told her, smirking.

Just as I sat down on my unmade mattress, a pretty girl with a cocoa brown complexion and long, wavy black hair peeked into my room. "Hey, y'all," she said with a pretty smile.

"What's up," I said, unconsciously smiling back at her.

"Oh! I'm so rude. I'm Jade, y'all," she said, stepping into the room. My eyes unintentionally roamed her tall body. Her long brown legs looked so smooth and shiny it was as if she'd bathed in nothing but baby oil. She was wearing some cut-off jean shorts and a thin pink tank top that showed her nipples.

I guessed my eyes must have lingered a little too long because Raina instantly walked over to me and started to clear her throat. "Oh, I'm Dame, and this is my girl, Raina," I said, pulling Raina down into my lap.

"I'm Raquel, and this is my man, Melo," Raquel said with a roll of her eyes. I let out a small laugh under my breath and shook my head.

"Oh, yeah. Hey, Melo. How you doing?" Jade asked with familiarity.

Raina and I snapped our heads back at the same time to look at him and Raquel.

"Oh! You two are already acquainted, I see," Raquel snapped, looking back and forth between the two. Melo simply tightened his jaw and hit the girl with a simple head nod. He didn't even respond to Raquel's crazy ass.

"Yeah, I'm Phillip's girl, so I'll probably be seeing you all around," she said, tucking her hair behind her ear. "Well, I just wanted to introduce myself and say hey, that's all. I guess I'll let you get back to your unpacking," she said before leaving the room.

"She's pretty," Raina said with a smirk.

"Not nearly as pretty as your pretty ass," I said before kissing her lips. True, Jade was a pretty girl, but Raina was beautiful. She was the most beautiful girl I had ever laid my eyes on. As I continued to kiss her lips, she let out an unintentional moan.

"Eww, y'all, get a room! Dang!" Raquel said.

"This is their room. Now come on, shawty, let's go," Melo told her before heading to the door.

As soon as they left, I started kissing all over Raina's neck, causing her to giggle. When she fell back on the mattress, I hovered my body over hers and looked right into her pretty, light brown eyes. "You love me?" I whispered.

"Stop asking questions you already know the answer to," she said with a smile. She grabbed the sides of my face and pulled me in for another kiss.

While our tongues passionately wrestled in each other's mouths, I heard someone approaching my bedroom door. *Shit, I forgot to shut the door.* I turned around, and there in the doorway stood a pretty, light-skinned girl with a big, curly Afro and big, doe-like brown eyes.

"Hey, guys . . . Oops, sorry," the girl said, noticing that I was lying on top of Raina. Before I even got a chance to say another word, she walked off down the hall.

I quickly got up from the bed and went over to shut and lock the door. As I was taking off my shirt, thinking of all the nasty things I wanted to do to Raina, she interrupted my thoughts.

"Is this a frat house, or do the sorority girls live here, too?" she asked, pouting her lips.

I let out a light chuckle in response to her jealous little comment before climbing back on the bed. Damn, she was so cute.

After sliding her T-shirt over her head, I quickly tossed it to the floor. Twirling my tongue across the flesh of her neck, I tried to quickly unclasp her bra. Once it was off, I took each of her breasts into my mouth one at a time. Reaching down, I hurriedly unbuckled her jeans while she undid mine. Slowly, I slid them down to her ankles, kissing her plump thighs along the journey. When they were off completely, I stood up, letting my pants and boxers drop to the floor. I watched her eyes widen with delight at the sight of my dick. Smiling, I noticed the desire written all over her face as she licked her lips.

"Damn, you eye raping a nigga, shit. What you tryin'a do?" I said jokingly, running my tongue across my bottom lip. I looked her beautiful body over once more and bit down on my bottom lip.

She bashfully looked away with a smirk on her face. I grabbed her ankle and pulled her closer to the edge of the bed. She squealed and giggled before I lifted her pretty foot to my mouth and began kissing it. Although I really didn't care for feet like that, I'd try anything once with her, and I'd do just about anything to please her. I looked down, taking in the soft pink polish on her toes that complemented her smooth golden complexion. After a quick smell check, I slipped her big toe right into my mouth.

"Mmm," she softly moaned with her eyes closed.

I guess she likes this shit. Gradually, I began running the tip of my tongue down her ankle and along her inner thigh. When my mouth finally connected with her pink lace panties, I let my tongue slither up and down her center just to tease her. Her back slightly arched, and a series of soft moans escaped her lips. My teeth lightly grazed her panties just before I lifted up and snatched them shits right off of her, ripping them at the seams. Once I threw them to the side, I lay down in between her legs and slid into her wetness with ease.

"Gah damn," I groaned low, closing my eyes. She felt good as fuck.

"Get a condom, Dame," she softly said, holding my face in her hands.

"Let me just feel you first, bae," I told her, still working my way in and out of her.

"Please. I don't want to get pregnant," she whispered, killing my vibe.

Just hearing the word "pregnant" reminded me of everything my brother Dre was going through. Now don't get me wrong, I loved Raina with all my heart, but a nigga was only 19, and I wasn't ready for all that. With a huff of my breath, I slowly pulled out and reached over to a box on my nightstand that had yet to be unpacked. I fished around in it with my hand until I finally found a condom. After unwrapping the gold package and sliding it up my length, I lay back down on top of her.

"Thank you," she said.

I didn't respond. Instead, I dove back into her with such unexpected quickness and force that she gasped and closed her eyes. Winding my hips, I began giving her long, deep strokes in and out. I looked down and studied her beautiful face, which was painted with nothing but pure pleasure. Stripes of light beamed across her face from the withering sun shining through the blinds. Although she remained silent, her mouth was slightly ajar, and her eyes were sealed tight. As I ground into her with more speed and intensity, I could feel her walls tightening around me.

"Ahhh. Shhh," she let out, trembling from her first orgasm this go-round.

"You're welcome, baby," I finally whispered, kissing her lips.

Chapter 24

Raquel

I let my head hang out of the window, catching the warm Cuban breeze on my face as we rode quietly in the back of the limo. It was our second day visiting, and we were out touring the narrow, rocky roads of Havana. The sunlight glistened down as I took in the city's historical buildings and old cement homes, which were vivid in colors of pink, yellow, and blue. If I listened carefully, I could even hear the faint urban sounds of Reggaeton echoing from a distance.

"And you see right there? That's where Anton and I grew up," Melo's dad said, pointing toward an old, run-down housing community.

"Wow," was all I could say, taking in the gray crumbling buildings, dirt roads, and poor-looking people hanging around.

"Yeah, we grew up poor," he said low.

"Is that why you guys got into the drug business?" I asked.

"Quel!" Melo growled through gritted teeth. He cut his hazel eyes over at me, wearing a scowl on his face.

Mr. Raul let out a light chuckle but never responded to my question. We rode around the city for about an hour more before we headed back to the house. Mr. Raul lived in an old mansion high up in the hills overlooking the blue beaches of Cuba. You could literally hear the waves crashing against the shore from his backyard.

"I told Juanita to fix your favorite for dinner tonight, Melo," he said as we all made our way into the house.

Once we got inside, I told Melo I had to use the restroom and rushed up the stairs. I started to head toward our bedroom, which had an adjoining bath, but something told me to walk down the opposite hall. Although I was given a tour of Mr. Raul's home earlier when we first arrived, this was the only part of the house I hadn't seen. While the house was huge, it was extremely old. It looked as if nothing had been updated in the last twenty, maybe even thirty years. All of the fixtures in the house were tarnished brass, and even the cracked marble floors had started to yellow.

One thing I did love about the house, though, was that there were no windows, only hurricane shutters. No matter where you were in the house, you could literally feel the warm air from outside swirling around and hear the movement of the water. As I continued walking down the long hall, I noticed that every door in my path was open, providing spotlights in the corridor. I made sure to pop my head into each door and be nosy. There were three bedrooms down this hall alone. I saw one bathroom and a room that looked like an office.

Then suddenly I noticed that there was one other door, and it was completely shut. Without hesitation, I turned the brass knob and opened up the door before looking inside. A strong, musty smell instantly burned my nostrils. When I looked in, it appeared to be an old bedroom, a master suite, to be exact. What caught me off guard was that everything in there was covered in a thick coating of dust with spiderwebs scattered throughout. Even the hurricane shutters were completely closed, giving the room a dim and eerie feel.

The room looked as if it hadn't been touched in years. The cherry-wood poster bed was covered in an old, dingy lace spread that was peeled back at the top corner. It was like someone had gotten out of bed and never made it back up. There was even a huge, round wooden clock hanging on the wall that read the wrong time. In between the hands of the clock were more fine strings of spiderwebs.

As I took one step farther into the old, creepy room, I suddenly felt a strong hand on my shoulder, causing me to nearly jump out of my skin. "Ahhh!" I screamed.

"It's just me, my dear," Mr. Raul said.

"Oh, I was just, uh . . . I was looking for the bathroom," I stammered.

He raised his eyebrows, and the look on his face told me he knew I was lying. "The bathroom is that way," he said, pointing down the hall.

"Oh, okay," I said as if I didn't already know.

"We don't go into Kizzy's room," he said in a serious tone.

"I see," I said softly.

He led me out of the room and closed the door behind him. "Dinner is ready now. Come downstairs when you get through," he said sternly. He pushed up his glasses to the bridge of his nose, watching me intently as I made my way down the hall.

After I went to the bathroom, I went downstairs to eat dinner as instructed. Ms. Juanita, their maid, had fixed empanadas for us, and I had to admit that they were absolutely delicious. After dinner was over, Melo and I decided to walk down the beach. We held hands and talked until almost midnight, trekking through the sand.

In the past two days, Melo had talked more to me than he'd ever had. I felt so close to him, and I was starting to think that maybe I was actually falling in love. Raina talked about being in love all the time, and usually I just let it go in one ear and out the other. However, there was something about the intimacy I was starting to feel with

Melo here in Cuba that made me see him differently. He was finally opening up and letting me in.

"I'm tired as fuck. You ready to call it a night?" he asked, stretching his arms out wide, cracking the muscles in his chest.

I didn't respond. I looked up, seeing a full white moon in the sky, and I smiled.

"Shawty, what you smiling at?" he asked with a confused smirk on his face.

I pointed up toward the sky and said, "It's a full moon tonight."

He looked up and studied the moon for a few seconds, then asked, "What's that supposed to mean?"

I shrugged my shoulders before he walked up close behind me. When he wrapped his big, strong arms around my waist, I instantly allowed my head to fall back against his muscular chest. We looked up at the moon together, just taking in the soft sounds of the ocean. Inwardly I laughed because I had no idea we could be this romantic.

"I don't know what it means. It's just beautiful out here," I told him.

"Come on, let's go inside. It can be beautiful in there too," he said with a little smile in his voice.

I shook my head because I knew that was code talk for sex. After we went in the house and showered, we had a full round of wild, passionate sex, followed by a little pillow talk. Shortly after, I could hear Melo's light snores, but for some reason, I just couldn't sleep. I tossed and turned for a good thirty minutes before I decided to get up and go get a glass of water. I threw my robe on and used the light of my phone to help guide me through the dark house.

After drinking a glass of water, I still wasn't ready to go to bed, so I decided to go back to Ms. Kizzy's room. Melo's dad was hiding something when it came to Melo's mother, and I wanted to know exactly what it was. As I tiptoed my way through the dark corridors of the mansion, hearing the wind shake the shutters throughout the house, I looked over my shoulders, making sure no one was behind me. Seeing that I was the only person up roaming the house, I found Ms. Kizzy's bedroom and took a deep breath before opening it up.

"Here goes nothing," I said to myself.

I cut the bedroom light on and quietly closed the door behind me. Slowly, I began looking over everything in the room. Initially, I was coughing every other second from the dust in there, but then I got used to it. As my eyes started to scan the room, the first thing I noticed was a picture of Melo and his mother, sitting on the wooden nightstand next to the bed. He looked to be no more than 3 years old in the photo. I let my fingers lightly skim the old golden frame, admiring her beauty. She had a pretty, deep complexion with light hazel eyes. I had to admit that Melo and his dad were right. I did resemble her.

After placing the picture back down, I checked the nightstand drawer. There were some old papers in there along with some romance novels. I smiled, thinking that Melo's mom and I also shared a love of reading. I went into the bathroom inside the room, and other than old dirt and stains, I didn't find much. I checked inside her closet, noticing the vintage clothes, most with tags still on them. Every pair of shoes she'd owned were heels.

I spent almost an hour in the room before finally getting tired. Although I learned a little bit more about Melo's mother, which was nice, I found nothing to support my theory. Just as I was ready to give up and settle on the simple fact that Melo's mother had committed suicide, I glanced over and noticed a tall wooden wardrobe in the far corner of the room.

"One quick look and then I'll leave," I said quietly to myself.

I opened up the wardrobe only to see more old clothes. At the top of the wardrobe, however, was an old blue shoebox. Standing on my tiptoes, I reached up high and grabbed it. Once I had it in hand, I took it and walked over to the bed. When I opened up the box, I noticed a bunch of papers and started reading them one at a time. Most of them appeared to be 20-year-old bills and legal documents. I thumbed through all the papers before my eyes finally landed on a torn envelope addressed to Kizzy Borrego. Quickly I opened it up and started reading a letter that was written almost twenty-two years ago.

> *Dear Kizzy,*
> *I hope this letter finds you well and in the best of health. After receiving your much unexpected news, I thought it'd only be fair to write you back a letter expressing exactly how I feel on the matter. The truth is, I now realize that our one drunken night of passion has caused a multitude of hard conse-quences for our family. That is, if we don't do what we both know is right. I love Calisa with all my heart, and no matter what you may think, I love my brother to no end. There's nothing I wouldn't do for either of them. What we did is so wrong, Kizzy, and the fact that you're now pregnant, carrying my child, I know for sure it would only cause hurt and pain to the ones we truly love. I'd never thought I'd live to say this, but you need to terminate this pregnancy and move on with your life. Please! I think that's the only thing to do in our situation to protect our family. You will always have a special*

place in my heart, but Calisa holds the key. Please forgive me if you were expecting any different of a response, but this is our only option. Let me know when it's done.

Sincerely,
Anton

Chapter 25

Dre

"Ro! Ro! Wake up!" I hollered, shaking Romi from her deep sleep.

Her eyes popped open wide as she clutched her chest, probably from hearing the panic in my voice. "What's wrong?" she asked, wiping the sleep from her eyes.

"We gotta go, shawty. Now! Brandi was rushed to the hospital," I told her, pulling up my sweatpants in a hurry. "Fuck!" I muttered.

"Do you know what's wrong? Is she in labor?" she asked, getting out of bed.

"She called her neighbor, saying she had a fever and didn't feel well. Her neighbor was going to take her to the hospital, but when she went over there, Brandi had a seizure and shit," I explained, running my hands down my face.

After quickly getting dressed and gathering li'l Armond's things, we all got into my truck and rode up to the hospital. The clock on the dashboard read 5:02 a.m., and it was still dark outside. On the way, Romi called her mother and asked if she would meet us up there to take li'l Armond for us. Of course, Ms. Ernie agreed. The car was completely silent as we drove, allowing every negative thought possible to seep into my mind. While at first I didn't want another baby, I now had my heart set on meeting her. I didn't know what I would do if I lost my baby girl. I clenched my jaw at the thought.

Romi reached over and gently grabbed my free hand, almost like she was reading my mind. "Everything's going to be all right, babe," she softly said. I simply nodded my head in response because I was too scared to even speak on that shit.

When we finally pulled up to the hospital, we met Ms. Ernie out in the parking lot and put li'l Armond in the back seat of her car. "Call me when y'all find out what's going on," Ms. Ernie said. "I'll keep praying for her and the baby, okay?"

"Thanks, Ma," I told her, leaning down in the car and kissing her cheek before she pulled off.

When Romi and I got inside the hospital, I searched for the nearest nurse's station. I walked up, seeing a fat white woman with blond hair and blue eyes sitting behind the desk. "How may I help you?" she asked, her eyes still down on her computer screen.

"I'm looking for Brandi Mitchell. She's pregnant and was rushed in for having a seizure," I said.

"How far along is she?" she asked.

"Around thirty-seven weeks," I told her with confidence, leaning forward on the counter.

"Are you the child's father?" she asked, glancing up with her blue eyes bouncing back and forth between me and Romi.

"Yes, he's the father. Now do your job and tell us where she's at!" Romi cut in.

The lady pursed her lips and looked at the computer some more before she finally said, "They took her to labor and delivery on the fourth floor. Room 428."

We rushed to the nearest elevator and headed up to the fourth floor. When we finally got to room 428, no one was in there except for a nurse. "I'm looking for Brandi Mitchell. The nurse downstairs told us this was her room," I said.

"Yes, they just took her in for an emergency C-section. Her fever spiked to one hundred and five, and her blood pressure was through the roof. They had no other choice. Are you the child's father?"

"Yes, I am."

"Well, come on. I'll take you to get prepped, and then you can head over to the OR to be with her," she said. I looked over at Romi, and she nodded her head, telling me to go on.

After I cleaned my hands thoroughly and put on a blue hospital cap and gown, the nurse led me straight to the OR as promised. I walked in the cold, sterile room to see Brandi lying there with weak eyes. All of the color had drained from her face, and her lips were bluish purple. While machines were beeping all around her, there were about eight doctors and nurses who scurried about the room, all similarly dressed in blue scrubs, caps, and latex gloves.

"You made it," she said weakly, giving a faint smile.

"Of course I did," I told her, sitting down on the stool next to her.

"I'm scared, Dre. I don't want to lose our baby," she cried softly, letting tears run down from the corners of her eyes.

I reached for her hand, which was cold to the touch, and gently began caressing the top of it with my thumb. "Everything's going to be okay. Just let the doctors do what they gotta do, a'ight?" I leaned down and kissed her forehead in an attempt to calm her down. Her eyes instantly closed when I began stroking back the fine curls of her hair.

All of a sudden, the machines started beeping louder and faster. I looked around the room, seeing a look of panic on the doctors' faces. "We gotta move now!" one doctor said.

"Dre, I'm scared," Brandi feebly said.

The nurses quickly put up a white curtain in front of our faces, allowing the doctors to begin their work. Meanwhile, the rhythmic sounds of the machines were still loud and holding steady. I thought both of us were a bundle of nerves in that moment.

"I'm making the incision," I could hear the doctor say.

I looked down at Brandi to see if she was in any pain, but she only looked scared. Her purple lips were now trembling, and her teeth were starting to chatter.

"Shh, Bran, everything's gon' be okay," I told her, still caressing her hand. More and more tears dropped from her eyes, but she didn't say another word.

"Her BP's dropping!" another nurse hollered out.

"I'm moving as quickly as I can," the doctor said.

"Ninety over fifty. Eighty-five over forty-five. It's dropping, Dr. Pratt," the nurse continued.

"Ms. Mitchell, hang on. I'm reaching in for the baby now. You're going to feel a slight tug and pull, but it should be painless," the doctor said.

I knew I shouldn't have done it, but I peeped around the curtain just so that I could see him pull my baby out. Brandi's abdomen was straight sliced the fuck open, and blood was everywhere. When the doctor reached up inside of her to pull the baby out, I winced like a straight bitch as if that shit were actually happening to me. All of a sudden, I could see him pull the baby's head out. She had a head full of black hair, which was coated in her mother's blood.

"She's almost out," I said, squeezing Brandi's hand. I couldn't take my eyes off of what the doctor was doing over the curtain because I had never seen no shit like that before.

The next thing I knew, he tugged a little bit harder, almost as if he was trying to rip the baby up out of her. I noticed every stretch and pull of her skin and the blood that was now dripping heavily on the floor. Only a few seconds later, I could begin to hear her little cry as he pulled her out completely. He then held our baby girl high up in the air, over the curtain, for Brandi to see. I looked back at Brandi, seeing her give a weak smile as she peered up at our baby. But within a split second, her body started seizing, and her eyes rolled to the back of her head. Suddenly the beeping sounds of the machines grew faster and faster.

"Yo, what the fuck!" I yelled, getting the nurses' attention.

"Get back, sir! Get back!" one of the nurses shouted, shoving me out of the way.

All of the beeping sounds were suddenly starting to fade. I watched as the doctor took two metal panels and began rubbing them together. "Let me get four hundred stat!" he yelled.

"Come on, Brandi. Please!" I begged just above a whisper.

He placed the defibrillator to her bare chest and tried to shock her back to life. I observed Brandi's body rise and fall, plopping back down onto the table. Her eyes were shut, and her lifeless arms dangled down by her sides. "Give me five hundred. Now!" the doctor barked. "Five hundred. Clear," he said, shocking her body again.

I stood there frozen with my hands on the top of my head, watching him shock her for a third time. As our baby girl cried in the background, only one steady beep on the machine could be heard, indicating that Brandi had flatlined. My heart instantly sank into the pit of my stomach.

"Time of death?" the doctor finally asked, shaking his head in defeat.

"Six forty-three a.m.," one of the nurses said just above a whisper.

"I'm so sorry, son," the doctor looked at me and said with tears pooled in his eyes.

"Fuck!" I screamed out in disbelief of it all. A nigga didn't even know I was crying until I felt water dripping down on my hands. I stood there staring at Brandi's unconscious body for another minute or so before I finally found the courage to walk over to her. I tenderly kissed the tops of her sealed lids and then the top of her head before saying my final goodbye.

"Best believe I'm gon' take care of our baby girl, Bran. Rest easy on that shit, a'ight," I said, kissing her lips one last time.

I ran my hands down my face, wiping the tears away before finally cutting my eyes over at my baby girl. Her eyes were wide open, and she was sucking on her thumb like she'd already been living in this world. That shit made me instantly smile. Sniffing back the remainder of my tears, I walked over to where she was in the bassinet and scooped her up into my arms. I looked over her perfect little face, taking in her small, dainty features that looked exactly like Brandi's.

"I would like to name our daughter Brandi Borrego," I told the nurse standing next to me.

"Brandi Borrego. I like that a lot, sir," she said softly, looking at me with sympathetic eyes.

Chapter 26

Melo

I stared quietly out the window, taking in the aerial view from 30,000 feet above. While Raquel and I were riding on a plane heading back home from Cuba, my thoughts were running rampant. We'd gotten the call late last night that Brandi had passed away giving birth. That was shortly after Raquel dropped this bomb of a letter on me. Truthfully, I don't know which situation had my head fucked up the most.

Could Uncle Anton really be my biological father? I thought about asking my father while we were back in Cuba and just showing him the letter, but since he didn't raise me, he and I were never really that close. Uncle Anton was more like a father to me, so I wanted to talk with him directly. He always treated me as his own and never showed any difference between me and the rest of his sons. That's why I always referred to them as my brothers.

So why the fuck would he withhold such important information?

After several hours of being on the plane, we landed and were finally getting into my car. I hadn't said shit to Raquel the entire plane ride, although she kept asking every so often if I was okay. I was a quiet nigga and really didn't say much. I wanted to just say to her ass, 'If you were me, would you be all right?" Shit! Although I didn't want to blame her for what she'd found, I really didn't like the fact that she'd been snooping through my father's home like that. Sometimes the things she did were just careless and too fucking reckless for my liking.

"Are we going over to Dre and Romi's first to see the baby and give them our condolences?" she asked, breaking the silence in the car.

"Nah, shawty, I'm gon' drop you off at your dorm. I'm tired as fuck, so I'll probably just chill," I told her nonchalantly, not even looking her way.

"You shouldn't be alone at a time like this, Melo. I'll just stay with you, okay?"

"Nah, I'm straight," I responded coldly. I knew that I was icing her out, but I had to get my mind wrapped around all of this shit so I'd know how to face it.

"Fine," she said with a little pout, crossing her arms over her chest.

When we pulled up to her dorm, she naturally leaned over the console to give me a kiss, but I tilted my head the other way, giving her my jaw. Yeah, I knew I was acting like a straight-up bitch, but a nigga just wanted to be left the fuck alone. She let out a loud sigh of annoyance, and although I wasn't looking at her, I knew she was most likely rolling those hazel eyes of hers. Despite the vibe I was giving off, she went ahead and gave me a simple kiss on the cheek before opening up the car door.

"Call me later, okay?" she said softly.

I finally looked over at her and hit her with a nod. That must have pissed her off because she rolled her eyes and slammed my car door so hard I thought my window was going to shatter. My Mercedes E-Class was less than 6 months old, and there wasn't a soul alive who didn't know I ain't play when it came to my baby. I was two seconds from getting out of my whip and putting my foot up her little ass, but the way I was feeling in that moment, I knew I was liable to really hurt her.

Still boiling inside from everything that had transpired, I sped off and drove back home to the frat house. On the way to my room, I passed Damien's bedroom but noticed he wasn't there. I'd figured that the whole family was probably over at Dre and Romi's place anyway. As soon as I entered my room, I dropped my luggage to the floor and flopped down on my bed. Mentally, I was exhausted and emotionally just drained from it all. With my hands resting behind my head, I lay back on my pillow, staring up at the ceiling, thinking. I stayed like that for the rest of the night, fully clothed, until sleep finally came over me.

After avoiding everyone for six days, I had finally come out of the dark hole I was in. Today was Brandi's funeral, and as much as I was stressed and confused over my own shit, I knew I had to be there for my brother. He was probably already cursing me out over the fact that I hadn't even met my niece yet, so I knew I had to at least show my face today. I gave myself a final look in the mirror, straightening my black tie and Armani suit before heading out the door.

When I pulled up to the church, I saw all of my family's cars out front but not many others. Brandi was originally from California, so I didn't know who from her family would actually be able to attend. When I walked inside hearing that sad-ass music play, I noticed that only the first four pews on each side of the church were full. All of the other seats were completely empty, and the church was huge. Slowly, I crept up the center aisle, taking in the sleek ivory casket that sat up front. It was surrounded by lots of colorful flowers, and off to the side was a huge framed photo of Brandi placed on an easel.

I could see Dre and Romi on the right side of the church in the front pew with the two babies in their arms. Aunt

Calisa and Uncle Anton sat up front with them while my brothers sat back in the next row directly behind them. Raina and Raquel, along with Mr. and Mrs. Brimmage, were with them as well. Even a few bikers I knew who hung out with Dre and Brandi were in attendance.

When I finally made my way up to the front, I leaned down to speak directly into Dre's ear. "Sorry for your loss, bro. Shit's all fucked up, but you know I've got your back. Whatever you need, just holla," I said, bending down to giving him a brotherly hug.

Pursing his lips, he cut his eyes hard at me with a pissed expression etched on his face. He glared at me like that for the next few seconds before finally pulling me in for a one-arm hug. I knew he was mad because I hadn't called or gone over to see him, but I honestly couldn't be there for him when mentally I had shit of my own to deal with.

When I looked down at the sweet baby girl in his arms, I couldn't do shit but smile, no matter how solemn the mood. She was tiny and so new. I was surprised they even had her out of the house so early, but given the circumstances, I understood.

"This is your niece, bruh. Brandi," he said, propping her up for me to see.

"Damn, she's beautiful, man. Just beautiful," I told him low, meaning every word.

Continuing down the front pew, I stopped to play with li'l Armond for a second before giving Romi and Aunt Calisa a kiss on the cheek. That's when I came eye to eye with my Uncle Anton. Totally oblivious to everything I knew, he reached up to shake my hand. I cut my eyes over to him and sucked my teeth before continuing.

As I kept walking, I could feel Raquel's eyes burning a hole in me. It was like whenever I was around her, I could instantly sense her presence. Against my better judgment, I glanced over at her and saw how beautiful she looked. She wore a pretty, black lace dress that clung to the curve of her breasts. Her silky brown hair was up high in a bun, and her makeup was soft and pink. Black and gold earrings dangled from her ears, complementing her long, beautiful neck. My baby was flawless. Damn!

When our eyes met, she immediately slid over in the pew, making a little extra room for me. I started to go sit next to her, but truthfully, I was still fucked up about the letter she'd found. No matter how gorgeous she looked or how much I longed for her touch, in that moment, my stubbornness just wouldn't let me succumb. I simply chucked my chin up to her before walking past the pew she sat in, only to sit down in the row right behind her. There wasn't a doubt in my mind that I was acting childish and insensitive, but I just couldn't get over it.

As the service began, I quickly found out that Brandi's family all sat on the other side of the church. I could literally hear her mother weeping all the way from across the room. Shit was sad as fuck. Throughout the course of the funeral, I found out a lot about Brandi though. She wasn't just some biker chick from Cali. She was actually a straight A college student who wrote children's books and was aspiring to be a doctor. I knew she was a good girl, but who would have thought that shit? Damn.

When the funeral was finally over, we all headed over to the banquet hall inside the church for the repast. While everyone was in line getting their food or giving Dre's and Brandi's families their condolences, I chilled with Micah in the cut. He was going on and on, talking my ear off about work, and while I'd usually be engrossed in whatever he was saying, I just wasn't feeling that shit today. I just kept nodding my head, pretending that I was actually listening. Truth be told, I was agitated as fuck looking over at Uncle Anton from across the room. The more I watched him acting like he didn't have a care in the world, the more heated I became.

I quickly tapped Micah on the arm, interrupting his one-sided conversation, and said, "Yo, I need to go holla at your pops about something right quick."

He gave me a confused look, probably because I referred to Uncle Anton as his pops. Usually, I just called him Pops too because he was more of a father to me than an uncle. Without even giving Micah a chance to respond, I walked off. With every step I took toward my uncle, the angrier I became. God had given me sense enough to know that this was neither the time nor the place for this conversation, but I couldn't hold it in any longer. I was like a hot, bubbling volcano, ready to fucking erupt.

When I made it over to where he stood talking with Aunt Calisa and Mrs. Ernie, I grabbed his arm to turn him around and face me. "I need to ask you something," I said abruptly. I must have had a little too much bass in my voice for his liking because he cocked his head to the side, and a scowl slowly crept over his face.

"It's gonna have to wait, son," he said, trying to calm himself.

"Son? Am I your son?" I asked, sitting on go.

"What are you talking about?" he asked, confused.

"You know exactly what the fuck I'm talking about! Am I your son?" I barked, pointing in his face. While everyone in the room had turned to where we were, Uncle Anton's eyes immediately lit up with recognition.

Aunt Calisa instantly came between us and put her hand up to my heaving chest. "What is going on?" she asked, trying to keep her voice low.

"Do you want to tell her, or do you want me to?" I asked, looking him dead in the eyes. The way his eyes spoke, I didn't need shit else to confirm for me what was in the letter. It was all true. Anton was indeed my biological father.

"Tell me what?" Aunt Calisa asked, looking at Uncle Anton. Uncle Anton didn't answer her at first. Instead, he walked us over to a quiet office in the back of the hall but left the door open.

"Stop all this craziness, Melo. We'll talk when we leave here. Show some fucking respect," he said.

"Respect? Show some fucking respect? Like you respected my mama when you told her to get a fucking abortion?" I roared in his face, split flying from my mouth.

"Anton, what the hell is he talking about?" Aunt Calisa tried asking again. She was so nervous and scared that I could see her hands literally starting to shake.

"Bruh, what the fuck's going on?" Micah stepped in the room and asked.

"Tell him, nigga. Tell everybody what the fuck you did!" I yelled, pointing in his chest.

By this time, Raquel had come in too and walked over to stand next to me, gripping my arm. In that moment, neither she nor Micah could hold me back, though. I was going to get answers today if it was the last thing I did. Uncle Anton just stood there speechless with this dumb-ass look on his face, shaking his head. The longer he stayed silent, the angrier I became. Before I knew it, I had pulled out the 9 mm that was tucked in the back of my waist and aimed it right at his chest. I hadn't carried that gun on me in over ten months, but today I needed answers.

"My mother killed herself over you, didn't she?" I asked with my voice growing weak. My mind was racing with all sorts of thoughts, trying to put the pieces of the puzzle together.

That statement instantly got his attention, though. He took a step forward, closing the space between us with the gun now pressed hard in his chest. "Son, that's not what happened," he said, putting his hands up in surrender.

"Then tell me what the fuck happened. Why the fuck did she kill herself? Why the fuck have you been lying to me? My whole fucking life, yo. My whole fucking life," I said, putting my hands on top of my head, gun in hand, my voice suddenly cracking with pain. All those pent-up emotions had finally gotten the best of me, and tears were now threatening to fall.

"One night, twenty-two years ago, Kizzy and I made a terrible mistake," he said, looking over at Aunt Calisa with regretful eyes. "It was only one night, but that was all it took for her to get pregnant."

Aunt Calisa gasped before slapping Uncle Anton hard across the face. He instantly grabbed his jaw and closed his eyes, taking in that stinging sensation. Before he could say another word, she stormed off out of the room, crying, with Mrs. Ernie following her.

"Damn, Pops," Micah muttered, running his hand over his head.

"And then what? When she didn't get rid of me like you asked her to, what happened then?" I asked.

"I found out Kizzy hadn't gotten the abortion when Raul called to tell me that they were expecting. She let him believe that you were his," he said, shaking his head. "And then several years later, the truth came out. Like it always does," he explained.

"And that's when she killed herself?" I asked, still trying to understand.

"Son, your mother didn't kill herself. Raul did. He sho—"

"Shot her in the head," I mumbled, completing his sentence. All the fucking nightmares I had been having were images of what really happened that night. It was all starting to make sense. "If you knew that, why the fuck is that nigga still breathing? Why the fuck have I been living with you for the past sixteen years of my life calling you Uncle! The fuck? Tell me something, bruh," I cried.

He shook his head again, looking away like there was more to the story.

"Tell me!" I yelled, finally jumping into his face and pushing him hard in the chest. Micah grabbed my arm and held me back.

"After he confronted me, we made a deal. When I told him that I wanted you to come live with me so that I could raise you with your brothers, he said that I had to turn my drug business over to him. If I didn't, he was going to tell Calisa. I didn't want to hurt her, so . . . I gave it all up. And in the process, I got to raise you with your brothers. I'm sorry, son, please forgive me," he begged with tears coming down his face.

Hearing the entire story, I was completely disgusted. I didn't even know how to respond to that shit. I pushed Micah off of me and turned to walk away.

"Melo! Please!" my father called out to me.

I turned back to look at him one more time, seeing that pathetic-ass look on his face, but there wasn't shit left for me to say. "Man, fuck you!" I told him low before leaving the room.

Chapter 27

Raquel

It was Halloween night, and it had been almost a month since I'd last seen or heard from Melo. Ever since the day of Brandi's funeral, when everything came out in the open, I lost all contact with him. It seemed like he'd literally fallen off the face of the earth. His phone number had been disconnected, and when I tried visiting him at the frat house, his brothers all told me that he'd moved out. I also went by some of his classes, and his professors told me that he hadn't been to class. Even Dre, Dame, and Micah said that they rarely heard from him.

These past few weeks without him had been really hard on me. I went through feeling guilty because I was the one who started it all, finding that stupid-ass letter. Along with the guilt, I also felt extremely worried. I prayed to God for Melo's safety every morning and every night. Now don't get me wrong, I knew he might have needed some time to digest everything, but him not letting me know that he was even okay and leaving the way he did just broke my heart in two. I was going through it so bad that I could barely eat or sleep. The only thing that was getting me through it all was writing these lyrics and singing more hooks on Traxx's new album.

"Are you coming out to the Halloween party tonight?" Raina asked, going through my closet. Thankfully, she and I shared a dorm room together at Clark this semester.

"No, I don't feel like it tonight," I told her. I was lying in my bed in my pajamas with the covers pulled up to my chin.

"Pleasse, Raquel. Pleasse," she whined. "You don't do anything fun anymore. I finally get here to Clark, so we're able to hang out like we used to, and you just want to lie up here and mope around."

"I'm not moping. I'm just tired. Plus, I don't want to be a third wheel with you and Dame. You know how mushy you two can be. Just cause y'all all in love and whatnot doesn't mean everybody wants to see that shit," I complained, pulling the covers completely up over my head.

"Stop hatin'," she said.

"I'm not."

"Fine. If you don't go, I'm calling Mama. I gonna tell her how you're not eating and how you're all depressed and stuff," she said.

She knew that was the last thing I wanted to hear. Once my mother got wind of that, she'd be on Highway 85 to Atlanta faster than lightning speed. I was already in my feelings dealing with this whole Melo ordeal. The last thing I needed was Mama coming up here, making things worse.

First she'd want to talk about what happened with Melo and Mr. Anton that day. That was a given. I'd then have to confess to the whole "finding the letter in Cuba" situation. For sure she'd make me feel guilty. Then she'd try to psychoanalyze him, rationalizing his behavior. "Maybe he just needs time. I'm sure he's just hurting, Raquel," I could already hear her saying. But when I'd tell her about my heart breaking a little bit more with each day that passed by, it would only be a matter of time before all that understanding went right out the door. She'd be cussing, saying, "Fuck him, shit! He didn't deserve you anyway." Mama was like that, though, when it came to us girls. She'd try to be as empathetic and impartial as she could, but not at the expense of her daughters.

"Fine," I groaned, putting the pillow over my head.

Raina got so happy she literally jumped her thick butt on top of me and started to tickle my sides. I squirmed and laughed so much under the covers until I ended up tossing her completely off my bed and onto the floor.

"Ouch!" she said, rubbing her bottom. "You're so mean," she pouted before laughing and trying to get up.

"Stop playing then," I told her, finally getting up from the bed and casting my covers to the side.

"So are you dressing up? It is a costume party, ya know," she said.

"I wasn't planning on it. What are you going as?"

"Me and Dame are going to be Beyoncé and Jay-Z," she said, smiling proudly.

"Uggh! Lame!" I said, sticking my finger down my throat, pretending to gag. She simply frowned at my dramatics.

I flipped through my closet, looking at my naughty nurse's outfit from last year that I never got a chance to wear. "What about this?" I asked, pulling it out of the closet and holding up in the air. *If Melo could only see me in this.*

"Cute," she said low with a shrug.

I guessed she was in her feelings about me calling her and Dame's lame asses lame. Yes, I was hating a little bit, but who could blame me? While they were still madly in love, carrying on with their normal lovey-dovey relationship, the man I had yet to profess my love to disappeared like a thief in the night.

"You know I was just playing with you, right? I mean, who the hell doesn't want to be Jay and Bey!"

Instantly that made her smile.

After we both got dressed and ready for the party, I looked my sister over from head to toe. You couldn't tell that girl she wasn't Beyoncé, but I had to give it to her. She had on a honey blond wig that cascaded down the length of her back. The sparkling turquoise leotard she wore hugged her curvy frame, while the silver stiletto heels she had on made her legs look long and lean.

"I see you, Bey," I told her, looking at her pretty face, which was beat to perfection.

"Thanks. And look at you. You look sexy."

Being silly, I twirled around so that she could get a better look. I knew for a fact that if Melo saw me in this outfit, he would have had a pure fit. The white skirt I wore barely covered up my ass, while the top was cut so low the little cleavage I did have was completely exposed. I guessed if I was going for the role of the slutty nurse, I had to go all the way. I brushed my long, silky hair down my back one final time and put on some cherry red lipstick to complete my look. After I slipped on my white pumps and placed the red and white nurse's cap on my head, we both walked out the door.

After a fifteen-minute drive over to the party, we both got out of the car. The Halloween sky was pitch-black, and the white moon was fatefully full. As we headed for the door, I could feel that cool October air whipping up my skirt, causing goosebumps to rise, covering my entire body. Dame's fraternity was cosponsoring the party, so we didn't even have to wait in line. Thank goodness, because besides it being cool outside, there were so many people in line I doubted everyone was going to make it in.

As soon as we entered, I bobbed my head to Cardi B's "Bodak Yellow," which was blaring throughout the building. The party was so crowded that we could barely even walk through without touching someone. Raina and I got a lot of stares as we made our way to the center of the dance floor, and even a few gropes, but I was used to that kind of attention nowadays. After just one year of college and taming one of the most desired frat brothers on campus, my confidence level was through the roof. As I looked around the party, everyone was dressed up in their Halloween costumes having fun, either dancing, drinking, or taking pictures. When the beat dropped on the song, Raina started twerking.

"Damn, Bey, what you doing over here?" Dame said, walking up with his perfect white smile. He had on a black sweatshirt, black Versace jeans, and a black Yankees cap that was turned to the back. Around his neck was a long gold necklace that had a small cross on it dangling down his chest.

"Boy, you ain't no Jay-Z. Where's your costume at?" I asked jokingly, punching him in the arm.

"As long as I'm standing next to her," he said, pointing to Raina, "that's all the costume I need." He kissed her on the cheek and ran his hand down her backside.

"Y'all, please don't start that mushy shit," I hollered over the music, cutting my eyes at Raina. She knew exactly what I was referring to. She and I had just had this conversation because the last thing I wanted was to feel like a third wheel tonight.

After the song was over and the next track started to play, I immediately recognized the beat. It was one of the songs I did with Traxx a couple of months ago called "Ride Wit' Me." I stood there frozen in disbelief for a second, listening to the crowd go wild over my music. Everyone was dancing and rapping along to the shit like they knew it. That completely threw me for a loop, because as far as I knew, it hadn't even made it on the radio yet.

"This shit fire right here," Dame said, waving his hands in the air.

"Oh my God, y'all. This is my song! The song I did with Traxx!" I yelled, making sure Raina and Dame could hear me over the music.

"Yo, this is you? The one you did wit' Traxx?" he asked, surprised.

I just nodded my head with my hands covering my mouth, still somewhat in shock.

"Damn, shawty. Y'all got a hit on your hands," he said, continuing to bop his head.

"This is my sister's song, y'all!" Raina started to yell at the top of her lungs. She began walking through the crowd, telling everyone she came in contact with that it was me singing on the song. I was completely embarrassed at first. That was until people started coming over to me, telling me how dope the song was and how great my voice sounded. I felt like a real celebrity in that moment.

Hearing my voice on that song and seeing everyone react to it the way they did totally made my night. For the first time in a good long while, I wasn't sad, and Melo wasn't at the center of my thoughts. I was actually smiling, just dreaming about my future singing career.

Chapter 28

Dame

"I finally got up with that nigga Melo last night," Micah said before taking a quick pull on his blunt. "Said he was probably gon' come through the club tonight."

He, Dre, and I had just arrived at Magic City and were already drinking, smoking, and ready to turn the fuck up. It was rare that we got together these days. Between Micah working like a madman, Dre spending time with his family, and Melo being MIA, I was actually looking forward to spending some quality time with my brothers.

"Where the nigga been hiding at?" I asked, looking at the half-naked girl twirl around the pole on stage.

"Went down to Miami for a bit, and now the nigga's back in town," Micah said, allowing the smoke to swirl from his lips.

"Back in town? Where he staying at?" Dre cut in.

"I'on know. I didn't even get into all of that shit. I was trying to make sure he was straight," Micah said, leaning back in his chair.

"Yeah, everything's fucked up. Ma's been staying over at Mrs. Ernie's house, and Pops is all depressed and shit. I don't know what to do," I said, running my hand down my face.

"Ain't really shit to do right now, baby bro. Time heals all wounds. We just gotta let that shit play out how it's gon' play out, ya feel me? I mean, in all honesty, I can't really blame Melo for the way he feels. If the shoe were on the other foot, I probably would have murked that nigga. Pops or not, you don't have that nigga in your house for umpteen years and never let him know that it's your blood flowing through his veins. That's fucked up no matter how you look at it. And Ma, man, I don't know if she'll ever forgive him for the shit he did," Micah said.

All I could do was nod my head because he was right. My whole privileged life, I had lived in a two-parent household. We never hit hard times, and my parents rarely fought, so this shit was all new to me. The only way I was even getting through it all was having Raina by my side. She had been the one and only person to calm all my fears. Whenever I felt weak, that girl made sure she was my cornerstone of strength. I had known for a good little while that I loved her pretty ass. But as time went on, I found out that my heart beat for her and her only. And as scary a feeling as that was, I wasn't fucking up what we had for no one.

"Do baby girl know you out here like this tonight, li'l nigga?" Micah asked with a smirk on his face.

I sucked my teeth and shook my head. "Yeah, she knows, nigga. She ain't worried about none of these stripper hoes," I told him.

"Hey, here comes that nigga now," Dre said, pointing through the crowd.

We all looked to see Melo walking in wearing the usual mug on his face. For a short period of time there, Melo's mood had begun to lighten up. He was actually beginning to laugh and smile on a regular basis. Nigga was even talking more. You didn't have to be a rocket scientist to figure out that Raquel had been the cause of his whole transformation, but that shit was short-lived. Finding out my pops was truly his father and that Uncle Raul had murdered his mother in cold blood definitely took its toll on him.

I looked over at my brother, seeing that his light eyes were puffy and red around the brim. Instantly I knew he was high. The hair on his head and face was so long it looked like it hadn't been cut in months. Even the natural Borrego swagger and sparkle we all seemed to carry was missing in his appearance. He didn't rock not even one gold rope or diamond that night, and that shit was completely out of the norm for us.

"What's up?" Melo approached us, slapping hands with each one of us.

"How you been doing? You a'ight?" Micah asked, cutting to the chase.

Melo sat down in one of the cream leather chairs and waved one of the cocktail waitresses over. "I guess you can say I'm making it," he replied somberly, running his hand down his thick beard.

"Yo, where you staying at?" Dre asked.

"At the W for now, but I'll probably get me a spot out there where you and Micah at."

"You mean you not coming back to the frat house?" I asked, disappointed.

"Nah, probably not, li'l bro," he said, shaking his head.

"Well, no matter what fucked-up shit Pops and Uncle Raul did in the past, I just want you to know that you've always been our brother. Ain't shit changed on that front. It's all love over here, li'l brother, ya feel me?" Micah said, slapping hands with him again before pulling him in for a quick brotherly hug.

When the cocktail waitress sashayed over and set our drinks down on the table, we all reached in and grabbed a glass. Looking to see whether Micah was eye raping her, I noticed that instead, his full attention was still on Melo. He was truly concerned about our brother, and it showed all over his face. I was completely surprised. Not so much by that fact that he actually cared about what Melo was going through, but more so because not once did he look shawty-girl over.

She wasn't by far a slouch. In fact, she was a beautiful brown-skinned girl with high cheekbones and big, doe-like eyes. Prancing around the club in a hot pink thong and a matching bra, shit, she'd definitely caught my eye. Her fat ass and muscular thighs, which were coated in oil, ran all the way down to her feet, which were arched in hot pink stilettos.

"Can I get you gentlemen anything else?" she asked, tossing her long ponytail back behind her shoulder.

"Nah, shawty, we good for now," Micah dismissed her with a crisp $100 bill in his hand, not even looking her way.

Smirking, I cut my eyes over at him.

"Fuck is you looking at me like that for?" he asked with his eyebrows scrunched together.

"Yo' ass done changed, nigga," I said with a chuckle.

"Changed? Fuck you mean?" he quizzed.

"He means you didn't get ol' girl's fine ass to go top you off in the bathroom like you did the last time," Dre reminded him with a laugh. The last time all four of us went out to the strip club together like this had to have been about a year ago, if not longer. I distinctly remembered Micah having one poor girl on her knees in the bathroom stall.

"Nah, I'm good on that shit," Micah said, taking a swig of his Hennessy.

"Have you talked to Risa lately?" I asked out of the blue.

He let out a deep breath of frustration before wiping his hand down his face. "We talk by text damn near every day, but I only talk to her on the phone maybe once or twice a week when she wants to talk to Zari."

"Damn," I muttered.

"Y'all gon' make that shit work or not?" Dre asked.

"I don't know. The ball is in her court. She's keeping me in the friend zone right now, so ain't much a nigga can really do at this point except wait."

"Shidd! The hell there ain't. Nigga, you better go get your girl if that's what you really want. I mean, while you sitting over here all sad and shit, the next nigga 'bout to roll up and scoop her li'l fine ass right out from under you. Watch," Dre schooled, turning his Atlanta cap to the back.

"Yeah, I hear you," was all Micah could say.

"Man, I'm serious. That's why me and Romi eloped," Dre confessed.

My eyes grew wide from shock while Micah instantly started choking and beating on his chest. "The fuck you just say?" Micah asked in between coughs.

"Yeah, one night a few weeks ago, we were just lying in bed, talking and shit. We were talking about everything that's happened between us over the past couple of years," he said, slowly shaking his head. "We came to the conclusion that we were meant to go through everything we've been through just to make us that much stronger in the end," he said, taking a small drink from his glass. "I love that girl, man." He let out a small snort, shaking his head again at the realization of if all. "Making her my wife was the best decision I could have ever made. The way she loves me, the way she loves my seeds . . . Bruh! Shit is unreal."

"Does Ma know?" I asked.

"Fuck nah!" he said, waving his hand in the air. "We went down to the courthouse one morning on some old sneaky shit and ain't tell nobody. We been married for like almost three weeks now," he said with his lips slowly forming a smile.

"Damn," Micah muttered. "Are you gon' finish school?"

"Hell yeah, ain't shit changed with that. I even hired a nanny to take care of the kids so we can both go to school."

"Well, congrats, bro," Micah said, raising his glass.

"Congrats," I joined in.

While the three of us toasted to Dre and Romi's top-secret marriage, Melo remained quiet in his seat. His eyes stayed fixed on a thick red bone working the stage. She was completely topless as she clapped her ass cheeks together to the beat of Juicy J's "Bounce It." He had this lustful look in his eyes as he stared at her, almost in a trance. That instantly made me think of Raquel.

"When's the last time you talked to Raquel, bruh? She's been asking about you," I leaned over and asked him.

He shrugged his shoulders nonchalantly, letting his eyes still linger on ol' girl before he finally said, "It's been a minute."

As if on cue, the DJ cut off "Bounce It" and began to play Raquel and Traxx's song, making the crowd in the club immediately go wild. While the strippers were twerking their asses every which way, dollar bills were flying everywhere, and glasses of liquor were being raised high up in the air. Their track was on fire, playing on every major radio station and in every nightclub in Atlanta. I had yet to meet a nigga who could deny how dope that shit was.

"You know this is Raquel's song, bruh? The one she made with Traxx," I told him over the music.

For just a second, I thought I saw a slight glimmer of surprise in his eyes. Perhaps it was even pride, but it quickly faded, and again he shrugged his shoulders as if he didn't care.

"Well, I'm glad you ain't really worried about her like that no more, because she and Traxx are going on tour, opening up for Gucci. I think she said they were leaving right after Christmas," I told him, knowing exactly what that would do.

Slowly he removed his cold hazel eyes from the red bone on stage and looked at me with the most serious expression on his face. Although he never opened up his mouth to say a single word, I knew exactly how my brother felt. Sure, he needed some space from the shit he had been dealing with, but everyone knew Raquel was his heart. If it was the last thing on earth he did, he was going to get his girl back.

Chapter 29

Risa

Christmas had always been my favorite time of the year, and although I was dog-tired, I was so glad to finally be back at home for the holidays. There was absolutely nothing that could keep me from catching that late flight from Boston to Atlanta last night. When I quietly slipped through the front door, I found Mama sleeping peacefully on the couch. Just the sight of her instantly made me smile because I knew she was trying to wait up for me. Careful not to disturb her, I gently covered her with a soft throw before tiptoeing up the stairs to my old bedroom.

I slept until almost two o'clock in the afternoon the very next day, which just happened to be Christmas Eve. It was the joyful smell of Christmas, along with Mama's seafood gumbo, that woke me up from my deep sleep. That was a family tradition of ours, seafood gumbo. Every Christmas Eve, we could always count on eating some of Mama's good old New Orleans–style cuisine.

Walking down the stairs, I noticed the green garland that neatly hung from the banister with care. The fresh aroma of pine and peppermint, combined with Mama's food, swirled around the room. When I reached the bottom landing, I took in the sight of our ten-foot tree, which was purposely placed in front of a large picture window. No matter what time of day it was, Mama made sure the Christmas tree lights stayed on. Always white lights, none of that colored mess, and always paired with silver tinsel and gold ornaments. It had been that way ever since I could remember. Strangely, I never got bored with Mama's decorations. Somehow in my mind, it was the image of a perfect Christmas. To me it had become what Christmas was supposed to look, smell, and feel like.

"Good afternoon, ladybug," Mama said when I entered the kitchen. The same old red tablecloth neatly covered the kitchen table, while a Christmas tree cookie jar sat on top of the granite counter. I hadn't checked, but I was willing to bet it was full of her homemade cookies.

"Good afternoon, Mama," I replied with a yawn. I walked over to where she stood by the stove and wrapped my arms tightly around her.

She leaned her head back and kissed me on the cheek. "I didn't hear you come in last night. How did you sleep?" she asked, stirring in her pot.

"I slept pretty well." Glancing at the time displayed on the stove, I asked, "What time is everybody coming over?"

"Everyone should be here around five o'clock," she said. Mama was having a small dinner party at the house for the holidays.

"What about Mr. Borrego? Is he coming too?" I asked in a whisper, looking back over my shoulder. Since Mrs. Calisa had been staying with Mama and Daddy for the past few months, I figured she was probably lurking around somewhere.

"Oh, she's upstairs in the shower, but yes, your father invited him," Mama said snippily, pursing her lips. Whenever she'd call Daddy "your father," I knew they'd had a disagreement.

"Well, does she know that?" I asked, concerned.

"Not yet, but I plan to tell her before everyone gets here this evening. And have you talked to Micah yet? He called the house phone looking for you. Said he just wanted to make sure you made it home from school safe, but you haven't been answering your phone."

"Oh, I had my phone on silent while I was sleeping. I'll call him back when I go upstairs," I told her.

"Ummhmm," she muttered, continuing to stir in her pot.

Mama knew everything that went down between me and Micah, play by play. Although she didn't like what he'd done to me last year, she knew just how much I still loved him. Through every conversation we had about that relationship, she would always encourage me to make a decision. "Either give him another chance or let him go, Risa," she'd say. However, that was much easier said than done.

"Have you talked to Tisa lately?" I asked, changing the subject.

A wide smile spread across her beautiful face, just hearing Tisa's name. Over the past several months, she and Tisa had grown very close. Mama even went out to Texas to visit her and her adoptive parents. They were in a good space, and I was truly happy about that. Not only had they begun to build a relationship, but Tisa and I did as well. We talked just about every day on the phone, and I could honestly say that I loved her no different than my other three sisters.

"Yes, I've already talked to her this morning. Her flight should land around four, and then she'll be here for dinner," she said, grinning.

"Well, I guess I'll just run up and get dressed," I said, grabbing a cookie on my way out.

When I got upstairs, I first peeped into Raquel's room. A four-piece Louis Vuitton luggage set was fully packed in the corner of her room. Her keyboard was also put up, which reminded me that she was going on tour. As my eyes continued to search her room, she appeared from her walk-in closet.

"Hey, how long have you been up?" she asked.

"Not long. Getting all ready for the tour, I see."

She shook her head and gave a closed-lip smile. "Yeah, Mama's a little upset about me taking a semester off, but this is my dream. I'd really hate myself if I didn't go," she said, flopping down on the bed.

"Well, I support you one hundred percent. Anyone with eyes and ears knows that you're a star. I want you to go out there and sing your heart out, okay? School will still be here when you return."

"Thanks, Risa."

I left her room and walked a little farther down the hall until I reached Raina's bedroom. After peeping inside, I noticed she wasn't there. I figured she was probably in the bathroom, so I continued. As I walked past Romi's room, where the door was shut, I could hear a sappy Luther Vandross song being played. I knew for sure that Mrs. Calisa was in there. I shook my head and kept walking.

When I finally got to my room, I collapsed down on my bed and immediately grabbed my cell phone. I quickly noticed that I had four missed calls from Micah and one text. I opened up his message and began reading it.

Micah: Thanks for letting me know you made it home safe. Call me when you get up, sleepyhead.

Smiling, I tossed my phone down on the bed and hopped up to go get in the shower. I figured he'd already been waiting this long to talk to me, so he could wait a little bit longer.

At exactly ten minutes after five, I heard the doorbell ring. Before I could make it down the steps, I heard Tisa coming in, talking to Mama. I rushed down the rest of the way until I was standing right in front of my twin sister. Smiling, she stood there with her awaiting arms out wide for me. As if I hadn't seen her in decades, I rushed to her like Celie ran to Nettie in *The Color Purple*. Our trip to New Orleans had been the last time we'd seen one another, so I'd truly missed my sister.

"I . . . I can't breathe," she squealed as I hugged her tight.

When I released her from my embrace, we both laughed at how silly I was acting. But before I could say anything else, I caught a quick glimpse of the ugly Christmas sweater she wore. It was by far the ugliest thing I had ever seen someone wear: a red sweater with a huge picture of Santa Claus's big-headed self on the front. His white beard was made of soft, fuzzy cotton that stuck out from the sweater, and off the tip of his hat was a dangling white knit ball. Shiny red sequins trimmed the collar and wrists of her sleeves, while the bottom of her sweater was bordered in bells. Basically, it was a hot mess, but then I quickly reminded myself that her parents were white. Not to be stereotypical, but I assumed it was most likely a tradition of theirs. I looked the rest of her over, seeing almost a mirror image of myself: the same silky black hair that had grown to drape slightly over her shoulders, and the same piercing dark brown eyes.

"Something smells so good," she said, putting her nose in the air.

"That's Mama's gumbo. You've got to try it," I said, pulling her toward the kitchen.

Before we could barely make it in, the front door opened again. Only this time, it was Romi and Dre with the babies. I left Tisa in the kitchen with Mama and ran right to li'l Armond, who was flailing around in Dre's arms. He was 10 months old and as fat as he could be. His bright green eyes glimmered against his beautiful brown tone as he drooled and smiled toothlessly at me.

"There's Auntie's baby," I cooed, taking him from Dre.

Baby Brandi instantly starting crying as Romi cradled her in her arms.

"I know. Auntie didn't show her other baby no love, did she?" I leaned down to kiss her the top of her head, which was now covered in the silkiest of soft brown hair.

We all walked into the kitchen and gathered around the kitchen table. When my mother's eyes met li'l Armond's, tears pooled in her eyes. She was used to seeing him every day, but when Dre and Romi decided to move in together, she didn't see him as often. So I knew she missed him something terrible.

She walked over and kissed baby Brandi's head, the same as I had done, before pulling li'l Armond out of my arms. "There goes Grammy's sweet boy," she said, kissing his chubby cheeks.

"There goes the sneaky little newlyweds I see," Mrs. Calisa said, entering the kitchen.

Romi and Dre just laughed. They had finally confessed to the entire family a couple of weeks ago that they had been secretly married. They were actually doing so good, balancing the two babies with school, along with being madly in love. So there wasn't anything anyone could say but congratulations. I was so happy for Dre and especially for my sister. After everything she'd been through, she'd finally gotten her happily ever after.

Mrs. Calisa grabbed baby Brandi's teeny body up from Romi's arms and took her over by where Mama stood with li'l Armond. When Raquel and Raina finally came downstairs and entered the kitchen, it was completely loud and chaotic, with everyone chatting and laughing about. The drowned-out sounds of Mama's *Motown Christmas* CD played in the background. Once Daddy came in and got the eggnog flowing, the house was rowdy.

In between all the chaos, I somehow managed to hear the doorbell ring. I jogged and quickly opened up the door only to find Micah, Dame, and Mr. Anton standing out on our front porch in front of me. Although I knew the others were there too, my eyes were solely fixed on Micah. I studied his smooth, dark, angular face, noticing just how handsome he was. With a fresh haircut and sparkling diamond studs in each of his ears, he stood there, lips slowly curving up into a boyish smile. He hadn't even said a word, yet he was making me blush. I turned my head to release the smile I had been biting back.

"I see you two need some alone time," Damien said before kissing me on the cheek and walking past me to get into the house. Mr. Borrego gave me a hug and went inside as well.

"Where's Melo?" I asked, noticing now that he was the only one missing.

"When he found out Pops was coming, he decided he would pass. He's still fucked up about everything that went down," Micah explained.

I simply nodded my head because I didn't know what to make of the whole ordeal with Melo and Mr. Borrego. I hated that Melo was the one excluding himself from the family, especially during the Christmas season, when none of it was even his fault. If anything, I thought that Mr. Borrego should have been the one shunned, but I remained silent, keeping my opinions solely to myself.

"Come out here and talk to me, shawty," Micah said.

"But it's cold, Micah. Just come inside," I whined.

"I got you a little something," he encouraged me, dangling a gold gift bag in front of my face. "You ain't gon' come out here and get it?" he teased, gently pulling me out of the door.

As soon as I stepped across the threshold, he firmly grabbed me by the waist and pulled me in close. Placing my hands up to his muscular chest, I could feel my pearl instantly starting to pulsate between my thighs. We stared deeply into one another's eyes with our lips so close I could literally feel the warmth of his mouth against my skin. In fact, I could see the fog from our breath floating up in the cool night air as we panted from just the anticipation of our first kiss in months.

I watched as he licked his lips and turned his eyes into lustful slits right before crashing his mouth against mine. Slowly, he eased his warm tongue inside my mouth and deepened our kiss. I instinctively closed my eyes and brought my hands up to the sides of his face, enjoying the sweet taste of him.

"Mmm," he said, almost groaning into my mouth. "I missed yo' ass." He pulled back from our kiss and looked me in the eye.

"I missed you too, Micah," I admitted, pecking his lips once more.

He took my hand and help me down to sit on the top step of the porch. Folding my arms across my chest, I rubbed myself vigorously to keep from shivering in the cold. "Here, take my jacket," he said, tossing it over my shoulders.

"Thanks."

He reached inside the gold gift bag and pulled out a big red box that was large enough to fit shoes in. There was a white satin ribbon neatly tied around it, and whoever wrapped the gift for him had done a beautiful job. He tossed the gift bag to the side and handed me the box.

"What is all this?" I said, smiling.

"Open it up and see."

I untied the beautiful white bow and began neatly unwrapping the present. When I removed the top of the box, I saw that there was another neatly wrapped box inside, only a little bit smaller, and instead of red wrapping paper, it was blue. I took it out and tossed the big box to the side. After removing the next white ribbon and all of the blue wrapping paper, I took off the lid only to see another beautifully wrapped box is. It was just a little bit smaller.

"Micah, what is all of this?" I asked, totally confused.

"G'on head and open up your present," he said, smiling.

I went ahead and unwrapped this box only to find another one inside. "Micahh," I whined. "What is this?"

"Just keep going, shawty. It's in there. You just gotta find it," he said with a chuckle.

After letting out a deep sigh, I unwrapped two more gift boxes that were both smaller than the one before until I finally got down to one that was ring-box size. It was Tiffany blue with a beautiful white ribbon tied around it like the rest. For sure it was a ring. *He isn't gonna . . . No, he's not gonna do that,* I thought until I looked up at his expression and saw him drop down to one knee on the step before me. His handsome face was so serious in that moment, and his dark eyes were so full of love.

"Risa, from that very night in the club when I first laid eyes on you, I knew you'd be the one," he said, licking his lips. He took the unopened ring box from me and took both of my hands into his. "Shit, a nigga didn't even say anything to you that night because I was so scared. You were by far the most beautiful woman I had ever laid my eyes on," he said with a shake of his head, recalling that night. "I don't know what it was about you, but a nigga knew he had to come correct. And when I saw you at the cookout that day, right here in your family's backyard," he continued, pointing with his finger, "I figured I needed to make my move. I probably shouldn't have even said shit to you that day, because my life wasn't in order, but I did anyway," he explained.

He reached up and hooked my chin with the tip of his finger, making me look him square in the eyes. Holding my breath, I felt my heart starting to sprint within my chest and tears beginning to form in my eyes.

"Since that day, you've been the one person I can't fucking seem to live without," he said just above a whisper.

"Next to Zari," I corrected him, feeling a tear slip down my cheek.

"Yes. Next to Zari, of course," he said, leaning forward to peck my lips. "I know I've fucked up in the past, Risa, in more ways than one. But I give you my word that I won't ever break your heart like that again. You have my everlasting love."

He pulled my hands up to his mouth and planted soft kisses on the back of each of them before releasing them back into my lap. Carefully he opened up the small gift, revealing a white leather ring box inside. When he opened it up, a large, sparkly yellow diamond set in a shiny platinum band appeared. I instantly gasped at the sight, covering my mouth and taking in all its beauty.

"Will you do me the honor, Risa? Will you be my wife?" he asked, now looking at me with tears of his own threatening to fall.

I swallowed hard, unsure of what exactly to say in that instance. My heart and my head were having an internal battle, and I was truly unsure of who would actually win. I couldn't deny my love for Micah, and of course, my heart wanted to say yes. But in my mind, I couldn't forget about everything I'd been through and all that he'd done. As a few seconds of silence passed between us, I could see his teary eyes starting to plead. Yes, I knew that he loved me, but was love really enough?

"Micah, I love you," I started to say.

"Don't do this, shawty," he held his hand up and whispered, somehow already knowing what was coming next.

"I love you, I do. But I can't marry you now," I continued, shaking my head. "I need to finish law school, and as much as I want to be with you . . . I just don't know if I can fully trust you," I confessed.

He stood up from where he was kneeling and dropped his head down in defeat. As he massaged the bridge of his nose, I watched him search for the right words to say next. "So what do you want me to do, Risa? You want me to just say fuck it and move on?" he asked, slicing his hands in the air.

I shook my head because I knew what that meant. I didn't want to lose him to anyone else, but I also didn't want to be hurt again.

"I know I hurt you, shawty. I know I fucked up, but right now, you playing wit' a nigga's heart."

"I know, and I'm sorry," I started to say, but before I could finish, a loud commotion came from within the house. The sound of glass crashing against the wall amid vulgar fussing and cussing could be heard. Instead of finishing up our conversation, both of us immediately rushed inside. With the family all gathered around the scene, we found Mr. Borrego standing in the kitchen, holding his head, which was gushing with blood, across from a chest-heaving Mrs. Calisa.

"Just sign the fucking papers, Anton! Please! I don't want to do this with you anymore!"

Chapter 30

Melo

For the past few weeks, I had been calling and texting Raquel like crazy but getting no answer. I even tried catching her on campus on a few occasions but would always seem to miss her. Damien and Dre didn't want to get involved, and I completely understood all that, but that didn't stop me from missing my girl. I would have swung by her people's house back in Greensboro to talk to Mrs. Ernie, but the truth was I wasn't ready to face Aunt Calisa yet. She had absolutely nothing to do with what my father did, but I knew if I saw her, she'd want to talk about everything.

If I didn't already know it before, today confirmed that Raquel was completely done with my ass when I sent her a text and was blocked. I guessed she was giving me a taste of my own medicine. "Fuck!" I yelled, slamming the phone down on the table.

"Nigga, the fuck wrong wit' you?" Damien asked, cocking his head to the side.

"Raquel blocked my ass, bruh," I told him, walking over to my stash.

"What? You tryin'a say goodbye to her and shit?"

"Goodbye? Nah, nigga, I been tryin'a holla at shawty for a few weeks now, but she's igging my ass," I told him, unfolding the paper for my blunt.

"Ahh, damn," he muttered. "I thought you knew she was leaving tonight," he said, looking down at the shiny Bvlgari watch on his wrist.

"Tonight?" I quizzed, finally remembering that she was about to go on tour. "Has she left already?"

He cut his eyes up at me from where he sat on the couch and shook his head. "I don't know. Let me shoot Raina a text."

After waiting for a couple of minutes, a text chimed through on his phone.

"Bruh, what she say?" I eagerly asked, pacing back and forth with a lit blunt dangling from my mouth.

"She said her flight leaves in about forty minutes. They're all there now, seeing her off," he said, looking down at his screen.

I quickly put the blunt out in the ashtray that was sitting on my end table before grabbing up my keys. Damien was quick on my heels when I rushed out of my condo, taking the stairwell to the parking garage instead of the elevator. After hitting the unlock button to my Mercedes, I slid inside and cranked up the engine. Damien looked over at me and decided to put his seat belt on just before I threw my car in reverse.

When we got down to the parking garage exit, I could see large flakes of snow falling rapidly from the sky. I first turned up the heat then the volume of French Montana's "Unforgettable" before speeding out onto the road. Pressing my foot harder on the gas, I immediately went into weaving in and out of traffic. A curse word flew from my mouth at every red light we hit. Well, at least the ones I didn't burn. Although it was getting harder and harder to see through the windshield with the weather, the only thing on my mind was getting to her in time.

I knew I couldn't stop her from leaving, but a nigga had to at least see her face one more time before she left. I wanted to apologize for icing her out these past few months, and most importantly, I wanted to tell her the three words I failed to express over the course of our relationship. It was true, her snooping around had caused my family a lot of hurt and pain, but deep down, I knew she wasn't the cause of any damage. My father and that snake-ass nigga Raul were. It would've only been a matter of time before the truth finally came out anyway.

"Bruh, slow down," Damien warned.

Instead of responding to him, I cut my music up and pressed my foot a little harder on the gas. After driving another ten or so minutes, we finally saw the green sign to the airport noting only two more miles. As I curved around the ramp with much speed, I noticed Damien grab ahold of the handle above the door to brace himself. "You good?" I glanced over and asked.

"Yeah, I'm good, just slow the fuck down," he said, looking pissed.

I was in such a hurry to actually see her face that I threw the car in park and hopped out all in one swift motion. When we got inside, I immediately looked over at Damien to point me in the right direction. He had been texting Raina on and off the whole ride over, so she knew we were coming. It was just a matter of making it in time.

"She's flying American, bruh," Damien said, pointing right.

I followed his lead until I saw the signs for myself. That's when my heart got to pumping, and the adrenaline started coursing through my veins. At first, I was jogging, but that quickly turned into a sprint. I was running, dodging people in my path left and right up until Raina, Romi, Mrs. Ernie, and Aunt Calisa finally came into my view. Just seeing them standing there without Raquel turned my stomach. I slowed down my pace and walked over to them.

"Did I make it in time?" I asked, completely out of breath.

"I'm sorry, baby. She just left," Aunt Calisa sadly said.

"Fuckkk!" I yelled, crashing my fist down on the top of my head.

I wasn't no soft-ass nigga by far, but coming all this way and not being able to look into her eyes one last time—those eyes that looked just like my mother's—did something to me. Sinking down into one of the airport chairs, I held my head down in my palms of my hands, feeling unnaturally overwhelmed. Every moment we'd ever spent together and every conversation we'd ever shared replayed in my mind in that moment. I kept thinking about all the shit I would have done differently if I could just turn back the hands of time.

After a few minutes passed, I started to feel the hands of the girls rubbing on my shoulders for comfort. They knew a nigga was crushed, and to be perfectly honest, I didn't know how I'd get through it. After acting like a jackass for the past couple of months, I'd officially lost my girl—the only girl, besides my mother, I had ever loved.

Chapter 31

Risa

I slid my keycard over the door handle only to see the little light turn green. When I opened up the door, I instantly noticed Romi and Raina lying back comfortably on one of the double beds. It was spring break, and we'd all decided to meet up in Miami at one of the Borrego beachfront luxury hotels. Massachusetts' cold weather had been brutal to me these past few months, so I was looking forward to some fun in the sun.

"I thought I was going to beat you guys here," I said, walking in as I rolled my suitcase behind me.

"Nope," Romi said, making her lips pops. "We've been here for almost an hour."

Raina stood up and came over to give me a hug. I hadn't seen any of my sisters since Christmas break, so it felt good to have my baby girl in my arms. "I missed you," she said.

"Missed you too." I then looked over at Romi, who still lying back on the bed. "You too good to give your big sister a hug now?' I asked with my hand on my hip.

She laughed, easing her way up from the bed. "No, I'm just tired," she complained.

Finally, she made it to me with her arms out wide. "Where's the diva at?" I asked while holding Romi in an embrace.

"Her flight should've landed about an hour ago," Raina said. Of all of us, the two of them kept in contact the most.

"Well, I don't know about y'all, but I want to hit the beach. A bitch is finally twenty-one, and I'm finna get my drank on," Romi said, shaking her ass to nonexistent music.

Raina and I both laughed.

While the three of us were changing into our bikinis, Raquel finally sauntered through the door. "Hey, y'all," she said. Dark shades were covering her hazel eyes, and her lips were painted a bright shade of red.

"Hey, my diva," I said. I went over and gave her a tight hug. "How are you? How was your flight?"

"It was okay, I guess," She dropped her luggage and went over to give Romi and Raina a hug as well. "Damn, y'all already in y'all's swimsuits? What, y'all were gonna leave me?" she asked, looking at the gold string bikini Romi had on.

"Yep, we sure were," Romi said. "Now hurry and put your bathing suit on so we can go hit the beach."

"Those kids must be tiring your ass out," Raquel said.

"You damn right," she joked.

As soon as we hit the beach, a flock of guys was following us, grabbing our arms, catcalling, and doing everything else to gain our attention. However, when we finally settled on the sand under the shade of an oversized umbrella, Romi grew tired of them. "Look, I'm married," she warned with a proud flash of her diamond ring. "Can y'all please move?"

"All y'all married?" one of the guys asked, looking us other three over.

"We're all taken," I spoke up.

When the guys left, Raquel said, "Who's taken? 'Cause I surely am not." She pointed to her own chest.

"Whatever." I rolled my eyes. "You mean to tell me that you still haven't talked to Melo? I thought you said that you were gonna reach out to him after you heard he came to the airport."

"I was, but Melo is so wishy-washy." She fanned her hand.

"Melo's the wishy-washy one?" Raina chimed in, her voice laced with sarcasm.

"Yes," Raquel sat up from her towel and leaned over me to look down at Raina on the other side of me. "Because I knew exactly what I wanted. He didn't. He kept ignoring my calls and avoiding me. I mean, I get that I fucked up by going through his father's things, but what eventually came out of it was the truth. A truth he needed to know."

"I think he just needed some time to himself, Raquel. That's a lot to process, ya know?" I told her.

"Well, I've decided that I'm not focused on having a man right now anyway, so it doesn't even matter. I'm on tour, and that's where my focus needs to be. My music career."

"I know that's right!" Romi exclaimed.

"How are things going out there on the road with Traxx anyway? I heard the show in Dallas was bananas," I said.

"So far, it's been fun. The groupies seemed to really love Traxx, though. I had to tell him that I wouldn't stand for him trying to turn our tour bus into the damn Bunny Ranch."

We all fell out laughing. "And what did he say?" Raina asked.

"He accused me of being jealous. Said I wanted him for myself."

I felt my eyes grow wide. "Do you? Want him?"

"Hell no! Traxx is cool and super talented, but nah," she said, shaking her head. "He's not even close to being my type."

"Why not?" Raina inquired.

"For one, he's too flashy. Talks all the damn time, and at night all I can see are his teeth and eyes. Shit is scary."

"Oh my Gah." Romi laughed. "Well, I love my black-ass nigga."

"Dark chocolate sure is the best kind of chocolate," I muttered, gripping the back of my neck as I thought of Micah.

Suddenly I felt my cell phone buzz beside me. I looked down to see I had a text from Micah. *Speak of the devil.* Surprisingly he was still pursuing me even after I turned down his marriage proposal. I swore that was one of the hardest things I'd ever had to do, but I knew I had to do what was best for me. I still loved him with all my heart, but I refused to let him distract me. If he took me through half of what he did last year, I didn't know if I'd be able to attain this law degree in one piece. But every day, it seemed Micah was working on building back my trust. He'd even come to visit me at school twice in the last four months. Both times we made love, but I wasn't ready just yet to reclaim the title of his girlfriend. Or fiancée, as he would have liked.

Micah: How's Miami, pretty lady?

Me: It's beautiful. We're all lying out on the beach right now.

Micah: What bathing suit are you wearing?

With a playful roll of my eyes, I sighed before typing my next response.

Me: My black one-piece.

Micah: Good girl. Call me before you settle in tonight.

Me: Will do.

Micah: Love you.

My fingers couldn't type back fast enough as my lips curled up for a wide grin.

Me: I love you too.

"And just who's got you cheesing like that?" Raquel asked, gaining my attention.

I looked up and tucked my lips inward, attempting to pull back the smile on my face. "Nobody," I said.

"Uh-huh," Romi said, pursing her lips to the side. "It's somebody all right. Just don't let Micah find out," Romi said.

"Don't let Micah find out what?" I heard his deep, raspy voice behind me.

With my eyes stretched wide, I looked back, seeing a bare-chested Micah Borrego approaching us. His smile was so bright that every tooth in his mouth was full on display.

"Micah," I gasped. "What are you doing here?"

He held out his hand and helped me up to my feet. "I came to see you, baby."

"Why you tryin'a ruin our girls' trip, Micah?" Romi asked. "My baby daddy ain't here, is he?" She smiled, looking around the beach for him.

"Nah, I'm solo dolo this trip. I'm only here for the night, though. I came down for some business anyway," he said, wrapping me in his arms.

"Yeah, right. Business," I said, peering up into his dark brown eyes.

"How you been doing, Miss Harvard?" His hands gently rested at the small of my back as his eyes remained on my lips with every word he spoke.

"Doing all right, I guess."

"I miss you," he whispered. Finally, his dark coffee-colored eyes lifted to meet mine.

"I miss you too," I told him.

He leaned in and pressed his lips against mine. Our tongues eased into a familiar dance as butterflies swarmed inside my belly and tingles traveled all the way down to my groin. "Awww," I could hear the girls all coo.

Micah pulled back and laughed. "Y'all a trip," he said. "Check it: let me borrow shawty for tonight. I promise she'll be all yours for the next three days. I'll even throw in a trip to the hotel spa."

"Fine by me," Romi said.

"That's fine," Raina chimed in too.

My neck instantly whipped back. "Well, damn. Don't I at least get a say in all this?"

Micah chuckled. "You right, baby. Go on, what you got to say?" he said, his hands still holding my waist.

I rolled my eyes up toward the sky and tapped my finger on my chin like I was thinking. "Hmm."

"What? You don't want to hang out with me tonight?"

"I do."

"So why you tryin'a front on me in front of your sisters?" he asked with a smirk.

My left shoulder hiked to my cheek in an effort to play coy. He simply shook his head. After gently taking me by the hand, he told the girls we would see them later. He then pulled me back across the sand toward the hotel.

"A black one-piece, huh?" he asked, looking down at the white string bikini I had on.

"Oh, is that what I said?" I innocently batted my eyes, playing stupid.

He and I locked eyes before we both fell out laughing. Without warning, he lifted me in the air and threw me across his shoulder. "Daddy gon' have to punish you for lying, you know that?" he said, smacking me hard on the ass.

Chapter 32

Micah

"Thank you for this," Risa half moaned. She was lying on the table next to me as the hands of some little Asian woman worked the muscles of her back and shoulders over with oil. We were side by side in a dim, candlelit room, getting a couple's massage. The sound of falling raindrops played in the background.

"You don't have to thank me, baby," I murmured in a trance of my own from my masseuse working on my lower back.

"Is this why you came all the way to Miami to see me? Just to take me to the spa?"

With my face lowered into the hole, I let out a light chuckle. "Nah, I came to spend time with you, among other things."

"Other things like what?" she quizzed.

"You'll see." I smirked.

I lifted up from the table, and with a wink of my eye, I silently asked the two masseuses to excuse us. After they quietly let themselves out of the room, I wrapped the white towel around my waist and stepped over to where she lay. Slowly I began kneading the flesh of her thighs, and she rewarded my efforts with a moan.

"Micah," she said, "that feels so good."

I released a snort of laughter. "How you know it's me?"

"I'd know your touch anywhere," she said, making me smile.

I slid the towel down from around her waist until she was lying completely naked in front of me. I leaned forward and began planting kisses on her ass cheeks. Whimpers of pleasure further escaped her. "You know why I really came all the way down here?" I asked.

She lifted up from the table and craned her neck back to finally look at me. "Why?"

"Because I wanted to taste you." I bit down on my bottom lip.

Her eyes instantly lit up. "Micah," she gasped, "you're so nasty."

"I am, baby. I'm one nasty muthafucka, especially when it comes to you."

I turned her body over completely until she was lying flat on her back. I leaned forward and took her pebbled nipple into my mouth. She caressed the top of my head as her back arched from the table. When her ragged breath heightened to the point of audibility, my dick swelled beneath my towel. My tongue dipped in the valley between her breasts, slithering all the way down to her belly button. Without further delay, I pulled her to the bottom of the table and planted myself between her thighs. She yelped, allowing a sharp breath to escape her lungs. I stooped down low, yanking her hips down to meet my face. I inhaled her sweet musk as I went in and planting a sloppy, wet tongue kiss right on her pussy.

"Ohhh," she moaned.

Her quivering thighs were draped over my shoulders as her hands continued to roam the sides of my head. My tongue continued to kiss, suck, and flick until her body nearly bucked off the table. "Oh God," she cried. Within mere seconds she was climaxing, trembling in my hands.

I stood up and dropped the towel from around my waist. My long, hard dick immediately sprung out like a jack-in-the-box. I spread her thighs and placed myself right at her wet slit. I slid myself up and down her center, teasing her.

"Micah, please," she whined.

Taking her out of her misery, I pushed myself into her warmth. She was so wet and tight, my eyes closed in delight as I bit down on my bottom lip. "Fuck," I breathed.

I worked my hips in and out of her as her fingers clawed against my abs. Her moans grew with the roll of her hips, faster and faster as her walls sucked me deeper and deeper into her soul. My thrusts grew rhythmic until I felt my balls drawing up. "Shit, baby," I murmured, feeling like I was about to burst. I looked down at her, seeing that her eyes were squeezed shut. Her brown-sugar skin glowed in the dimly lit room, and as she clenched her teeth, stifling her lustful sounds, she never looked so beautiful. Suddenly her pussy tightened around me, and within a matter of seconds, her body was convulsing.

"Micah," she cried, allowing real tears to escape the corners of her eyes.

Although I'd kept the momentum, seeing her climax pushed me over the edge. I drove in and out of her with determined speed until my body finally locked up, filling her insides with my semen. I jerked and pulsed inside of her for what felt like forever until my body eventually fell weak. When I collapsed on top of her, she quickly took me by the lips.

"I love you," she confessed through a whisper.

"I love you too." I looked her in the eyes.

Her heart was still beating wildly against my chest as I dipped down to kiss the curve of her neck.

"I think I wanna try again," she said.

My heart, already beating fast, somehow picked up speed. "You wanna get married?"

She shook her head. "No. I wanna be your girlfriend." She giggled.

I smiled. "Shawty, you never stopped being my girl. But whatever makes you happy, baby. I'm in this with you for life."

"You promise?"

"You got my heart, baby. That's my word."

Chapter 33

Melo

The Cuban wind whipped across my face as I eased down the dark hall of my father's home. It was well past midnight, and besides the lull of the ocean outside, the place was completely quiet. I screwed my silencer on my .45 and creeped toward his bedroom. Sucking in a deep breath, I slowly turned the brass knob. However, when I entered, I was completely caught off guard. From the moonlight pouring in the window, I was able to see my father sitting up on the edge of the bed.

"I was wondering how long it was gonna take you to come, son," he said with his back facing me.

Although my heart pounded inside my chest and my throat constricted, I kept moving forward, one foot in front of the other with my finger already on the trigger, gun aimed and ready.

"Your mother was so beautiful, Melo. Those eyes," he said, shaking his head at the memory. "By far the most gorgeous creature I've ever seen. And her laugh, my God. She could laugh at something on the TV or be laughing on the phone, and whoever was around her would start laughing too. That's just how infectious the sound was. And boy, did she love you."

"I'm not here to talk, Raul. I'm strictly here for retribution. You took away the best part of me, something I'll never be able to get back. I can't let that kind of violation go unpunished, no matter who you are," I told him, sliding back the .45 with a gloved hand.

When his head suddenly dropped between his shoulders, I knew it was an act of defeat. "I know, I know," he cried. His shoulders shook as he began to sob.

I walked around directly in front of him with my gun trained on his head. "On your fucking knees," I commanded.

As he nodded in surrender, the light of the moon highlighted the wet tears glossed across his face. He was crying. Good. Slowly he kneeled down to the tiled floor, and I didn't wait, not even a fucking second, before pressing the gun to his skull. I closed my eyes, remembering the painful sound of my mother begging for her life. It wasn't a dream. Within the blink of an eye, I squeezed the trigger.

Pow!

Brain matter flew across the room before his lifeless body collapsed face-first to the hard floor. I let out the shaky breath I'd been holding as a single tear trickled down my cheek. I swore I wouldn't be emotional over killing this motherfucker, but I'd been completely wrong. He was the man I believed to be my father for the last twenty-plus years. The man I believed loved my mother more than life itself. I looked down at Raul one final time before backing out of the room. On the way out of his estate, I walked down the pier and took a cleansing breath before tossing the gun into the ocean. I knew from this point on, life would never be the same.

By the time I made it back to my father Anton's private jet, Micah was coming down the stairs. "I was starting to get worried," he said.

"It's done," I told him, climbing the stairs. "It's over."

After we both boarded the plane, Micah didn't even ask what happened. He simply wrapped his arms around me and pulled me in for a brotherly hug. After taking a seat, I sat back and closed my eyes, waiting for the plane to take off. We were in the air when I decided I couldn't sleep. I connected the Wi-Fi and instantly went to Raquel's Instagram, @Hazel_Rock762.

It was something I did often because it was the only way I could see and hear her since she wasn't talking to me. Somehow just the sight of her beautiful face relaxed me. After looking at her pictures in Miami last month during spring break, when she got over 10,000 likes just for her bikini shots, I went to her latest post. It was a picture of her performing on stage with Traxx at the Barclays Center in New York. For that one pic alone, she got over 20,000 likes. My shawty was becoming a celebrity overnight, and as much as it hurt that we were no longer together, I was truly proud of her.

After liking her picture, I put my phone down and tried to fall asleep again. By the time I woke up, sunlight was shining through the windows of the plane, and we were landing. After we got off the plane, we walked over to Micah's ride, where I hopped in the passenger seat. We rode in silence for a while until I noticed we weren't headed back to my place.

"Where you going?" I asked.

"Oh, um . . ." He hesitated, scratching behind his ear. "Pops needs to talk with us. All of us," he said.

Feeling like I'd been set up, I clenched my teeth. Not only was I dog tired, but I'd also just finished killing the man I'd believed my entire life was my father. I wasn't ready to face the real one. "I'm not talking to that nigga."

Micah let out a deep breath of frustration. "Look, I'm not trying to get in the middle of this, bruh. All I know is he asked for all the family to get together. That includes you and Ma Dukes."

"She still staying with Mrs. Ernie?" I asked.

He nodded his head with a somber expression, his gaze still on the road ahead. Although we were all grown, the realization of our family falling apart saddened us. The bond Aunt Calisa and Pops shared as husband and wife, as the heads of our family, was something we all strove for. Their separation had been a blow to us all. And especially me, since I'd been the cause.

After another twenty minutes on the road, we were finally pulling up to the family home. Dre's and Dame's cars were already parked out front, but I didn't see Aunt Calisa's car. When we made our way inside, we could hear everyone talking in the kitchen. When we walked in, I was surprised to see Romi sitting there next to Dre. I guessed she was technically family now since they were married. She and I were first to lock eyes when I entered the room. She gave a soft, unassured smile and waved at me. After that small gesture, we got the attention of everyone else.

"You came," my father said, looking at me.

"Yeah, I'm here. What the fuck is this about?" I flopped down in a chair at the kitchen table before running my hand down my tired face.

"I'd like to give Calisa just a few more minutes. I still haven't lost hope that she'll join us," he said.

"Good luck," Dame chimed in with a shake of his head.

We all sat in silence for the next few minutes before we heard someone coming through the front door. Within a matter of seconds, Aunt Calisa, Mrs. Ernie, Raina, and Risa were all entering the kitchen. Micah immediately hopped up and took Risa into his arms. He kissed her like they were the only two in the room, and she let him. Immediately I felt some type of way seeing all the girls there without Raquel, but there wasn't shit I could do about it.

As I looked Aunt Calisa over, I noticed she didn't look as stressed as she did the last time I saw her. In fact, she had a glow about her. Her dreads were freshly twisted, and she had on a form-fitting maxi dress that showed off her youthful shape. Judging by the way my father looked at her, I wasn't the only one to notice.

"Dear God, you came," he said. His eyes held the same sentiment they did when he first saw me.

"I'm here, Anton. Now, what is this about?" Aunt Calisa sassed, placing her purse on the counter.

His eyes immediately went over to Ms. Ernie.

"Ernie and the girls aren't going anywhere, so you might as well spit it out," said Aunt Calisa. "We have plans after this."

He cleared his throat and nodded. "Fine," he breathed, throwing up his hands. "I've brought you all here because I want to apologize for my betrayal. I lied to all of you, keeping buried some really dark secrets from my past that I knew would hurt you. I know that I don't deserve any of your forgiveness, but I have to try."

He then looked at Aunt Calisa, who was standing next to Mrs. Ernie with her hand on her hip. "My darling, my love." He placed his right hand over his heart. "That one night with Kizzy was the biggest mistake of my life. I don't expect you exonerate me of this charge but . . ." He moved in close to her, attempting to take her by the hand, but she resisted. However, when she yanked away, Mrs. Ernie nudged her back toward him. "I promise you that the emotional torture I've endured all these years has been enough punishment to last me this lifetime and well into the next. I don't want to get a divorce, Calisa. You are my everything."

When Aunt Calisa's face remained defiant, my father surprised us all by dropping down to his knees. "Please," he begged, wrapping his arms around her legs. "I love you so much, I won't survive in this world without you."

Aunt Calisa's hand flew to cover the gasp floating from her mouth. Her eyes glossed over as tears began to roll down his cheeks. "Anton," she said softly, "don't do this to me."

"I'll die without you, baby," he croaked.

She shook head back and forth. "I can't. You killed my sister."

He peered up at her with a tearstained face. "I didn't kill her. Hell, I didn't even know what really had happened until months after. You know me, Calisa. I would have never condoned that."

"I don't know anything anymore," she whispered.

"Please, baby," he begged. "I miss you so much." He hugged her legs even tighter, not giving one single fuck that we were all there.

Then, just above a whisper, my aunt said, "I miss you too."

My father's eyes doubled in size from shock. He quickly rose to his feet and pulled her into his arms. She didn't refuse his touch this time. Instead she cried with her face buried in his chest.

I looked around the room, seeing that all of the women in the kitchen were crying. Even Dame, the baby boy, had tears in his eyes. I stood up from the chair and began to make my exit. When I finally began to exit through the entryway of the kitchen, he called out to me.

"Melo," my father said. I turned back, seeing a pained expression on his face. "I know I don't deserve it, son, but if you can ever find it in your heart—"

I didn't even give him a chance to finish. I threw up my hand, cutting his words short. I gave him a single head nod, which was all I could muster in the moment before heading for the door. The only thing sparing Anton's life was the fact that he had actually been a good father to me. A true dad in every sense of the word. He'd been there for all the times I was sick and each time I'd gotten hurt. He'd never missed a game and was present for every graduation since I'd passed the fifth grade. I didn't exactly know how, but deep down I knew that I would eventually have to let this go. No matter the pain I was feeling, my wounds would ultimately heal with time.

Chapter 34

Romi

Three and a Half Years Later

As Dre, Brandi, and I all walked in the church holding hands, I watched as li'l Armond ran full speed ahead of us. He was now 4 years old, while Brandi was still 3. The two of them had taken our lives by storm these past few years, filling our lives with so much joy and excitement. Although we were only 24 and 25 years old, we often acted like an old married couple, planning date nights and turning in early.

After finally getting accepted into Clark and getting my degree, I was officially a registered nurse. I chose to stay home with the kids, though, at least until they both had to go off to school. Dre got his bachelor's degree, too, and went on to work as the chief operating officer of the Borrego luxury hotel chain as planned. I was so proud of him, not only for making that cheese but also for just handling his business like a man.

These days, my man wore nothing but the finest Armani suits and Prada shoes. They looked damn good on him, too. He even moved us into a six-bedroom brick home right outside the city. We were definitely doing big things to be so young. Looking back on everything that had transpired to get us to this point in our lives, I honestly didn't know if I'd change a thing other than Brandi's unexpected death. That was something that none of us would ever be able to get over. Currently, I was a proud mother of two beautiful children and married to one of the sexiest and most successful men in Atlanta. What more could any girl ask for?

"Watch them, babe. I'm going up to see her," I told Dre before puckering up my lips. He leaned down and softly pecked my lips before slapping me hard on the ass.

"Ouch!" I said with a playful pout.

Lustfully, he looked my body over, taking his bottom lip in between his teeth. I knew exactly what that meant. He'd be dicking me down until I cried before the night was over, and I was more than okay with that. That's right, I was one lucky girl.

When I made it up the stairs into the church's bridal suite, my eyes finally landed on her. Even from behind, fixing the pins in her hair, she looked absolutely stunning. As I entered, everyone was either still getting ready or snapping pictures. I snuck up behind her and kissed her on her cheek.

"Oh my God," she gasped, looking at me through the mirror. "You made it."

"What do you mean I made it? I wouldn't have missed this for the world."

Chapter 35

Raina

"Can you suck in a little bit more?" I asked my sister Tisa, struggling to zip up her dress.

"Hey, I'm doing the best I can here," she said, attempting to hold her breath.

"Nobody told you to run off and get pregnant right before this wedding. You knew you had a dress to fit in today," I teased.

"I know, right," she said with a laugh. Tisa and her husband Robert had been married for over two years now, and after months and months of trying, she was finally four months pregnant.

"There," I said, jerking up to close her zipper.

"Thanks, sissy."

After she looked herself over in the long mirror, she walked over to where my other sisters were standing. I twirled around in the mirror, admiring my curvy frame, which was covered in the gorgeous mermaid dress my sister had picked out. It was a soft shade of teal and strapless, exposing my beautiful caramel shoulders. These days, I was more confident than ever, and I had Damien to thank for that. He told me just how beautiful I was each and every day of our lives.

Just as I tucked a wispy piece of hair behind my ear, I felt his soft lips against the crook of my neck.

"Dame. What are you doing in here?" I turned around and asked.

"Shh," he whispered with his finger over his mouth, knowing good and well he shouldn't have been in here with us girls.

I looked him over, seeing the expensive cream tux tailored to fit his muscular physique to perfection. Straightening up the silk tie wrapped around his neck, I noticed his eyes looking down into my cleavage.

"Eyes up here," I said.

He bit back the sexy smile that threatened to spread across his face. Over the past few years, Dame had truly made me happy. We weren't married, or even engaged for that matter, because I was only 21 years old and in my last year of college. He had just started working for his father, and I was putting together a business plan to start my own majorette-style dance company.

Although Dame asked me to move in with him, I declined. Mama always said, "Why would he buy the cow if he can get the milk for free?" He'd just suck his teeth and wave me off when I told him that. But the truth of the matter was I was deeply in love with him and perfectly happy with the stage we were at in our relationship.

"Boy! What are you doing in here?" Raquel fussed from across the room.

"Nice to see you too, superstar," Damien said sarcastically. He ducked just in time when she pitched a bouquet of pink roses right at his head.

"I'll see you see downstairs, beautiful," he said, winking at me. I smiled and shook my head, watching him chuck up the deuces to everyone else before slipping out of the door.

Chapter 36

Raquel

After going on tour with Traxx, I had become a hit in the music industry. I did a few more hooks and features on other rappers' songs before I was finally signed to one of the biggest record labels in the game. Although I never did finish college, I was content with the decision I'd made. Currently, I was living in California and living out my dream.

I wasn't on no Beyoncé-type status yet, but you definitely saw my face on TV and could hear my melodic voice on radio stations all across the nation. In fact, I won my first BET music award last year for Best New Artist. I was so proud of that. No, I didn't have a man in my life, but I was in grind mode, making them coins. I ain't need no man, or at least that's what I told myself on those long, lonely nights I found myself curled up with a book.

Just as I heard the wedding music starting to play, the double doors of the church opened wide. I peeped my head around and watched Tisa walk down the center aisle first. The church was filled to capacity, both the first and second floors. With all of the celebrities invited, this had easily become one of the biggest events in Atlanta this year. Even paparazzi were lingering outside.

Next in line to walk was Raina. She gracefully sashayed down the aisle, swaying her wide hips to the melody. I watched Dame down at the other end, looking like he just wanted to eat her alive. I couldn't do anything but shake my head and laugh at those two. They were still so in love after all these years.

From behind, I spotted Mrs. Calisa and Mr. Anton sitting in the front pew, side by side. They'd been back together for the past few years and genuinely seemed to be happy. Next, it was my turn, and my heart started to race. I had been on stage in front of millions before, but never once had I gotten this nervous. Even my palms were growing sweaty, and I could hardly breathe.

"Go on, dear. You're next," the wedding coordinator whispered, giving me a little shove.

As soon as I stepped foot on that aisle, I looked down at the other end, and my eyes instantly locked with Melo's. I hadn't seen him in over three years, and yet he stood there looking just as handsome as the day we'd met. I'd heard he was now living in Miami, working for some large tech firm there. On the occasions I'd come home to visit, I'd always wonder if I'd run into him, but I never did.

As I continued to walk down the aisle, my focus remained on Melo. Dre stood next to Micah, then Timo, then Dame, and on the very end was the one and only man I'd ever given my heart to. My mind started to flood with each and every memory we'd created, and all the moments of passion we had ever shared. I knew beforehand that I would most likely have to face him today, and I wondered if we'd talk. I even practiced exactly what I'd say, but in that moment, I was scared. Scared of all those old feelings he'd stir right back up out of me.

When I reached the top of the aisle, I swallowed hard, breaking the connection between our eyes. I went and stood in front of Raina, waiting for Romi to walk down. As soon as she started walking, I noticed from the corner of my eye that Melo had broken form and was coming toward me.

"Hey, man," I heard Micah say, putting his hand up to stop him in his tracks.

Melo cut his eyes hard over at him and spoke in a silent language that only the brothers knew. Micah nodded his head and motioned his hand for him to proceed, almost as if he was giving him his blessing. When he finally stood right in front of me, I let out the breath that I was unconsciously holding in. I stared into his beautiful light eyes and licked my lips, pondering what I should say.

When he grabbed my hand, just the warmth of his familiar touch made me feel some type of way. The shit was indescribable.

"I know it's taken me three long-ass years just to say the shit, but I love you, Raquel. That's some shit I should have told you a long-ass time ago, I know," he said, letting out a small snort of laughter. "I'm sorry for cutting you off at a time where I felt like my life was falling apart," he explained.

Holding my index finger up to his lips to stop him, I simply shook my head. "I love you, Mel—" Before I could even finish professing my love, he grabbed me tight and planted a long, movie-style kiss on my lips, taking my breath away. Nigga even bent me back and everything. Before I knew it, the whole church was clapping and cheering at our dramatic display of affection.

"Now get back in line, nigga. You fucking up my wedding," Micah barked through gritted teeth. At first, I thought he was mad, but when Melo walked past him to get back in line, Micah dapped him up and whispered something in his ear. They both smiled before he continued to get back in place.

I didn't know how we'd make this long-distance relationship work, but I was definitely giving it a try regardless. The music industry was popping in Miami, too. So, hey, you never knew. As I stood there planning it all out in my head, I didn't know what was making me smile more. It was between the taste of Melo's kiss that still remained on my lips and the sight of Zaria and little Brandi walking down the aisle, throwing rose petals directly at the people sitting in the pews.

Chapter 37

Risa

Today was finally the day I got to marry my soul mate. Although I didn't accept Micah's proposal that Christmas Eve three years ago on my front porch, that didn't stop him from trying again and again. In fact, he proposed two more times before I finally accepted. He was a persistent man, to say the least. I loved Micah, and I always knew that I was going to marry him, but I wanted to finish school first. I had big dreams of becoming the district attorney one day, and I didn't want anything, or anyone for that matter, to get in the way of that. After officially passing the bar a few months ago, I was more than ready for this next phase in our lives.

Despite the trust issues I had with Micah after he cheated, we ended up doing the long-distance relationship thing while I was away at Harvard. He had gone above and beyond to prove his love for me. So that very last time he'd gotten down on his knee with that same beautiful canary diamond in his hand, I didn't hesitate to say yes. The same way Micah knew that I was his wife when he first laid eyes on me, I too knew that he was my husband. I just never wanted to admit it out loud for fear of getting my heart broken all over again. Lord knows Zo had done enough damage.

Speaking of Zo, one week after Christmas three years ago, the police had finally arrested someone for his murder. It had been my dear friend Sabrina. Before her court date, she confessed to me that she was, in fact, the one to kill him. She said that she too was once in an abusive relationship, and she just couldn't continue to sit idly by, watching me go through that.

"I went over to your place because you'd left your chemistry book in my car. I remember you saying that you wanted to sell it back before you went home for the summer," she had explained. "When I got there, Zo had another woman in the apartment. I tried to turn away and leave, act like I didn't see anything, but he grabbed me. He pushed me up against the corridor walls and threatened my life. He slapped me hard across the face several times and said that if I told you about ol' girl, he'd kill me. I went back to my car, crying, shaking, and boiling over with anger. I knew that he'd been hitting you, so his cheating had only made my view of him that much worse. And when he put his hands on me"—she'd shaken her head—"that brought back memories of my ex, Kevin. That jackass used to use me as his full-time punching bag. I went inside my glove compartment and pulled out my gun. I had bought it for protection because of all those rapes that had been happening across campus. You remember?"

I had nodded.

"Well, it wasn't registered, so that's one charge." She'd shrugged. "The next thing I remember is going back up to the apartment and knocking on the door. The whole event was like an out-of-body experience. Although he was confused, he let me in. The girl was now gone. I attempted to seduce him until we were back in the bedroom. He fell for it." She'd snorted a somber laugh, recalling the events. "I pulled out the gun, and before I even knew what was happening, I shot his ass."

"What about Timo?" I had asked, confused, wondering if it was all a setup.

"I love him."

The police had reviewed the footage from the surveillance tape in the parking garage of the day Zo got murdered. Of course, it showed me going in and out close to his time of death. That's why they arrested me. But as soon as Sabrina found out that I'd gotten arrested, she anonymously sent them the surveillance tape that she'd stolen of herself, showing her going in just moments before me. That's what had gotten me off so quick. Sabrina was disguised, dressed down in all black, which was why I guessed it took them so long to figure out that it was actually her on the tape.

Timo was so broken by it all because he had really begun to fall hard for Sabrina. Once we found out that it was, in fact, Zo's brother she was dating, I immediately told her to break it off because he was still angry at me, but she said that she just couldn't. She would say that as soon as she'd try to call it quits, they'd be right back together again. They had that same undeniable chemistry that Micah and I had, so I tried not to judge.

The evidence they had against her was minimal, and even though they were able to get a conviction, her appeal went through, and she had another trial coming up soon. I told her that I'd be right there to support her, and I truly meant that. Over the years, as a part of my study, I'd been researching the holes in her case. I'd recently reached out to her attorney and even given him a copy of all my notes.

"Wow, you look absolutely gorgeous," my father said, walking into the room.

"Thank you, Daddy," I said, smiling at him through the mirror.

"They're all waiting for you," he said.

"Yes, sir, I'm coming now."

I looked myself over one more time, taking in the $200,000 Carolina Herrera dress I'd chosen. It was off-white with sparkly Swarovski crystals throughout. Just the way the dress clung to my slender frame and how the silky material felt against my skin made me feel like a royal princess. My hair was in a soft, elegant updo, and I wore a small tiara, covered in the same Swarovski crystals, on my crown. I looked at my face, making sure my makeup was perfect, before grabbing my train in one hand and my father's arm in the other.

Feeling my emotions already surfacing, I took one big breath before the doors of the church opened up wide for us. Everyone was standing up with their eyes focused on me. However, my eyes were only on Micah. I'd picked out the song "The Point of It All" by Anthony Hamilton to walk down the aisle to, but I didn't know Micah would actually have him here singing it for me in person. Just hearing the lyrics and how befitting they were instantly made me cry.

> I can't stay away from you too long
> Even if I do I'll always call
> Checkin' on you make sure you're OK
> Be the one to brighten up your day, yeah yeah

When I finally reached the top of the aisle, my father kissed me on the cheek and placed my hand in Micah's before sitting down next to my mother. I looked in Micah's handsome face, seeing tears already in his eyes. He leaned down and kissed me as though we were already pronounced husband and wife.

"Ahem," the pastor cleared his throat, and everyone in the church cooed and laughed.

We went on with the ceremony, reciting traditional vowels to one another, both saying, "I do." Afterward,

Micah kissed me so deeply that my knees buckled beneath me. When we were finally introduced to all of our family and friends as Mr. and Mrs. Micah Borrego, we jumped the same broom my mother and father did twenty-three years ago. As we walked back down the aisle, heading out of the church, I leaned over to Micah and whispered, "By the way, husband, you're gonna be a daddy again."

He looked at me with a confused look on his face, letting his mind register what I just said. As soon as the light bulb went off in his head, a huge white smile spread across his face, and he swooped me up in his arms. "She's having my baby, y'all!" he yelled throughout the church. That's right, all my dreams had come true.

Epilogue

Raquel

"What time was their flight supposed to land?" Melo asked, hand rubbing my belly as the warm summer breeze whipped across our faces.

"They should be here soon," I murmured.

We were lying back in a hammock by the pool, waiting for everyone to arrive. I hadn't seen my sisters in months, so I invited everyone down to celebrate Raina's birthday as well as share with them our good news. The chefs we hired for the occasion were finishing up on the grill, and the fireworks were all set and ready to go. The only thing missing was our family.

Suddenly the French doors leading to our backyard opened. I looked up to see Raina stepping out with Dame behind her. "Hey there, big mama," she teased, walking over with her arms out for a hug. I got up off the hammock and wobbled over to hug them both. Her hands immediately went to my pregnant belly. "Wow, you've gotten so big!" she said.

"Damn, look like you 'bout to bust," Dame reaffirmed with a smile.

I waved him off and rolled my eyes. "No, actually, I've got two more months." Shamefully, I'd already gained twenty pounds and was expected to gain at least fifteen to twenty more.

Melo came over and clapped hands with Dame, then pulled Raina in for a hug. "Where's everybody else?" he asked.

"They were pulling up behind us. We rented our own car because Dame wants to hit the clubs tomorrow night down in South Beach," Raina explained.

After months of dating long-distance, Melo and I finally settled in Miami. We bought a beautiful 8,000-square-foot home right in the heart of Coral Gables. With the checks I'd saved from my tour with Traxx along with a single I'd put out of my own, I was able to contribute financially. That gave me a sense of pride.

Although we'd gotten pregnant fast, Melo still wanted me to pursue my dreams. He even paid for studio time that wasn't even scheduled for a couple months after I was to give birth. In fact, Melo was my biggest fan. He knew all the lyrics to my songs by heart and would even listen to me sing out the new ones I'd often write. After Micah and Risa's wedding, he came out to one of my shows in L.A., and it seemed we'd been inseparable ever since.

"How the dance company coming along?" I asked Raina.

"Great." She beamed. "Actually, we've got more students than I can teach right now, but I've already started looking for a second location as well as doubled up on the staff," she said.

"That's awesome."

Suddenly I heard the back door opening up again. "Whadup, whadup, whadup!" Dre said, stepping out into the backyard. Romi was right on his heels, green eyes sparkling in the sun and her long black hair blowing in the wind.

"I thought this was a party. Where the music at?" she asked with a laugh.

Melo and I both went over to greet them as well. While she was filling me in on the kids, telling me how she'd left them behind with our mother and father, Micah and Risa also stepped out from the house.

"Oh my God, sissy, you're glowing," Risa said with a pleased smile. Her eyes were stapled to my belly.

"And what about you? You look so good, Ris. I hope my body bounces back just as quick as yours," I said, looking her over. She'd given birth just six months ago to a little boy, and already her trim figure had returned. Risa, having such a modest personality, simply gave a coy shrug.

"Did y'all bring y'all's shit inside, or is it still out in the car?" Melo rudely asked.

Risa laughed. "We brought it all in. We already took our stuff up to our room," she said. They'd all been here a time or two before. However, Risa and Micah felt the most at home, always claiming the largest guest suite as their own.

I looked around and was so happy to have all of our siblings back in one place. Tisa wanted to come all the way from Texas but had been on bedrest for the past month while pregnant with her second child. First, they'd had a little girl named Elizabeth, and their second one they'd planned to call Katherine. Her due date was exactly two weeks before mine, and we were so elated. Although it wasn't planned, it seemed we were all having our kids close together. We could only hope it meant that their bond with each other as cousins would be that much stronger.

The butler we'd hired for the weekend, Roy, came over with a tray of champagne flutes in his hands. "Ma'am, could I please offer your guests a glass of champagne before dinner?" he asked. "I have sparkling cider for you."

"Why certainly, Roy."

We all grabbed a glass, and before I could even make the toast, Melo did the honors. Everyone looked totally surprised. Melo had always been a man of few words, but for the right occasion, he always could find the perfect things to say. "First, I'd just like to thank all y'all for coming down here to visit me and my shawty. I'm so thankful that, even with the distance, we all still trying to remain close. I know I speak for the both of us when I say that we're so thankful to have y'all's support as we bring another mini me into this world."

"Sis," Micah said, placing his hand on my shoulder, "day in and day out, I swear I've been praying for you." With a serious expression on his face, he shook his head.

We all fell out laughing. Melo and I were having a little boy, and the joke was that he'd be just as rude as his daddy.

"Yeah, whatever, nigga," Melo said. "So anyway, back to my toast." He raised his glass, silently commanding all of us to do the same. "I want to toast to my queen, my heart," he said, looking down at me, "the mother of my unborn child, and my soon-to-be wife—"

"Wife?" Risa asked in shock, eyes immediately locking in with my left hand.

Up to this point, no one had noticed the four-carat diamond engagement ring I'd been wearing. Melo had proposed two weeks ago. We were both lying in the hammock outside one night, looking up at the stars. Then out of nowhere, he pulled out this little black box. As I opened it, with my breath stalled in my lungs, he said, "Shawty, you know you got my heart on lock. Ain't another broad in this world who can do for me what you do, make a nigga feel inside how you make me feel. I want you, this," he said, placing his hand on my pregnant belly, "forever. Will you do me the honor of being my wife?" Of course, I said yes. Melo and I were imperfectly perfect together.

"Wow, man. Congrats," Micah said.

"So once again," Melo said, "everybody raise your glasses to the Borregos."

"To the Borregos!" everyone cheered.

"But wait, my last name isn't Borrego," Raina chimed in.

Dame took her softly by the chin and gazed down into her light brown eyes. "No worries, beautiful, it will be soon."

The End